SAVING LADY ABIGAIL
A Historical Regency Romance Novel

ABBY AYLES
FANNY FINCH

Edited by
ELIZABETH CONNOR

Copyright © 2018 by Abby Ayles

All rights reserved.

No part of this book may be reproduced in any form or by any electronic or mechanical means, including information storage and retrieval systems, without written permission from the author, except for the use of brief quotations in a book review.

ABBY AYLES

♥ Historical Romance Author ♥

BE A PART OF THE ABBY AYLES FAMILY…

I write for you, the readers, and I love hearing from you! Thank you for your on going support as we journey through the most romantic era together.

If you're not a member of my family yet, it's never too late. Stay up to date on upcoming releases and check out the website for all information on romance.

I hope my stories touch you as deeply as you have impacted me. Enjoy the happily ever after!

Let's connect and download this Free Exclusive Bonus Story!

(Available only to my subscribers)

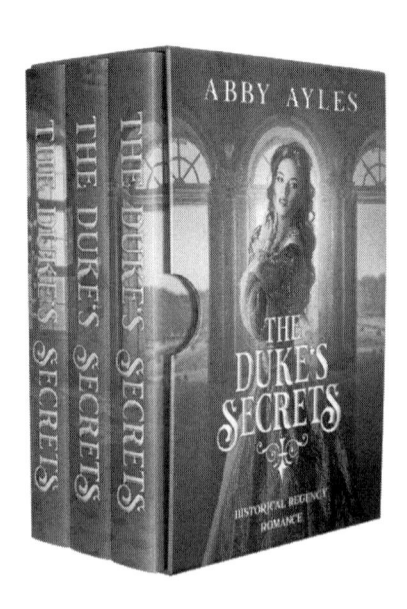

Click on the image or on the button below to get the BONUS

BookHip.com/XNVQAW

ACKNOWLEDGEMENTS
THANK YOUS

Thank you to my parents for their ongoing support. You have turned the world upside down and inside out in order for me to pursue my dreams. I love you.

Thank you to my beta readers Robert & Eris Hyrkas, Barbara Pierson, Kim Elliott and Danielle Carpenter. Interacting with you is so fun and I am so thankful to have you in my corner rooting for me every step of the way.

Thank you to my editorial team for helping bring my words to life in the exact way I envision them to be said. You push me to be better.

Thank you to the authors who inspire me. There is no

world without love, and your books are the reason I'm here now.

Most importantly, thank you to my readers! Whether you are new to my work, or a loyal fan, thank you from the bottom of my heart.

A MESSAGE FROM ABBY

Dear Reader,

Thank you for reading! I hope you enjoyed every page and I would love to hear your thoughts whether it be a review online or you contact me via my website. I am eternally grateful for you and none of this would be possible without our shared love of romance.

I pray that someday I will get to meet each of you and thank you in person, but in the meantime, all I can do is tell you how amazing you are.

As I prepare my next love story for you, keep believing in your dreams and know that mine would not be possible without you.

With Love

ABBY AYLES

Historical Romance Author

INTRODUCTION

Saving Lady Abigail

The Earl of Gilchrist has just returned home from his time in the Napoleonic Wars. His departure was to his families disapproval, and his return is no less covered in shadows.

After great battles, and a near-death injury Colton Frasier the Earl of Gilchrist has significantly been changed by the ghost that haunts his every step.

Lady Abigail is more than ecstatic to be returning to London for the season. Accompanying her is her brother, the Duke of Wintercrest and his pregnant wife, Isabella Watts. Lady Abigail is free-spirited and unconventional.

Lady Abigail is also anticipating the meeting of an Earl that is much loved by her sister-in-law, the duchess, and notorious for his own mischief-making. For Lady Abigail it is a gross misrepresentation when she finally meets Colton Frasier, not only is he horrendously scarred down the left side of his body with boiled flesh, he also seems to be just as mangled on the inside.

Colton is irritated and perhaps even jealous of Lady Abigail's youthful enthusiasm. If she would only learn from his mistakes that a reckless path will only lead her to heartache. Lady Abigail is disappointed that the man didn't live up to the tales, but none the less she doesn't let it hamper her fun in town.

Lady Abigail finds the Earl's words to be true when her own unconventional actions lands her in the hands of a Lord with less than admirable intentions.

Now Colton must decide if he is willing to set aside his own pride to face his demons and save Lady Abigail before it's too late.

PROLOGUE

"I just don't understand how you could have done this without discussing it with me first," the Earl of Gilchrist said to his only son.

"I am twenty-six years of age, Father; I don't need your permission to purchase a commission," Lord Colton Frasier, the Viscount Dunthorpe, responded.

"But how could you have possibly purchased a lieutenant's commission on the allowance given? I understand that it would normally be rather sufficient, but you so often spend yours at the gentlemen's club or on races."

Lord Gilchrist was not the type of man to be angered or raise his voice. The most emotion he ever showed to others was the furrowing of his soft blonde brows and declarations of the impossibility of an action he didn't agree with.

"As you said, Father, my allowance is sufficient. I have grown bored with both the tables and the races. I want to experience some of life. I would have thought I chose a noble course."

"Noble? Are you not aware that we are in the midst of a war with Napoleon? What is so noble about my only son dying on the battlefield?"

The Viscount softened his demeanor. He certainly knew this announcement to his father would stir up mixed emotions. He had yet to tell his sister or mother. Lord Dunthorpe would have liked to at least have his father on his side before that time came.

"I am aware of the battle, Father. I can assure you that as a lieutenant, and with an earldom in my future, I will be sure to take the proper precautions necessary."

Lord Dunthorpe got up from his leather seat and paced his father's office.

"I want to see some of the world, Father," he said, waving his arms around him. "I want to have experiences and adventures. It is not fair that such things should be taken from me purely because I am your only son. Had you another son, it would not have mattered what adventures I wished to embrace."

"But you are my only son, and very dear to me for that matter," his father retorted, still seated behind his desk.

Lord Gilchrist knew his son was a spirited man, always hungry for the next excitement. He somewhat wished he was more like his sister, Lady Louisa. She was perpetually quiet and reserved. Where Lord Dunthorpe jumped before he thought, Lady Louisa always profoundly considered before she even spoke.

"I suppose what is done is done," Lord Gilchrist said, laying his weathered hands upon the oak desk in front of him. "I will never say I agree with this choice but, as you said, you are a grown man and able to make your own decisions."

Lord Dunthorpe sat down in relief. Perhaps with his father now surrendered to his choice it would be easier to tell the rest of the household.

"I thought perhaps that I might announce it to Mother and Louisa this evening at dinner."

"Why so soon?"

"I leave at the end of the week, Father. There is a great need at this time for willing and capable men."

Lord Gilchrist gave out a long sigh. He would have rather liked some time to adjust to his son's new course in life.

In all honesty, Lord Gilchrist rather hoped that Colton would be forced to consider the choice he made before going straight into it. So often, his only son was prone to making rash decisions, but he would soon see rational reason if given the time.

"I suppose you hoped that with coming here and telling me first in private, I might ease the blow to the others," Lord Gilchrist said with a shuffling of papers on his desk. "I cannot promise that will be the case."

"But think of Mother," Lord Dunthorpe said with an ease of charming manipulation. "She will be so frightened at the prospect. If you support me, she will be assured that it is safe. I would ask for your agreement only for the sake of her nerves."

"You are using the delicate nature of a lady to support your own devilish devices, and I don't think I particularly like that," Lord Gilchrist retorted.

He softened into a smile, however. There was much of himself he saw in his son.

"But because I do care so dearly for your mother and her constitution, I will give in to your demands."

Lord Dunthorpe eased into a smile. He had overcome his first hurdle. With his father now on his side, the next would be much easier.

Lord Dunthorpe was well aware that his father, and no doubt the rest of his family, would see his choice to join the Regulars as a rash decision. He, on the other hand, found it to be the most promising course of action he had ever taken in the whole of his life.

He knew that soon the time would come for him to have to settle down, take a wife, and continue the legacy of his father's earldom. He had enjoyed the prospects of the peerage and the social discretions that came with it.

He was now finding himself a grown man, no longer enamored of the artless pleasure of a gentleman's life. He wanted to have some importance attached to his life. The constant revolutions of seasons at his family's country estates no longer seemed worthwhile or meaningful in Colton's mind.

That evening at dinner, Lord Dunthorpe tried his best to be a perfect son for the sake of his mother. Anything to help ease the blow he was about to give was worth the sacrifice.

"Mother, I have just received a letter from Isabella. I can

scarcely believe the words she wrote," Lady Louisa Frasier said to her mother across the dinner table.

"Oh, does that mean she has given birth? Do tell me quickly! Are both Isabella and the babe doing well?"

"Well," Lady Louisa said, not usually the one excited to be in the limelight. Her news, however, was just so fantastical that it made her forget her normally timid demeanor. "She told me first that everything went wonderfully and that she is recovering very quickly.

"She also reported that not only did she have a healthy baby boy," Lady Louisa paused for dramatic effect, "but also a beautiful baby girl."

The Countess of Gilchrist raised both hands to her face in shock.

"Twins?"

Lady Louisa nodded in the affirmative.

"She also inquired if we all might be able to visit her at Wintercrest Manor at our earliest convenience. Won't that be wonderful to go and see both beautiful babies?"

"How very exciting. We will have to find the time to go before the winter storms settle in. It is already very near to autumn."

"I am sure she would be more than happy if we stayed the whole holiday season through," Lady Louisa added.

"What do you think, Lord Gilchrist? Shall we all go up north to see the Duke and Duchess's new babies?"

Lady Gilchrist turned to her husband at the other end of the table. His eyes flickered on each member seated before saying anything.

"I think it would be a lovely diversion to spend the holidays up north," Lord Gilchrist agreed.

The Frasier household rarely left their London home, all finding it to be comfortable and inviting. From time to time, as it suited their fancies, they would spend short occasions at their country seat. It was along the western coast of the country and boasted beautiful views of the Bristol Channel very near to the fashionable retreat town of Bath.

"Colton, you must come with us too," Lady Louisa said, turning to her brother. "I know you and the Duke of Wintercrest got on very well. He will no doubt be most happy to have your company."

Both Lord Dunthorpe and his father exchanged a nervous look. This was no doubt the right window of opportunity for Lord Dunthorpe to tell his sister and mother of his alternate future to that of Wintercrest Manor.

"It seems like a charming diversion, but I'm afraid I won't be able to join you," Lord Dunthorpe said, doing his best to ease into his own arrangement.

"Why ever not?" Lady Louisa asked, raising one of her mousey brows as she lifted some cured ham casually to her mouth.

"I am afraid I have my own announcement to make. The cause of it will keep me detained for quite some time."

"Don't tell me you bought another racing horse," Lady Gilchrist chimed in. "The last one you got, you spent a whole year with the trainers and we scarcely ever saw you."

Lord Dunthorpe recalled with fondness that particular diversion a few years back. He had grown tired of just watching the gig races and wanted to try his hand at it himself.

Lord Dunthorpe was never one to do something halfway. For that reason, he searched the whole country over for the most outstanding racing horse stock and the fastest gig. Then he spent every waking moment training with his horse and buggy.

He had to admit it did pay off in the end. He had won almost every race. It was entertaining at first. However, winning continually quickly soured Lord Dunthorpe's taste for racing. What was the point if there was no fear of losing?

"I have not purchased a horse. In fact, I can promise you that I won't even be attending any races for quite some time. I have bought a commission."

He looked back and forth between his sister and mother. Poor Lady Louisa held a boiled potato mid-air, with her mouth agape, unable to move.

"I don't understand," Lady Gilchrist finally said.

It was enough to wake her daughter and Lady Louisa set down her fork, suddenly put off her meal.

"I will be joining the Regulars, Mother. I have bought a lieutenant's commission and will be doing what is necessary for king and crown."

Lord Dunthorpe couldn't help but hold his head up high as he said these words. It was not for pride, but to show that he was confident in his choice.

"Did you know about this, Lord Gilchrist?" the Countess asked, turning significantly pale as she faced her husband.

"He informed me earlier this afternoon in my office, my dear."

"And you are in agreement with it?" she struggled out.

The Earl of Gilchrist looked between his wife and son. He would not lie for one, nor would he willingly bring more unease than necessary on the other.

"I am settled to the fact. Colton is old enough to do what he wishes with his own life. If this is the course he chooses, I will not stand in his way."

"But Colton," Lady Gilchrist said, with a visible shake to her voice, "what of the danger?"

"I promise I will be very considerate of my actions, Mother."

Lady Gilchrist promptly excused herself from the table, too overcome with emotion to stay much longer.

The room was silent as she left. Soon after, Lord Gilchrist went to console his wife. This left the two siblings alone in the dining room.

"You are very set on this, then?" Lady Louisa finally asked.

Colton felt his first pang of regret. Their whole lives, Colton had made it his mission to take care of and protect his younger sister. She was not only younger than him, but of a very meek nature. Between this and her moderately plain-featured looks, she had often been an easy target for a cruel miss.

"I am very set on this," he said softly.

"Then you will promise to write me often?"

Lord Dunthorpe and Lady Louisa may have had a few years of age between them, but they were still very close siblings. Lady Louisa had counted on him on a number of occasions to be her champion in times of distress. Not only that, but he had also brought much light and laughter to what might otherwise have been a very dull life for her.

"Of course I will," Lord Dunthorpe said, reaching across the table and taking his sister's hand. "Every day, if you wish it. So much, in fact, it will be as if I am still here and you wish me gone."

Lady Louisa gave a soft smile of relief at this promise. She had been at her brother's side so much of her life, she feared how she would go on with him away. What brought an even colder shudder to her was the thought that this endeavor might result in losing her brother permanently.

CHAPTER 1

"James, you little rascal. Where are you hiding?" Jackie called out down the long hall of Wintercrest Manor.

She took her slippered steps very carefully with her little cousin, Elisabeth, holding her hand. They paused for a moment, as Jackie was sure she heard a giggle.

Sure enough, the sound came again. It was the soft laughter of a three-year-old who couldn't contain himself. Elisabeth gave her own toddler laugh in reply, covering her mouth with her free cherubic hand.

"We've caught them now," Jackie said to her partner.

Jackie slid open the door to what seemed like an empty bedroom. She could, however, hear the rustle of bedding.

Jackie put a finger to her lips and pointed under the bed for Elisabeth's benefit. They both snuck over and got down on their knees before the long bed covering.

With a swift movement, Jackie lifted the bedding to reveal Elisabeth's twin brother hiding under the bed.

"Got you!" Elisabeth called out to him.

"Where is Aunt Abigail?" Jackie asked as she helped pull the three-year-old from under the bed.

It wasn't a room that was often used, and his clothes and dark hair were now covered in a light coating of dust.

James promptly sneezed as Jackie attempted to brush it off. Mrs. Murray wasn't one to rise to a temper, but she would be very unhappy to see the boy in such a state.

Elisabeth decided to search the room as Jackie did her best to brush her brother off. She knew her Aunt Abigail couldn't be far away from her hide-and-seek partner.

"Found you, too," Elisabeth called out as she poked behind a privacy screen.

There, she did find her Aunt Abigail, much too old for silly games, but still happily playing with her two nieces and nephew.

"Oh, dear. I thought I really had you fooled that time,"

Lady Abigail Grant said as she was led by the hand from behind the curtain.

"Aunt Abigail couldn't fit under the bed," James said with a giggle.

"I could so fit," Lady Abigail retorted with a hand on her hip. "I just didn't want to get all dusty like you."

The children all happily laughed with their aunt before she returned them all to the nursery. It would soon be time for Lady Abigail to dress for dinner.

"May I come down with you too, tonight?" Jackie asked.

"I am afraid not. We are to have Captain Jones and a few of his officers from the militia with us tonight."

"But I am almost twelve years old. Certainly that is old enough," Jackie retorted.

Lady Abigail knew that her niece was now at that age where she no longer wanted to be treated as a child left in the nursery. She had struggled with the same frustrations as a young girl.

"I know it doesn't seem fair now, but you would not want to come anyway. "Captain Jones is an ancient, very boring man. I fear you would fall asleep during your first course and never want to come to dinner again," Lady Abigail added, trying to make it seem less enticing.

"I don't care, I still want to go," Jackie grumbled.

"I know, my dear. Very soon you will and wish you didn't have to."

Lady Abigail would have been more than happy to stay the night in the nursery with the twins and let Jackie go in her place. Not only was Captain Jones incredibly unentertaining, he was also very long-winded.

It was going to be a very long night of pretending to be interested. Lady Abigail's only hope was that at least one of the three lieutenants that would be joining the captain would be of some interest.

Lady Abigail was now nineteen years old and of a marrying age. She thought the prospect of finding a gentleman who would interest her very unlikely. They all wanted a quiet, prim, proper lady. That was not Abigail at all.

She much rather fancied the idea of marrying an officer instead. Though he might not have been one of the peerages, he was undoubtedly considered a gentleman. Men of this social standing would also be less likely to be put off by a less than gentle manner.

Lady Abigail had of course been bred to be an entirely proper lady by her parents, the Duke and Duchess of Wintercrest. They also had, however, given her the freedom to grow into her own personality.

Lady Abigail hoped to marry someday. She wished to find that love that seemed to defy any barricades of social standards, as her brother, the current Duke of Wintercrest, had done when he first met his wife, Isabella.

She, however, did not want to marry solely because social graces dictated that she do so. If she did marry, she had long ago determined it would be someone she loved dearly and who would care for her just as she would them.

Sadly, Lady Abigail was sorely disappointed with the night's dinner guests. Captain Jones had brought three of his lieutenants and a colonel. The colonel was much too old for Lady Abigail's liking, two of the three lieutenants were already married, and the third betrothed.

Lady Abigail half wondered if her brother had purposefully only invited the otherwise unavailable to dinner that night.

The duke often had the high-ranking officers from the

militia come to dinner when they were in the area. It was an important gesture for him to give, but it also allowed nostalgia for his own days in the Royal Navy.

The duke was aware that Abigail was now of the age when courtships became pressing and engagements were on the horizon. He rather overprotected her when it came to opportunities of meeting gentlemen.

"You know he did it on purpose," Lady Abigail said softly to her sister-in-law after dinner.

The whole party was now seated in the drawing room. The men were by the fire talking politics while Lady Abigail, Isabella, the Duchess of Wintercrest, and the dowager duchess played a game of cards.

"I am quite certain he did do it on purpose," the duchess agreed.

"What a rotten thing it is to do," Lady Abigail said, setting down her cards rather exaggeratedly.

"What is it you two are whispering about?" Lady Abigail's mother asked over her own hand of cards.

The dowager duchess was now deteriorating quickly in her older age. Lady Abigail suspected, with the loss of her husband a few years back, her mother had since lost much of the light in her life.

Lady Abigail's parents could not have been more opposite creatures. Not only were they different in manners and personality, but there was a very vast age difference. For an outsider to look in on their marriage, it would have been assumed the arrangement was made for practical purposes.

It was well known, however, by all the late duke and dowager duchess's children that their parents did, in fact, have a deep affection for each other.

"Abigail is not very happy to see that the gentlemen invited tonight are not of her preference," the duchess explained to her mother-in-law.

"Your brother hopes better for you than a common militiaman," Lady Abigail's mother explained.

Lady Abigail didn't like this response, nor did she look forward to the idea of her overly protective brother choosing dinner guests in the future.

"Don't worry," the duchess said, taking her sister-in-law's hand and patting it softly. "Soon, the season will be upon us. You will have more suitors than you know what to do with."

It was an accurate statement that, due to Lady Abigail's beauty, she caught the eye of many potential suitors during her time in London each year. What was upsetting to her was that, so far, no one had caught her eye in return.

Lady Abigail brushed a rust-colored ringlet back from her shoulder. It was an act of irritation that both the duchess and Lady Abigail's mother knew well.

"I have to say, I am surprised that His Grace is allowing you to go at all," Lady Abigail said with emphasis on her brother's proper title.

The duchess patted her belly that was beginning to show the swell of life beneath.

" I have plenty of time before this little one comes. I have been away from London for so long, I could not bear to spend another season away. And as for the duke," she said with a raised brow, "I did not ask. I merely announced my intentions."

All three ladies laughed at this. They had become quite a close trio with all the time they had spent together over the last four years.

Though up until now the duchess had chosen to stay home with her young children, Lady Abigail and her mother had still attended the season at their lavish city house. They always came home in time to spend the remainder of the year with the duke, duchess, their ever-growing family, and the late Lord James Grant's daughter, Jaqueline De'belmount.

"You will give my best to my sister, won't you?" Lady Abigail's mother asked after they all contained their rather girlish giggles.

"Of course I will," Lady Abigail assured her mother.

Lady Abigail rather looked forward to her time each year in London, less for the prospects and more for time with her favorite cousin, Lady Fortuna Rosh. She dearly loved this extension of her family and, in times past, had spent many weeks visiting with her uncle and aunt, the Marquess and Marchioness of Huntington.

"I do wish you would come though, Mother," Lady Abigail added.

"I am not feeling at all up to it this year. Plus, with all three of my grandchildren staying here at Wintercrest, I dare say I will be much happier to have them about than the ladies of the town."

"I must confess, I am happy to have you here with them too," the duchess added. "It will be my first time away from the twins. I didn't think I could do it but knowing you will be with them brings me comfort."

"Remember you said that, my dear, for when you return, you may find them entirely spoiled," Lady Abigail's mother said with a happy glow around her aging face.

Lady Abigail couldn't help but notice that, despite the wrinkles that now curled around her brown eyes and the large amounts of silver hair that glowed in the light of candles, her mother was still a gorgeous woman.

CHAPTER 2

"I still don't think it's a good idea for you to go," the duke said the following night as the whole household sat around the fire.

"Don't worry, my love," the duchess reassured her husband. "I will be able to go to town and return home at the end of the season all before this little one is even ready to come out."

"But the twins came early. What if that happens again?"

"It has only been two months since we discovered the pregnancy. I can't imagine that this child will make its debut so vastly early as to arrive in London."

"Still, all this traveling in your condition makes me

nervous," the duke said, taking his wife's hand and kissing it gently.

"I don't want to go to town just for myself, but also for Abigail. With your mother not feeling up to it this year, she will need a chaperone."

"I can be her chaperone," the duke retorted.

Isabella had to smile at this idea. Protecting Lady Abigail from having her brother as her chaperone was what she had meant. She loved her husband dearly, but he was far too protective of his younger sister.

Not to mention the fact that there would be many instances where Lady Abigail would be in need of a female chaperone to make her way among afternoon parties with other ladies. Finding your place was just as much dependent on these social gatherings as the more commonly thought of balls and large evening events.

"I think it will be more to her comfort if I am there with her," the duchess tried to explain as efficiently as possible to her husband.

She watched the fire glow reflected off his red hair as he swiveled his look from his wife on the couch to his sister sitting at a distant table with the twins. His angular face darkened as he tried to make sense of her meaning.

"I am not that horrible," he said once all the lines connected in his head.

"My love, were you not there at last night's dinner party? Could you not have invited at least one gentleman for Abigail to have found even an ounce of interest in?"

"She is far too good for a militiaman," the duke retorted.

"I didn't mean for her to marry, though I would be happy for her no matter what vocation the person she chooses to marry has. She is young and in want of some excitement. I fear, with just you taking her to London, her whole season would be much like that dinner party."

"It's just hard for me. She is my little sister, after all."

"I know," the duchess said softly, touching her husband's cheek. "I fear the day that Elisabeth comes of age. Even Jackie, for that matter," Isabella added with a smile.

The duke looked at the whole of his family in the drawing room. Though Jackie was his niece, he had treated her as if she was his own daughter and not just his ward to take care of. He could scarcely imagine his own behavior when the time came for either Jackie or his darling little Elisabeth.

Lady Abigail couldn't help but sneak a peek at her brother and his wife as they spoke on the couch by the fire. Though their relationship had begun on unsure waters, it had blossomed into something wonderful.

As Isabella ran a soft hand along her husband's face, Lady Abigail felt that pang of wistfulness deep inside her heart. She wondered if she, too, would ever find someone that she could look upon with such love and admiration as her sister-in-law did on her brother.

"Lord James, Lady Elisabeth," the children's governess, Miss Smith, called from her seat. "It is just about time to retire to bed."

The announcement woke Lady Abigail from her wishful thinking. Her young niece and nephew's governess was a very time efficient lady. Everything seemed to run on an exact schedule.

Lady Abigail expected it was a necessity when dealing with two children of the same age. Not only did that mean double the mischief, but they also seemed to have a unique connection between them that often led to more trouble.

Miss Smith had taken over the task of educating Miss Jackie after the previous governess had found a better situation. That, of course, was the Duchess of

Wintercrest. Though the twins were still too young for formal education, Miss Smith had happily taken on the task of including them whenever possible.

"Aunt Abigail, will you read to us before we have to go to bed?" James asked in his sweet voice.

Lady Abigail saw that Elisabeth already had a book in hand for her to read to them.

"We only have but a moment. I would hate to make Miss Smith cross," Lady Abigail said, taking the book from the little hand.

"Do come read it over here, so we may all hear it," Lady Abigail's mother called from her seat close to the fire.

Lady Abigail did as she was bid. With a child on either side, she walked over and sat before the fire.

Jackie, too, who was at first playing the piano, also stopped to come and listen. She happily took the spot next to her grandmother.

Sitting on the floor near the warm glow of the fire, Lady Abigail began to read. It was an enjoyable pastime that the family participated in each night.

The twins, and even Jackie, though she felt herself now too old to admit it, loved when Lady Abigail read to them.

She always did it with the most animated of voices and emotions that it quite nearly brought the stories right off the pages of the book.

By the end of the week, matters between the duke and duchess were all settled and the pair, along with Lady Abigail, were setting out on the long journey to town.

The duchess tried her best to hide her tears as she kissed her children goodbye. Though it might have been a very usual thing for a duchess to leave her children to see to social duties, it was not something Isabella did.

Of course, though the duchess knew that her children would be more than well cared for in the hands of her mother-in-law and Jackie, she was still torn by the thought of leaving them. The added emotions that came with her pregnancy didn't seem to help the matter much.

"I received a letter from Fortuna yesterday," Lady Abigail said once they were all seated in the carriage and away down the road.

Lady Abigail hoped that some exciting conversation might help distract her sister-in-law from her sorrowful feelings.

"How lovely," the duchess said, doing her best to put on a brave face. "Did she have anything of interest to say?"

Isabella was happy for the distraction, just as much as Lady Abigail was for giving it.

"They have already arrived in London. With the weather being so warm, they went early this year."

The duke and duchess both looked out their windows at this, almost to confirm that it was, in fact, unusually warm for the time of year.

"Aunt Amelia has invited us all over for dinner at our earliest convenience."

"That was very kind of her," Isabella responded. "I have been looking forward to meeting these relations that I have heard so much about over the years."

"You will really like Fortuna, I think," Lady Abigail continued, now falling into an ease of conversation. "She is very much like Lady Louisa."

"How so?" the duchess asked, intrigued.

They spent the remainder of the day describing every last detail of the relatives Isabella was soon to meet. The duchess was always happy to meet the family of her husband, as she was very limited in her own.

Lady Louisa Frasier and her family had often taken Isabella under their wing as her only family, since her father, the Baron Leinster, had often been away attending to business before his passing. The Frasiers were the closest thing that Isabella had ever had to family dynamics.

When she and the duke had married, she was joyful to find that she was welcomed with open arms into not just his heart, but the whole of his household and family.

"Perhaps we should plan our own event," Lady Abigail said, after a time. "We could invite Lord and Lady Gilchrist, as well as our aunt and uncle. I think we would all get on as such a happy party."

"I think that would be a splendid idea," the duchess agreed.

"It seems to me," interjected the duke, who, for the most part, had kept to observing the scenery as they went along the road, "that it might be a lot of work for someone who promised to take it easy."

The duchess waved him off as a silly man.

"It will give me something to occupy my mind with."

For the next three days, as the trio traveled from the estate up north to the prestigious house in London, Lady Abigail and the duchess were hard at work making plans for a beautiful dinner party.

Arriving, finally, at their destination, both women could

honestly say they would be happy never to sit in another carriage again. They made their way into the home already opened and prepared for their arrival, ready for a peaceful day of relaxation and recuperation.

"Perhaps both you ladies should retire early for the night," the duke said as the carriage arrived at the house at dusk.

"I promised Louisa I would send her a note as soon as I got here."

The duke didn't like his wife's answer to his suggestion, but allowed it nonetheless. He therefore had some tea brought into the evening sitting room so she could write her letter and regain some energy from the refreshments.

"I thought I might call on my aunt tomorrow," Lady Abigail said between sips of tea. "I'm sure she would be happy to see you, Christian, and meet you, Isabella, if you're feeling up to it."

"Well, I think after talking about them for three days, I can't bear to go much longer without meeting them," Isabella said as she finished her letter and folded it for a servant to deliver.

Normally Isabella would have just waited to put it with the post, but since Lady Louisa seemed most anxious to know that Isabella was safely in London, she thought it best to have it taken to the Frasier household right away.

"And perhaps we could take a walk around the park, too," Lady Abigail added.

"Perhaps it's best to stick to one event at a time," the duke admonished.

"You're a ball of fun," his sister retorted back in a teasing fashion.

"Yes, well you know how much your brother loves to spend the season in town," the duchess added to the jeering.

"Well, I would guess that you just want to catch the next gig race," the duke retorted to his sister with a raised red brow. "I am not at all certain that it's a very good idea for you."

"Why, because ladies should be abashed by such behavior?" Lady Abigail retorted.

"No, because I fear you might climb into one and show them all up. Then I would have to write to Mother and explain why her daughter is now a pariah."

"You wouldn't do that, would you?" the duchess asked Lady Abigail.

It was not at all shocking to hear that Lady Abigail wanted to attend a race, but to be a part of one seemed like an even more drastic line to cross than she could imagine for her sister-in-law.

"I may have done it, once before. But that was at Fortuna's house and in a basket, not a gig," Lady Abigail corrected her brother.

"Yes, well, things are different when you are in London. You are also a very prestigious member of the town, whether you want it or not, and that comes with more judgmental appraisals."

"This is not my first time, Christian. I am well aware of the conduct I must follow."

" I don't think you do fully understand," the duke retorted. He should have uttered it in a reprimanding tone, but instead, he wore a smirk of pride.

The duke detested the time in town because, unlike his sister who still had a bit of leeway to enjoy herself, he had to act exactly as expected of someone of his social status.

"Do try not to make too big a spectacle of yourself this year, Abigail," the duke finally sighed.

"Of course not, dear brother. Plus, Isabella will keep me in line, won't you?"

It was right that, of the trio, the duchess was the one most keen to sensibility and propriety. She sincerely hoped that she could instill some of those values in Lady Abigail without disrupting her free spirit too much.

CHAPTER 3

Lady Abigail couldn't have been more excited to see her cousin. Though it had scarcely been a year since seeing Lady Fortuna Rosh last, it still seemed too long to Lady Abigail.

The two cousins had grown up as close friends since childhood. There was not much that happened to one that the other did not know about.

The Duchess of Wintercrest was a little nervous to meet the family she had heard such great praise about, from both Lady Abigail and her husband.

"Oh, Abigail, I've missed you so," Lady Huntington said as she hugged her niece. "And Christian, look at you," she added, raising a hand to a plump, rosy cheek at the appearance of her nephew. "You have grown into quite a man. How long has it been?"

The duke happily took his aunt's hand and kissed it lovingly. Lady Huntington blushed an even more profound crimson as the small ringlets encircling her face shook with her giggles.

"And Your Grace, of course, it is lovely to finally make your acquaintance," Lady Huntington said as the duke introduced his wife.

"I must confess, poor Isabella must feel as if she knows you already, dear aunt," Lady Abigail said as they all entered the home and came to sit in the morning room. "I about chewed her ear off the whole way from Wintercrest."

"Where is Fortuna?" Lady Abigail asked when her cousin did not greet her or appear in the sitting room.

"She went out already this morning. It was a little early if you ask me, but she insisted on going with Josie to pick out the fabric."

"Fabric for what?" Lady Abigail asked as she took a seat on a mint-colored couch.

The whole room was decorated in a soft green color with gold accents all around. Between that and the excellent light coming in through the window, it gave the room an air of freshness that would brighten even the saddest of moods.

"I will have to let her tell you. She is quite excited about it," Lady Huntington said before beginning to pour the tea set before them.

Lady Abigail enjoyed the company of her aunt as she drank her delicate morning tea and ate moist muffins. The whole party, including her brother, seemed utterly at ease as they shared stories of memories from the past.

Lady Abigail was just picking at a loose thread coming off the embroidered cuff of her morning dress and wondering where her cousin could be when Lady Fortuna finally returned home.

Immediately, Lady Abigail rose to greet her cousin, forgetting all about the rose-colored cuff. It also didn't escape her eye that behind Lady Fortuna's entrance into the party was a maid heavily weighed down with a massive amount of fabric.

"Now, before you do anything," Lady Abigail said after new introductions were made between the duchess and Lady Fortuna, "you must enlighten me on your mysterious morning endeavors."

Lady Fortuna, who sat perfectly next to her mother,

looked more akin to a china doll than lady. She seemed far too fragile to be traveling about in early morning dew.

She was always one to think things through before speaking, so instead of starting right in, as Lady Abigail might have done, she instead smoothed the folds of her cream morning dress as she collected her thoughts.

As Lady Abigail waited, she wondered over the color of her cousin's dress. It somewhat made her look more pale and fragile. She thought to perhaps tell Lady Fortuna that cream was not a preferable color for her. Certainly, a soft blue would do better to bring out the little color in her cheeks and azure color of her cousin's eyes.

"Well, upon arriving in London last week, I was determined to find a good use of my time. While at home, I have been very fortunate to have a large amount of work for myself, under the request of Reverend Brown, attending to the needs of our local girls' school."

She took a deep breath of air. Lady Abigail couldn't help but wonder why her cousin always looked about to faint from weariness when she knew Lady Fortuna to be a lady of many talents and busy hands.

"He recommended, before our leaving for town, that I get in touch with a very good friend of his, a Mr.

Thomas Bloomsbury. Mr. Bloomsbury is a rector at the Foundling Hospital here in London."

Lady Abigail was familiar with the Foundling Hospital. It was a place for children whose parents had, unfortunately, had to surrender them. The hospice was used to care for the children, as well as give them a good education and means for apprenticeship when they came of age.

It had already been around for several decades and had received not only high praise for its work but had also been replicated a few times in different areas of the country since.

"Mr. Brown informed me that his friend was concerned about the constant need at the hospital. They have more children than required funds for the necessary provisions."

Lady Abigail knew that helping less fortunate children was very dear to her cousin's heart. She had been given the Christian name Fortuna because she had been a miracle in her parents lives. For many years they had tried unsuccessfully to have children, and then when they were finally able, their plans seemed destined for heartache and pain.

They buried four of Lady Fortuna's siblings before she

was born. With her sickly demeanor, they had expected her to go the way of all her predecessors. Lady Fortuna had grown and thrived, however. Her parents instilled in her the deep gratitude of her survival.

For Lady Fortuna, this gratitude showed in her constant willingness to help all other children as much as she could. She felt that if she were able to help one sick child get better, or perhaps give one impoverished child a better start in life, she would be doing the work that God had preserved her for.

"I wrote to Mr. Bloomsbury and asked to help in any way they needed. I met with him and toured the hospital. He explained to me that, more often than not, the funds they receive go to clothing and bedding, making it difficult for them to buy supplies for educational purposes. He wondered if I might be willing to donate clothing and the like so that their funds could be used for a better cause."

"Which explains the need to go to the fabric store so early in the morning and to burden your maid so heavily," the duke said with a teasing smile.

"I thought perhaps I could start with making nightgowns, uniforms, pinafores, and bonnets for the children. They are also in need of proper bedding and winter garments."

"That is quite a tall order for just beginning," Lady Abigail said. She often feared her cousin took on more than she was able to adequately cope with.

"Well, I rather hoped to start a sewing group. This is where I was hoping you could help me, Abigail," Lady Fortuna continued. "You are so good at making friends. I hoped you would help me organize a group of ladies to meet a few times a week."

"Well, I have your first candidate right here," Lady Abigail said, pointing to the duchess. "I have never seen anyone embroider as finely as Isabella."

"I would love to join if you would have me. The idea sounds wonderful," Isabella agreed.

"Oh, Your Grace, I would appreciate that very much if you would be willing."

"I also might suggest another addition if you would let me," the duchess continued.

Lady Fortuna nodded in encouragement.

"My friend Lady Louisa Frasier is a very talented seamstress. I am sure she too would be happy to join your worthy cause."

"Oh, this is so exciting," Lady Fortuna said, clapping her hands with delight. "To already have so many potential ladies, I do not doubt that we will make a wonderful improvement to the Foundling Hospital and its residents."

"Well, just two besides yourself," the duke said with a little laugh.

"Three you mean, dear cousin," Lady Fortuna countered. "There is your lovely wife, possibly her friend, and Abigail, of course."

The duke struggled to hold back his laughter.

"Oh, Fortuna, I would be happy to rally to your cause, but you know I have no ability when it comes to sewing. I am dreadful at it, in fact."

"I know it isn't your strong suit," Lady Fortuna said, always trying to see the light through the clouds. "I thought perhaps we could just start you on something very simple like the bedding or pinafores."

"Oh, yes, Abigail. That would be easy enough," the duchess added encouragingly. "You could make the pinafores; it's just a simple stitch. Then when you are done, I could embellish them just a little to give each girl her own special pattern."

"Maybe you should have Abigail start with a handkerchief instead. That way if it goes wrong, at least it will spend most of its time in a pocket or up a sleeve," the duke said with a hearty laugh.

Lady Abigail gave her teasing brother a pointed look. She knew Christian meant his words all in good fun. To be completely honest with herself, she partly agreed with him. But Lady Abigail also was not one to shy away from a challenge.

So often, Lady Abigail found sewing and embroidery too dull to catch her attention for very long. She would much rather be out and about exploring the beautiful earth.

She was sure the image of children wearing comfortable, warm clothes and having the tools necessary for their education would be more than sufficient inspiration to put her whole focus to the task.

"I would be more than happy to help," Lady Abigail said, wrinkling her freckled nose at her brother.

CHAPTER 4

As decided earlier, on the way home from their aunt's house, the party paused to take a ride around the very popular Hyde Park. It didn't escape the duke's attention that his sister's whole intent behind this diversion was not to be seen as most fine ladies wished, but instead to peek her own glance at the notorious activity.

"Come now, let your sister have some enjoyment," Isabella said to her husband when he seemed to be steering their open carriage completely clear of the route.

What had once been the King's private road was now more commonly used by daring gentlemen in gigs with fast horses.

"It is not as if she is asking to witness dueling. You, yourself, told me that on occasion you drove your witnessed races along that course. Do not deprive her of a small amount of fun."

The duke seemed to roll this over in his mind, before finally turning down the desired path. With any luck, no one would be there. It was, after all, just starting to be the fashionable time for turns around the park. More often, races occurred toward the end of night.

Much to the duke's disappointment, and his sister's excitement, there was, in fact, a group of gentlemen preparing for a friendly race.

Lady Abigail sat up immediately in her spot to scan the crowd for familiar faces. She was acquainted with several of the ladies who stood off to the side as the gentlemen prepared their steeds.

Lady Abigail was happy to see that the race at that moment would be between three men on horseback. She found this to be far more exciting than gig races.

Without hesitation, she hopped down from the carriage and made her way over to some familiar ladies.

"This seems like it will be quite the exciting event," Miss Mary Johansson said after Lady Abigail made her introductions and inquiries to friends since last they met.

Miss Mary was the daughter of a Baron who had not much more than the title to his name. She was, however, a beauty in the extreme and Lady Abigail did not doubt that she would marry up in life.

Though they were not entirely close friends, they were, however, acquaintances that often frequented the same groups and less than desirable events for ladies such as this.

Lady Abigail looked over the riders. Two she knew well. They were usual contestants here on the King's private road. Though they had long since outgrown the age of young pups, they still seemed to wish to prove themselves.

The third rider was a man she had never seen before. She couldn't help but let her eyes linger on him as he checked his saddle and the condition of his horse.

He was dressed very finely in a velvet riding jacket and matching brown trousers. His high boots looked to be of excellent black leather, and the crop in his hand was held with an air of confidence.

"Who is that gentleman in the middle? I don't think I have ever made his acquaintance."

"Why, that is Lord Franklin Stuartson, Earl of Heshing, Lady Abigail," Miss Mary instructed, happy to have a bit of information to dole out.

"Heshing," Lady Abigail thought the name over. It did have a bit of familiarity to it.

"I believe this is one of his first seasons in town. He has just taken his father's seat in the House of Lords this year."

Lady Abigail figured the name was only familiar to her by way of passing word from her father or brother. She took a mental note to perhaps ask the duke about the gentleman when he was slightly less of a vexing older brother.

The riders mounted their steeds and prepared for the long stretch of road ahead of them. The small crowd clapped in excitement.

"Have you placed a bet?" Miss Mary asked, motioning to Lord Fenton, who was the usual orchestrator of such events.

Lady Abigail looked over at her brother. He had just finished helping Isabella down from the carriage and together they were making their way over. Had she been here without him, she would have happily placed a sixpence on Lord Heshing.

It was not at all proper for ladies to witness such events, let alone bet on them. She decided it was best, with her brother present, not to do so.

Lady Abigail couldn't help but notice the gasp and whispers that surrounded her brother as he escorted his wife over to witness the race. It made more sense to her now why he had been so uptight over the course of their trip. People undoubtedly thought differently of him now that he was the Duke of Wintercrest.

"I have never seen one of these before," the duchess said, coming to Lady Abigail's side. "It does seem rather exciting."

She leaned closer to Lady Abigail's ear, "Don't tell Christian, but I put a bet on the chestnut mare."

Lady Abigail looked at her sister-in-law with shock. The Duchess of Wintercrest, for the most part, was a very proper lady. It was no surprise that this was her first race, but slightly scandalous that she had placed a bet.

Lady Abigail looked over the chestnut mare and rider. It was Lord Heshing, spoken of before. She certainly hoped he won and told herself it was for the reason of the duchess's bet.

Within a flash, the race was on, and the three men went speeding down the road. The goal of the race was to travel the whole length, turning just before Kensington Gardens, and making the full length back. The first rider to cross the line drawn at the start would be the winner.

Not only would he have the pride of winning the race, but he would also get to take home his companions' steeds.

For many gentlemen, the time-consuming act of training, purchasing well-bred horses, and racing was merely to pass the time. For a select few, such as Mr. Shawn James, second son to Viscount Sheffield, who now pressed his horse with every ounce of strength, the gamble of a race was a chance to make something more of oneself.

The crowd quietly chatted together as the riders disappeared from view. Each member had their own opinion of who was in the lead and the prospect of the return trip.

It wasn't long before the loud sound of hoofs again reverberated on the gravel road. All eyes watched and bodies leaned, to get the first glimpse of the rider first to come into view.

Lady Abigail held in her cheer on seeing that it was Lord Heshing in the lead. Mr. James was quickly gaining on the earl and Abigail was torn with nerves. She knew it would be more right for her to wish Mr. James to win the race, as he was sure to need the win more than an earl, but she couldn't help but wish the champion to be the intriguing new lord.

Finally, the last seconds of the race were upon them. Some in the crowd began to shout or cheer in the final moments. It was just barely by a nose of the horse that Lord Heshing won the race.

Lady Abigail couldn't help but cheer along with her sister-in-law who had won the bet, but with no experience, had no idea what that meant, exactly.

"Your Grace," Lord Fenton said, coming up to the duke, having not yet been introduced to his wife, "here are your winnings. Congratulations."

"I thank you, Fenton," the duke said, "but I did not place any bets."

Lord Fenton looked between the duke and the rest of the trio, a little unsure what to do.

"Was this your doing?" the duke turned on Lady Abigail.

"It was mine, actually," Isabella said with an upturned chin. "I've always wanted to bet on a horse race. I must be very good at it as well, seeing how I won my first try."

She promptly removed the money from Lord Fenton's hands as they were introduced to each other by way of her husband.

The duke smiled softly at his wife and, with a shaking head, laughed.

"I believe my sister has been a bad influence on you," he said.

"Not at all. If anything, my love, it is you that has been the influence. In fact, you seemed to know Lord Fenton very well for someone shaming his sister for attending such adventures."

"It is one thing for a man to be present at races, a lady is entirely different."

"And what of a duke and duchess?" she retorted with a smile on her lips.

"I suppose we will discover that tomorrow in the gossip column. Come, you two. Let us be off before we are noticed any more than we have been."

"Oh, please may I go congratulate the rider first? You said you know him," the duchess asked her husband in her sweet way.

SAVING LADY ABIGAIL 61

Lady Abigail's heart did a little leap at the thought of meeting this handsome man who seemed to be the champion of the hour.

The duke led the two ladies over to Lord Heshing. He was gratefully taking the congratulations from others as he stroked his beautiful steed.

"Your Grace," he said, with a bow to the duke.

"Please let me have the pleasure of introducing my wife, the Duchess of Wintercrest, and younger sister, Lady Abigail Grant."

Lord Heshing politely bowed and greeted both ladies.

"It was fortunate you happened to stop by today," Lord Heshing said to the duke. "I would have hated to lose a race in front of Your Grace."

"If I heard correctly the rumors swirling around the crowd of onlookers, losing doesn't happen too often for you," the duke retorted.

"Though I suspect that would not be the case if it were still your day of horse races."

Both Lady Abigail and the duchess looked at the duke in utter shock.

"His Grace was quite a legend," Lord Heshing said in

answer to their expressions.

"And here you were giving me such a hard time," Lady Abigail said. "And you used to actually race horses yourself?"

"It was a very long time ago, when I was just a young pup without a dukedom to consider."

"Still, you teased me all morning long," Lady Abigail said with hands on her hips.

"Unfortunately, Lord Heshing, I may never speak to you again as you have just ruined my image in front of my wife and given my sister sufficient cause to vex me for many days," the duke said in a teasing fashion.

"Oh, absolutely not. I think I rather like Lord Heshing's honesty about your youthful years. I think we must have him over for dinner soon to hear more of your galivanting tales," the duchess retorted.

"I would be most honored by such an invitation, Your Grace," Heshing said with a slight bow.

Lady Abigail couldn't help but notice that though he spoke the words to Isabella, he did it with eyes on her. It sent little chills of excitement up and down her spine as his soft brown eyes seemed to see deep inside her inner self and find it of interest.

CHAPTER 5

The following day, Lady Abigail accompanied her sister-in-law to visit the Gilchrist family.

It was a very small gathering, as Lady Abigail had expected. Lady Louisa's oldest brother, who she had heard much of but never met, was still away with the Royal Army. Her father had passed away just over a year ago, very unfortunately.

Lady Abigail thought fondly of the late Earl of Gilchrist as they walked up the steps to the white London house. Though she had only met him on a few occasions, she had found him to be a very kind and loving gentleman.

Lady Gilchrist opened the door, still completely covered in a black dress though it had been over a year since her husband's passing. It was a stark contrast to her pale skin and blonde hair of almost the same pale sheen.

"My dear Isabella," she said, taking her daughter's closest friend in a motherly embrace.

Lady Gilchrist paused to rub a hand over Isabella's small belly. It was, after all, the closest Lady Gilchrist had to a grandchild.

Soon they were joined by Lady Louisa in the drawing room. Unlike her mother, who chose to still dress in mourning, Lady Louisa had decided on a slightly lighter navy-colored dress.

Very often, young maidens would choose muted and pastel colors, as Lady Abigail and Lady Fortuna had worn the day before. Lady Louisa, however, was now reaching past the age of a possible match.

She had resigned herself to the thoughts of spinsterhood in the care of her mother. With that decision, she happily turned from creams and florals to much darker colors of dress. She had felt it an acceptable turn for not only her age, but the loss of her father.

"I was so glad to hear your whole party was able to return to London safely," Lady Gilchrist said as tea and a small sandwich tray was placed before them, having just arrived in time for luncheon.

"I was so concerned for your condition. Jostling about in a carriage cannot be good for your constitution," the lady continued.

"I can assure you that the duke saw to my every comfort as we traveled. I rather felt like a princess escorted across her country in his company," Isabella assured Lady Gilchrist.

"How is His Grace?" Lady Louisa asked.

"A right pain in the side, if you ask me," Lady Abigail said before another answer could be given.

The Duke of Wintercrest had not ceased in teasing his little sister over the course of the last day on the matter of her sewing skills. She, however, had some jabbing words of her own with the knowledge from Lord Heshing that her brother used to be one of those rake gentlemen who raced on the King's road.

"He is doing very well," the duchess corrected. "However, there is a bit of sibling squabble going on at the moment."

Lady Louisa had a far-off look, as if she too remembered a time when she enjoyed the companionship of a sibling held dear to her.

"How is Colton?" the duchess asked her dear friend, sensing her turn of mind.

Isabella knew that the Frasier family had not had just the hardship of losing a father but had also been struggling with the condition of the newly instated Earl of Gilchrist.

Several months ago, Colton Frasier, Earl of Gilchrist, was severely injured while serving the crown in endeavors against France. The duchess was not entirely sure of the details, but she was aware that, since that time, he had been recovering in a hospital.

She often wondered if it was the news of his son's severe injury that caused the Earl of Gilchrist to lose his health, because he passed not long after receiving news on his son.

"In his last letter, he seemed very hopeful to be returning home shortly. He explained to me that he has been healing well from his injuries and is again feeling the strength to travel."

Both Lady Gilchrist and Lady Louisa's faces fell with a sorrowful countenance at the reminder of recent life events.

"How exciting it must be for you, to have your dear

brother returned to you," Lady Abigail said, doing her best to brighten the mood.

"Will he be returning here to town for the season?" she added, to encourage pleasant conversation.

"I do hope so," Lady Gilchrist said.

"Well, after hearing all the wonderful tales about the earl, I am more than excited to meet him myself," Lady Abigail continued. "We must throw a party in his honor when he returns.

"I think that would be a wonderful idea," the duchess agreed. "That is, of course, if you think he will be up to it?"

"It's hard to say," Lady Louisa said with a furrow of her brow. "He has not very clearly explained all that has occurred. Instead, he constantly repeated that his injuries are little and of no consequence."

"But then, he has been in hospital for so long," the duchess continued for her friend. "Surely that must mean his injuries were very serious to need so much time before he could leave."

"I will just be happy when he is finally home," Lady Gilchrist said with a dark shadow over her face.

"Of course," the duchess said, taking Lady Gilchrist's hand in hers for comfort.

"Let us talk of other things. Words of my son's condition makes me so uneasy," Lady Gilchrist finally said.

Lady Abigail took the opportunity to propose the primary purpose of their visit that day. It was no surprise that Lady Louisa was more than happy to join their little seamstress cause. It was decided that, twice a week, all the ladies would meet together to socialize and work on their notions.

At first, the duchess encouraged the ladies to meet at her exceptional London home for these gatherings, but in the end, it was decided it would be more entertaining if each meeting was held at a different lady's house on a rotation.

Lady Abigail later reflected on the mysterious Lord Colton Frasier, Earl of Gilchrist, as she dressed for dinner. Not only had the Duchess of Wintercrest talked incessantly of him but also her brother, who met him the last season before his military departure, had spoken of his high character.

She suspected, from all the stories and descriptions, he was much like her own brother. Lord Gilchrist was always spoken of as a Cheshire cat type of character with a charming smile, wit, and excellent humor.

She couldn't help but want to meet the man who had been so connected to her society for the last several years, and yet was always away.

It was at dinner that Lady Abigail discovered her chance of meeting the gentleman had come.

"I have just received a note from Lady Louisa," the duchess said excitedly to her husband and sister-in-law at the dining table. "You will never guess who arrived on their doorstep, without so much as a message in advance, right after we left?"

Isabella paused to take a breath, "It was Colton!"

"How wonderful! I'm glad to hear the fellow will be in town. It might be nice to have someone to converse with during all these tedious events," the duke answered.

Though the family had just arrived in town two short days ago, Lady Abigail was finding her social calendar to be quickly filling up. Apparently, with the Duke and Duchess of Wintercrest both in attendance this season, just about everyone was hoping for them to grace their social event.

"We must start at once to plan a dinner party to

celebrate his return," the duchess continued. "I thought something small with just our families would be appropriate."

Lady Abigail had to smile at her words. Though the Frasiers were not Isabella's biological family, they were still very much family to her. It only increased the already high opinion Lady Abigail had of them all.

The following day, Lady Abigail and the Duke and Duchess of Wintercrest returned to Lady Louisa's house by invitation for an afternoon of socialization before they were to attend a ball held at the home of the Duke of Northingshire.

It was the first significant event of the season for Lady Abigail and she was happy to know that she would be accompanied not only by her sister-in-law, but also Lady Louisa's family.

With every meeting she had with the Frasier household, she felt more and more endeared to them.

She also couldn't help but hold a little anticipation in her stomach for finally meeting the earl she had been told so much about.

"Where is the earl?" Christian asked as he sat down in the drawing room, with only the ladies of the house to greet them.

"I am sure he will be down presently," Lady Louisa said with an unease about her.

The duchess picked up on this instantly. They were such great friends, it was hard for one to feel something that the other didn't immediately notice, even in written form.

"Is everything alright with Colton?" the duchess asked with her own worry in her throat.

"Yes, of course," Lady Louisa attempted to ease the mood. "He is whole and home again and that is all that matters."

Lady Abigail had the strangest feeling that Lady Louisa was more convincing herself than informing them. Her thoughts were confirmed when Lady Gilchrist suddenly removed herself from the party, so overcome with emotion.

Lady Abigail couldn't help but wonder what had both ladies in such distress. Lady Louisa said he came home whole, but perhaps that was not entirely the case. She had heard that so often while in the heat of battle, men would be injured by musket or cannon.

Though they would survive the attack, they would often lose an arm or leg in the process. Lady Abigail wondered if this was now the case with the earl.

The sound of a thumping cane resounded down the hall outside the drawing room and all heads turned to see the Earl of Gilchrist enter.

Every lady in the room seemed to lean back in shock at the appearance of him. Even Lady Louisa, who unquestionably already knew his visage, was still taken aback at seeing it renewed.

Only the Duke of Wintercrest had his wits about him. He stood and walked forward to shake Lord Gilchrist's hand.

"It's good to see you again, finally," the duke said as he shook hands heartily.

Lady Abigail could not take her eyes off the man. He was of a muscular build, most likely due to his years in battle, and was smartly dressed in a well-fitted tux. Even the cane he leaned heavily on with his left hand was of exquisite dark wood with a silver embellished top.

His hair was worn in a long, straight, dark blonde tie back. It was easy to see that his crystal blue eyes were his crowning trait. They seemed as if they could radiate their own energy if allowed. At the moment, however, he entered with them entirely concentrated on the ground before him.

It was his face that Lady Abigail couldn't seem to pull

her gaze from. The entire left side of his face was covered in deep red scars from just under his eye all the way down to the top of his collar. The wounds, no doubt, traveled even farther below.

What had once been a strong chin was now a mess of healed gashes and lines. With his hair tied back, it was apparent that most of his left ear was also missing. It left nothing but a hole with small fragments sticking out.

It was so grotesque that the duchess had to look away in sorrow. She loved the earl like a brother and couldn't imagine the pain such markings had caused him.

Lady Abigail, on the other hand, couldn't seem to peel her eyes away from him. It was a fascinating sight. She couldn't help but itch to ask him what had caused such marks.

"Have you been recovering well?" the duke continued.

Lord Gilchrist met the duke's words a little surprised. Up until this moment, people had rarely spoken to him, and even when they did, it was not while looking him straight in the face.

Even the nurses who attended him this last year often looked away from the raw flesh across almost half his body. His own mother had burst into tears at his homecoming and hadn't been in the same room as him since.

Louisa, bless her heart, had done her best to see the man he was before and not the monster now before her as she spent time with him since his return. Even with all her best efforts, however, he could still see the pain in her eyes every time she looked at him. More often than not, she seemed to busy herself so as not to need to look in his direction.

"It has been a prolonged recovery," Lord Gilchrist said simply.

"Well, come and have a seat and join us," the duke motioned toward the ladies. "We are just having some refreshments before leaving for tonight's events. I assume, by your dress, you will be joining us. It will certainly be an honor to have a war hero in our midst."

Gilchrist came to sit by his sister on her sofa, figuring it to be the safest place. He was now keenly aware of the effect he had on women.

Where before, his mere presence could bring rosiness to a lady's cheeks, he now made them pale in fear. He did his best to turn his frame so that the worst of his scars faced the fireplace and not the party present.

It burned his still very tender skin to have the heat of the fire on it, but the pain was of little consequence to him now.

"Do you hurt much?" Isabella looked at him with pity.

Though Gilchrist knew her heart was in the right place, he could no longer stand pitying looks and fear.

"There were many others who got it far worse. I am happy enough I survived."

His words came out much more curtly than he had hoped. Gilchrist shifted uneasily in his seat. He was already regretting being convinced to attend the ball by his sister.

CHAPTER 6

The ride over to the Duke of Northingshire's ball was not a very comfortable one. Though the duke kept up a conversation with Gilchrist on matters of the war, politics, and other gentlemen they knew in common, the tension was still high.

For Lady Abigail, she could not see how this scarred man before her could possibly be the Colton Frasier she had heard so much about over the years.

This man seemed to be quiet and reserved. When he did speak, he was short and very coarse in his manner. It didn't match well with the image of a playful gentleman who always seemed to win over crowds with humor and charm.

When they entered the hall, even Lady Abigail felt embarrassed for the earl. The number of stares and pointed whispers were frankly rude. One elderly woman actually screamed and, in a very loud tone, told her companion how frightfully garish the earl looked.

For his part, Lord Gilchrist did his best to ignore it, as did the rest of the party. His mood significantly soured with each look and whisper, however.

Lady Abigail usually enjoyed the spreading of news that others might call gossip and even rather liked when it was her in the limelight. This type of attention was not to her taste, though. To make matters worse, as the earl lost his temper over rude looks, he began to give his opinion vocally.

It came to a head when the elderly woman spoke so brazenly for the whole room to hear.

"Perhaps if you don't like it, you should look the other way," he said to the room on the whole.

This, of course, only caused more whispers.

"My dear, Mrs. Henderson was just surprised," Isabella cooed to calm him. "She is so hard of hearing; I expect she thought she was whispering."

"I don't care about the old crone's hearing," the earl spat back tartly.

"Perhaps a turn on the dance floor might lighten your mood," Lady Louisa suggested. "You used to love to dance."

Lady Abigail thought Louisa added these words in a desperate attempt to find the brother she once had.

He simply tapped his cane to the floor, a little louder than necessary, and said, "I can't imagine many ladies would find it enjoyable to dance with this, or this," he motioned to his face with his free hand.

Though she was ashamed to admit it, Lady Abigail feared that she might be volunteered for the job. All she had seen of the earl thus far was a rude, crabby man with no manners at all.

That image was not lost on all the others in attendance at the ball. If she were to dance a set with him, what would that say about her hopes of securing any prospects?

"Even if I could find a willing partner," he added, seeing that his words had hurt his sister, "my leg would be far too weak to keep up."

"Come, old chap," the duke said, motioning to Gilchrist. "Let us leave these ladies to their socializing while you and I join the gentlemen in the smoking room."

Lord Gilchrist couldn't help but be thankful for the friendship of the duke. He was the only one who had honestly looked at him no differently than before and wasn't put off by his sharp attitude.

For the latter, he tried his best to curtail it. There was so much anger boiling up inside him since he joined the Regulars that he scarcely thought he would ever keep his words down at a proper level.

It was not just that he had gone off to battle and seen things that no others in his company, with the exception of perhaps the duke, could even begin to imagine. It was also that so much had been lost in the process.

Because of his ridiculous need for adventure, he had changed himself permanently, both inside and out. What nagged at him even more was the genuine possibility that not only had his father been right in calling his commission a poor choice, but it had also led to his father's death. It was something that Gilchrist could never forgive himself for, nor did he expect his mother or sister ever would either.

He was happy to leave the company of the women. Both

his sister and Isabella seemed so keen on putting him in some kind of a happy mood or creating enjoyment in the event when it was impossible for him to find any.

Then there was the duke's younger sister. Naturally, she was the most distant from him of them all, as they had yet to meet each other before that night. Nothing had pained him more than the look on her face when Louisa had suggested dancing.

It was a look of pure terror that she would be the likely candidate. In years past, a beautiful young lady such as Lady Abigail Grant would have been happy to turn the floor with him. Now, she looked at him with pure fear and horror that doing so might ruin her reputation forever more.

He was glad for the duke's suggestion to escape from his sister's presence and hoped he wouldn't have to ever see her again. Gilchrist knew that wouldn't be hard since, from the moment he entered the ball, he determined it would surely be his last.

Gilchrist would not run from the party and let the gossipers know that they had gotten to him. He would also not subject himself to such ridicule ever again. If that meant staying within the confines of his home, then he would do so.

Lady Abigail felt the evening take a turn for the better once the men left them. She observed herself visibly relax at their departure. She hadn't even noticed how tightly she was holding herself for nerves.

At first, the ladies stayed in their own trio and talked about the preparations for the Foundling Hospital project. Soon, Lady Fortuna joined them and they began to plan in earnest when they would meet and what they would accomplish first.

All felt that warm, thick nightgowns and quilts were of the utmost importance. Making sure the children had comfortable beds and warm clothing seemed to be the wisest use of the ladies' time.

Lady Abigail, of course, was given the task of collecting fabric scraps and cutting them into proper shapes for the desired quilts. Perhaps if she did well enough at that, she might graduate to sewing the patches together.

Both Lady Abigail and the duchess determined to make the quilts first. Isabella was excited at the prospect of turning out the most creative decorative bedding time would allow her.

Lady Fortuna and Lady Louisa, therefore, determined to make nightgowns for both the girls and boys.

As the night progressed and the festivities continued, Lady Abigail quickly got swept up in the excitement of a ball. She danced several sets with young men she knew well, including Lord Fenton.

He stayed with the ladies after the set and happily told stories he had heard of the duke's younger years. He was such a pleasant, diverting man to have around, Lady Abigail almost forgot altogether the discomfort she had felt earlier in the earl's presence.

The mood shifted when the duke and Gilchrist returned to the party toward the end of the evening. They both smelled of rich tobacco and brandy, and it even seemed the earl's spirits were higher than before.

"I was hoping I might take you for a turn, if you are up for it, my dear?" the duke said to his wife.

He always felt her to be so delicate in her condition but, in reality, she had been secretly hoping for the good exercise of a dance to get her blood pumping after standing in one place for so long.

"It is good to see you, Lord Gilchrist," Fenton said with a slight bow. "I heard the news that you are back in town."

Unlike the duke, who was man enough to see Gilchrist

as the gentleman he once was, the earl found his old friend Fenton lacking in that department.

Suddenly, the relaxation of drinks and cigars with the duke in a leather easy chair melted back to the reality surrounding him.

Because of Fenton's faltering, Gilchrist only gave him a curt nod in return. Seeing that he was not about to converse, Lord Fenton turned back to the ladies.

"I was rather hoping to invite you to join me in the park tomorrow evening, Lady Abigail, before your brother returned. I do not doubt that he won't allow such a thing."

"No, I would not. I am all too aware that you will not only plan to take her to another gig race but maybe even allow her to be in one."

"Thankfully, my brother has no say over what I do during the day," Lady Abigail said pointedly. "Therefore, I would be happy to accompany you on a carriage ride around the park. Should we find ourselves at an impromptu race, all the better."

Before the duke could retort, his wife drew his attention to a new set about to start and his promise to dance with her.

"How about you, Lord Gilchrist?" Fenton said, turning to his old friend.

He was moderately put off by the look of Lord Gilchrist, but another body at the race meant more bets and a more significant cut for himself. He may have been sensitive next to Gilchrist now, but Lord Fenton was not above taking his money.

"I find racing to be an altogether waste of one's time. It is merely entertainment for those too simple to find actual substance of interest."

Lady Abigail opened her mouth in shock. Not only had he insulted Lord Fenton, but her as well.

"You didn't used to feel that way," Lord Fenton said, partly under his breath.

"Yes, and then I realized that life has more to offer than these useless pastimes."

"Yes, and how did that work out for you?" Lord Fenton spat back, no longer hiding his distaste behind civility.

The look on Gilchrist's face was altogether terrifying for the women. Lady Louisa was half worried that her brother might actually start a fist fight, right there and then.

He may have always been an energetic man, but he was never prone to letting anger get away from him. It was an entirely new side she was seeing of him and she didn't like it.

CHAPTER 7

Lady Abigail had been completely put off by Lord Gilchrist. It no longer mattered the types of praise Isabella or Louisa had given him in the past; in Lady Abigail's mind, he was a horrible person.

Between his coarse words, loud, brazen comments, and the insults he threw directly at her, she found him to be just as ugly a person on the inside as the scars had turned him on the outside. She would rather never cross his path again.

She soon forgot about the earl who seemed to worry her sister-in-law to no end when, the next day, Lord Fenton arrived in time for an afternoon carriage ride.

He was a pleasant enough fellow to ride along with and,

in many ways, a good friend of hers. Like Mr. Shawn James, races were a means for Lord Fenton to make a little something of himself. He came from a family of four brothers before him.

The first had taken his place as Earl of Dovenshire, the second a clergyman, the third a militia officer, and Lord Fenton the youngest. Lady Abigail felt deeply for the man. Where she still had the opportunity to marry back into the peerage, if desired, his lot in life was set at birth.

Whether it was because he was the youngest of sons, or the fact that each brother had already claimed all the other reasonable careers, Lord Fenton was left with studying the law. It was not something that he took to well and he was very vocal about his distaste of it.

Lady Abigail assumed his adventures with gambling were to ensure that he still held the life of a gentleman without having to work for a living. She didn't fault him for this desire. It was a hard thing for someone to grow up in the peerage, only to be removed from it as an adult.

"Do you know Lord Heshing well?" Lady Abigail asked as she shielded her face from the sun with her mint green parasol.

As promised, Lord Fenton had arrived at the

Wintercrest home in a fetching open carriage to take her around the park. Lady Abigail had chosen to wear the mint green silk walking gown that had a white stripe pattern and delicate lace cuffs.

It was her favorite to wear in the sun because it matched well with her warm skin tone and accentuated the vibrant red of her hair. She didn't dress so meticulously for the benefit of Lord Fenton. Though he was a good friend of hers, kind, and relatively handsome, he was not the one who occupied her mind as she dressed this morning.

Fenton gave Lady Abigail a sideward glance as he directed the horses at a leisurely pace.

"Having one's lady speak of another gentleman on a carriage ride is slightly off-putting," he said with a smile.

She was irritated that he dodged the question.

"I am certainly not your lady. Though I do cherish your friendship, I rather thought you had an eye on Miss Mary Johansson?"

Lord Fenton measured his words carefully before speaking. It was well known that he was drawn to Miss Mary. She was a great beauty. The match, however, would not do well for either of them. Both would be in need of a spouse with significant funds. This was something neither of them had.

"She is a very sweet girl, isn't she?" he finally said in return. "So, you find Heshing quite a beau, then?"

"I wouldn't say that, no. I only met him the one time. He seemed very nice though."

"And handsome, charming, a favorite of the racing circuit, oh, and not to mention an earl," Fenton teased.

"You are not the only one who has an eye on him," Lord Fenton continued when Lady Abigail refused to give into his teasing.

"I never said I had an eye on him," she replied exasperatedly, but still blushed all the same.

Much to Lady Abigail's satisfaction, Lord Heshing was, in fact, present when they came upon the King's road. Even better was the fact that he would not be racing that day. It would give Lady Abigail a chance to have a longer conversation with him.

Though Lord Heshing was not dressed in his riding clothes, he still looked just as handsome as ever in his blue velvet jacket, cream pants, and high boots.

Lord Fenton, ever the kind friend, made sure to park the carriage close to where Heshing was standing. As was customary of a gentleman, Lord Heshing came up to the side of the ride to help Lady Abigail down.

"It is a wonderful day, is it not, Lady Abigail?" Heshing said as he took her hand. "I know most women are not as happy for bright sunny days like this, but I must confess that they are my favorite."

"I must agree with you, Lord Heshing. Where I live up north, we don't have many sunny days, and when we do, I refuse to take them for granted."

"And how do you spend those few days? Perhaps attending races like you are now?" Heshing said as he walked Lady Abigail over to the start line.

Lord Fenton was already hard at work collecting bets and cared not a whit that his companion had been taken by another.

Lady Abigail smiled up at Heshing, gauging how much she should say. Typically, when meeting a gentleman for the first few times, she would hold herself back and try her best to be more of the timid lady that gentlemen seemed to enjoy.

Looking at the fiery spark in Heshing's brown eyes and knowing him to have as high a need for adventure as she did, she didn't feel the need to hold back today.

"There are not very many races at Wintercrest Manor. Instead, I rather like walks in the park surrounding the estate. It gives me a chance to soak up some sun."

"No doubt the cause of those freckles," the earl said with a nod to Lady Abigail's nose.

She covered it, embarrassed, with her gloved hand.

"Don't worry, I rather like them on you," he said in a lower tone, causing Lady Abigail to blush profusely.

"I find ladies that sit inside all day long, painting screens or sewing pillows, so dull. Life is meant to be experienced, not merely watched through a window," Lord Heshing added.

"I couldn't agree more," Lady Abigail ventured to say.

He smiled down at her then, satisfied with her reply. Lady Abigail couldn't help but feel the tingle of excitement as his brilliant white teeth shone down at her.

They stood next to each other, swapping tidbits of information as they watched two gig races in consecutive order.

Lady Abigail was happy to see that Mr. Shawn James was present for the first race and, in fact, won. It made her feel slightly better for wishing against him earlier.

"James was a good sport," Lord Heshing said after the final race. "I thought he would have been quite sour, losing to me again."

"Again? Have you been doing much racing this season already?"

"I have," he said casually, "but that is not how he lost to me. On occasion, I frequent White's and try my hand at faro when I have the time. I happened to be there the night before the race and so was James. Let's just say he lost far more than the cost of a horse that night."

"Poor Mr. James," Lady Abigail said, watching the now champion receive his congratulations.

The prize for a gig race was a small purse. Lady Abigail was sure the amount was not even enough to cover the cost of a horse, let alone more losses at a gentlemen's club.

"Well, that is the cost of taking a gamble. You shouldn't put down a bet unless you are willing to lose it all," Lord Heshing said firmly.

"What an interesting idea. I am sure most here would say the opposite. Why take a risk if you don't think you will win more in the end?"

"I suppose it is the heightened sense of the risk, knowing

that I might lose it all, and whether I am willing to part with it, that gives me the encouragement I need to see the win in the end."

"I always felt like card games were more chance than anything else. Are you saying you believe your pure determination and drive is what sets you on top of others?"

"Well, I don't win every time, I must admit," Lord Heshing said with a hearty laugh. "But I must also admit that I feel my drive does help me to find myself the champion at the end of the night."

Lady Abigail thought about Lord Heshing's words over the next few days. She had plenty of time to do so, as she was, in her mind, trapped indoors.

She was doing her best to make a counterpane covering for one of the beds of the Foundling Hospital. Each lady had set her goal last they met and were to work through the week before collecting items to be delivered to the hospital.

It was now the day of meeting at Lady Louisa's house and Lady Abigail was frantic to finish the last few stitches of her quilt. It was, by far, the simplistic bed covering that could be made.

Using a simple linen fabric for the top, wool batting for

the middle, and soft wool fabric for the bottom, she had stitched all the corners together. It was a slow, painstaking task to do such simple sewing.

Even still, she couldn't help but notice how her thread line seemed to lean whenever she was distracted. Even worse were the stitches much larger than the others every so often as she became impatient with the task.

Once the three pieces were sewn together, no matter how poorly, Lady Abigail then worked on creating a simple design on the top layer. She did the simplest stitching through all three layers as she created the design. She hoped it would add to the covering's sturdiness and prevent the woolen batting from moving too much.

Where applique or delicate embroidery were often used on the top of the covering, Lady Abigail had settled on the simple outline of a spring tree with pink blossoms and a bird nesting on a limb.

In the week she worked, she had just about completed the whole project. Currently, she sat in the morning room finishing the last few stitches of the bird's nest when the duchess came to join her.

In her hand was a large wicker basket filled with several

neatly folded blankets. They were beautiful to see even in their hidden state.

Each blanket had a different fabric applique pattern of cotton dotting the front. Isabella had even gone back over the applique adding details to the design with embroidery. Looking in the basket, Lady Abigail guessed there had to be at least six.

She let her own work fall to her lap as she gave a sigh of defeat.

"How is it possible that you have done all that in such a short time?" Lady Abigail asked, full of admiration.

"Well, I have not been as busy as you. With His Grace not allowing me to do much past sitting in the drawing room day and night, it is a necessity to keep one's hands busy," the duchess answered.

"Yours looks very lovely. I expect you will make your brother eat a helping of humble pie if he sees it. We must leave shortly, however, for the carriage is ready."

"I am not done yet," Lady Abigail said, feeling disheartened to not even have one finished.

It was accurate that she had been out of the house for much of the past week. She had attended various dinner parties and private receptions. Even with the knowledge that she had been busy with other engagements, Lady Abigail still felt very pitiful at her small accomplishment.

"I am sure we will have time to finish up at Lady Louisa's. We are to have luncheon first, after all."

Lady Abigail was resigned to that fact and got up with her own meager wicker basket of one blanket and some notions.

It had been decided that each week when they met, they would have a luncheon together first and then they would take a carriage over to Foundling Hospital to deliver their creations. The idea had been that they would get to experience some of the joy on the children's faces.

Lady Abigail was sure whichever child received her covering would more likely struggle to hide disappointment compared to the others that would be given out today.

CHAPTER 8

The luncheon at Lady Louisa's went smoothly for Lady Abigail. Happily, she wasn't the only one to have a few stitches to finish while they talked, and no one had as much done as the duchess.

"How is Colton doing?" Isabella asked with concern.

"I am deeply worried about him," Lady Louisa confessed. "He has not left the house once since the ball. He is very short-tempered and even snapped at Mother once. She has taken his changed appearance very badly. One evening at dinner, he told her that if she found him so grotesque, he would no longer join us for dinner."

"Since then, he has taken all his meals in Father's office. I fear he plans to stay locked up in that office forever."

Isabella was visibly concerned to hear such a report on the Earl of Gilchrist. She wished there was something she could do to help him, as Lady Louisa did.

Lady Abigail, on the other hand, sooner preferred not to think of Lord Gilchrist at all, and felt the mood was soured by talk of him.

"Perhaps if he was given a cause to help him forget his problems," Lady Fortuna suggested, always willing to help another in need.

"I have thought the same thing, but I fear he will do nothing that will require him to leave the house. He refuses to be seen by society at all," Lady Louisa replied.

"There must be something he can do in the safety of his home. Then, once he is feeling comfortable with himself again, he might be more willing to venture outward," Lady Fortuna said, deep in thought.

"I know," she finally said after a moment's contemplation. "Many of the boys at the Foundling Hospital are prepared for life as military men. Perhaps when we go today, we could ask the headmaster if there are any questions they might have for a returned war hero. Lord Gilchrist could spend the week writing his advice and answers and return them with us."

"It would be nice to have an escort as well," the duchess chimed in. "I know His Grace would be much relieved to hear that we did not go alone each week."

It was not exactly the best part of the city that the ladies would be traveling to. Lady Abigail was aware of this fact but also didn't like the idea of having to sit in a carriage with Lord Gilchrist each week.

She was far more offended by his manner and speech than by his scars.

"I am not entirely sure he would even leave the house for this," Lady Louisa stated frankly.

"It wouldn't hurt to ask, though," Lady Fortuna replied.

It was finally settled that, for that day, the ladies would go on their own. Lady Fortuna would discuss the idea with the headmaster of the boys' portion of the school. If he found it a favorable idea, the ladies would return that night with letters to be delivered to the earl.

All the party, except Lady Abigail, hoped that the earl would feel inspired by the task and accompany them next week. For this reason it was decided that, from that moment on, each meeting would be at Lady Louisa's for the comfort of the earl.

Lady Abigail was not without compassion. She fully understood that the trial Lord Gilchrist had experienced over the last year was likely more than she could imagine. The fact that he had just barely told the duke only the circumstances around his injury told Lady Abigail that it was still a very sensitive subject to him.

Compounding that with the normal stresses of war was much for a single man to carry. Lady Abigail knew this all with the logical side of her brain. The rest of her, however, couldn't seem to forgive the blatant slight he had given her or his coarse behavior to even those who cared for him and tried to help, like the duke, duchess, and his family.

Happily for Lady Abigail, the rest of luncheon and the carriage ride conversations turned away from the earl.

Lady Abigail was happy that her cousin insisted they all go to give out their projects. In the girls' school, there were just under forty children ranging from five to thirteen. The same could be said for the other school that was designated for the boys, though they ranged up to the age of sixteen.

Whereas most of the girls were apprenticed out to

seamstresses and the like at the earliest age possible, the boys who chose the military life stayed behind until they were of age to join.

Luckily, Lady Abigail's bed covering went to a small boy who had just joined the Foundling Hospital. Though all children there were accepted at infancy, they were sent away to be fostered until school age.

The boy who received the linen had just recently been removed from his foster home with nothing but the clothes on his back. He was so happy to have the luxury of a soft blanket, he cared very little for the unevenness of stitching or the simple pattern on top.

Seeing the children there, many in clothes or shoes too small or worn, gave Lady Abigail the desire to take this project more seriously. If that meant giving up some engagements and invitations, she would be willing to do so. It would be well worth it to see even more children with smiles on their faces.

Along with their baskets of linens, the ladies had also stopped along the way at a bakery to pick up currant rolls with icing for each child.

In that way, even if a child didn't receive a gift of clothing or bedding, they would still have the joy of a sweet, warm roll in their stomachs.

By the looks on their faces when the basket of bread was presented, Lady Abigail guessed that treats such as this were few and far between.

The ride home in the carriage was a quiet one as each lady seemed to contemplate the vast blessings of their own situation. In Lady Louisa's hand sat a stack of letters written by the boys of the school.

The headmaster had found the idea a marvelous one. He hoped that the Earl of Gilchrist would come in person to give his own presentation, as well as some finer points needed for preparation in the military.

Lady Louisa promised nothing more than the returned correspondence and hoped to be pleasantly surprised when the idea was placed before her bother.

That night, as the duke and duchess sat before the drawing room fire of their London home with Lady Abigail, conversation seemed to turn again to the status of the earl.

"I just worry for him so much," the duchess said to her husband, after giving a detailed account of Lady Louisa's report on the earl's health and situation.

"Honestly, I don't blame him. I am certain that if I were in Gilchrist's situation, I would shut myself up as well."

"That is not helpful, my dear," Isabella said to the duke. "I need to find a way to help him out of this sour mood he is in."

"It's quite a sour mood," Lady Abigail said under her breath as she worked on the first of what she hoped would be many pinafores.

Much to the duchess's disappointment, and Lady Abigail's satisfaction, they had been instructed that all clothes should be made per uniform requirements, void of any embellishments. It was disappointing for the duchess not to give each girl a unique touch to her outfit as she had hoped.

For Lady Abigail, it meant simpler patterns and not worrying about a disappointed little girl who got her much less ornate work compared to the abilities of the others.

"He was not always like this," the duchess tried to insist to Lady Abigail. "He used to be so much fun. Such a tease too." She smiled at the memory.

"Perhaps the injury has affected his head as much as his body, for the man you described to me seems irreconcilable with the one I met."

"I hope not," the duchess said as she wondered if it could be true.

"War can do a great many things to a man. Some of the mental strains are irreversible. I knew an admiral who refused ever to step foot on the bow of a ship. One time, in his past, he was thrown overboard in a storm and taken captive by the Spanish. He always associated his horrible ordeal with that portion of the deck and refused to ever set foot on it again, come rain or sunshine."

"But it didn't make him so quick to temper," Lady Abigail continued. "Lord Gilchrist was so rude at the ball, I could scarcely believe it. You can't possibly tell me that his disposition is due to an association of social events to battles?"

"I was just giving one example. The results of battle are just as varied as the men who experience them. I think Gilchrist is not only wracked with the scars but also the realization that he is now seen as vastly different than who he once was."

Lady Abigail tried her best to feel compassion for the man. He had suffered a lot; she knew that. But, for some reason, all the logic in the world that told her to give him a chance to grow into a better man seemed to fly straight out of her head as soon as it came in.

"I think if we invite Colton and the rest of his family over for dinner it might help him. Maybe starting with smaller crowds, with people he knows love and care about him, he will be able to begin the process of becoming whole again," Isabella suggested.

"I am more than happy to get behind that idea," the duke said to his wife. "But please be aware that the Colton you know now may be the one he is to be always. Some things are too hard to ever fully recover from. No amount of feminine meddling can change that," he added with a teasing gleam in his eyes.

The duchess tisked at her husband for being called meddling. It was, however, precisely what she planned to do. She knew that Louisa, too, would do anything and everything in her power to help heal what had damaged Colton on the inside.

CHAPTER 9

Colton struggled with his guilt as he sat in his office, the office that should still belong to his father. After losing his temper with his mother, he hadn't found it safe for him to leave again.

He never meant to snap at Lady Gilchrist, but he just couldn't stand the fact that she could no longer look him in the eyes. Surely, she had to know how much he already hated himself for his father's death. To recognize that his own mother held it against him was unbearable.

He hadn't spoken a word to his mother since that night. Instead, he locked himself in this room, never really knowing if it was day or night.

Even worse were the nightmarish fits that seemed to

overcome him during the twilight hours. It left him not wanting to sleep at all. Over and over again, he relived the action that led to his disfigurement and his father's ultimate death.

Gilchrist felt he kept himself busy enough but apparently his sister didn't agree on that fact. Instead, after an evening of listening to Louisa's voice resound around the house mingled with the other ladies, she came to him announcing a project which she insisted he take on.

It was an intriguing one and he couldn't help but at least read over the small stack of letters before him. Many of them were just to express their desire to join the Regulars or militia to make something of themselves.

It sent waves of anxiety through him as he read many of the emotions he had felt before taking up his commission.

Lord Gilchrist was also keenly aware of what awaited these boys. With nothing to their names or to support them, they would enlist in the lowest ranks of the military. He knew well what hardships and dangers lay ahead of them.

He toiled away in his office wondering what to do with such letters. As a military man, the right thing to do would be to encourage them. Tell the boys all the best of the military and what it entailed.

Another part of him wished to tell the boys to find a better lot in life. He knew, however, that this was not possible for many of them. It was poverty or enlistment.

He determined instead that he would tell them the whole truth. He would explain the brotherhood and camaraderie that was found in no other place. He would also suggest tools and training they could learn now to prepare for advancement and, frankly, survival.

He sat down and began to compile a list of things the boys should train in before they became of age. Many of these things were not considered proper schooling for boys. One such business was basic sewing.

Often men of the lower ranks couldn't afford to have buttons or hems tended to. It was far too high a cost for their meager salaries. For this reason, many either had to risk the reprimand of not having their uniform up to snuff or learn the art of mending themselves.

The Royal Military was not only full of rules and organized ranks, but also had a very keen eye for details. The slightest hem not suitably tended could end in severe consequences.

A soft knock on his door interrupted the earl's work.

"Come in," he said, slightly more irritated than he had meant.

He didn't fret over this too much as it was likely just a servant with a tray of some sorts. The rumble in his stomach told him that dinner must shortly come to pass.

Instead, he saw his sister enter the room. She was dressed in a delicate silk gown of ruby red. He did not doubt that Lousia must be going somewhere this evening from the way she looked.

"You might want to hurry and ready yourself," she said softly as she looked him over.

Colton looked down at his own clothes. He had not slept the last two days and therefore had not changed his clothes. His jacket was slung in a heap on the floor, and his shirt was severely wrinkled.

"Whatever for?" he asked his sister.

"Do you not remember? The Duke of Wintercrest invited us to dinner this night and you accepted."

The earl leaned back in his chair. He had reluctantly accepted because of the pleadings of his sister. Now that the night was apparently upon him, he was no longer feeling capable of gratifying her wishes.

"You must come," Lady Louisa said, sensing his

thoughts. "It is just the small group of us," she added by way of reasoning.

"Louisa," he started.

"No, I won't hear any excuses from you," she interrupted, more forceful than ever before.

"You have locked yourself away in here like you are some kind of prisoner."

"I stay here for others' comfort," he retorted.

"We are your family," she countered, exasperated. "We love you, no matter how you look. Your face offends no one."

"Tell that to Mother, who can't seem to look me in the eye," he mumbled under his breath.

"She hurts for many reasons and because of it has a weak constitution. She can bear little these days. You refusing to attend dinner with us will only make her worry more," Lady Louisa added with hands on her hips.

Colton thought over his mother. Her weak constitution and hurt were all his own doing. He had basically murdered his father and broken his mother. His sister's guilting tactic had its effect. He would not cause his mother any more pain than he could help.

"I mean it, Colton," Lady Louisa continued when he didn't at first respond or move. "I may be your little sister, but if I have to, I will grab you by your good ear and pull you all the way to the Duke of Wintercrest's house."

Lord Gilchrist relaxed into a smile. It was a rare thing for his little sister to be so passionate about something as to threaten force. He was sure this small dinner, and his presence at it, was something significant to her. He wouldn't let her down.

Standing up, he put one hand over his whole ear, pretending fear at her words.

"How dare you threaten him so," he said, finding some of the old humor he once had. "The poor fellow lost his mate and now you want to tug him around."

He smiled softly down at his sister. Seeing his good nature briefly return, Louisa gave out a long sigh of relief.

He took her hands in his and kissed them softly.

"I know I didn't come back right, old girl," he said softly. "I'm trying to fix it. I would prefer not to be gaped at, but I can see this is important to you so I will change presently."

"No one will gawk at you, Colton," Lady Louisa encouraged him.

For so much of their lives, Lord Gilchrist had to protect and encourage his little sister. It seemed that now it was her turn to give some of that courage back.

"Lady Abigail certainly will," he added as he walked over to pick his jacket up from its crumpled pile.

"She doesn't know you as well as the rest of us do. It didn't help, either, that you were a right terrible monster when she first met you."

Lord Gilchrist thought over his behavior at that ball. He probably had been what his sister said.

He was sick of being looked at like a spectacle, though. Just about every moment of that evening had utterly irritated him and the earl had not held back his opinions.

It was clear to Gilchrist that Lady Abigail was a very young lady. She was enjoying the thrills of the seasons of her youth. He couldn't fault her for doing the same things that he had once done. He supposed it was more a pang of jealousy.

He wasn't so much jealous that she was free to walk around, attend events, or even enjoy a stroll in the park without pointed stares. It was more the fact that Lady

Abigail still held her innocent bliss that he once had. The joy of the season without the knowledge of what life was really like outside of the peerage.

He did figure that perhaps he had been too harsh on Lady Abigail. He was determined, as he went to his room to quickly freshen up and dress, to attempt to make a better impression on her this evening.

He wasn't sure why it mattered so much to him that Lady Abigail thought better of him, but it did. Perhaps his goal to win over her favor would help bring back the part of him that he had lost over the last few years.

Lord Gilchrist did his best to be considerate and kind to his mother as they made the short ride over in the carriage. It still irritated him so that she would never look at him again.

He was torn with the turmoil of wondering what the cause was. Was Lady Gilchrist truly so disgusted by her own son's face? Or was looking at the man who caused her beloved husband's death unbearable?

Part of him wanted to berate the woman. Insist she forgive him for his crimes. He was, after all, her only son.

He knew that these feelings stemmed from his desire to relieve his own guilt. Perhaps, he thought, if his mother could love him despite his faults, he too would find a way to do so.

But for the most part, he sat in the carriage, silently contemplating his own disgust for himself. The earl didn't think he had the right to desire forgiveness from his mother.

He had taken his own selfish course with no regard of the consequences. He was a horrible person who didn't deserve the lavish life he lived.

If Lord Gilchrist was truly honest with himself, he wished he had never returned home from that fateful night that left him permanently scarred. At least then, he would not have to look into the faces of the ones he had let down.

"Everything will be wonderful," Lady Louisa said from the seat next to him.

She laid her delicate gloved hand on top of his and patted it gently. It was something that he had often said and done to her. Lady Louisa was usually the one overcome with nerves when it came to social gatherings.

She had often feared misstepping or misspeaking. Worse was that many of the social events that they attended also included ladies who seemed to deem it necessary to persecute her for her average looks and meek personality.

In times past, he would sense her discomfort and give her the same words of encouragement. He looked over at her to see the smile on her thin lips. She was well aware of the memories that now played through the earl's mind.

He looked her over, seeing much of her for the first time since his return home. He had initially thought Louisa the same little sister he had left. Indeed, like himself, she had seen much sorrow since his departure and the result showed on her face.

There was, however, something else about her. It was an air of bravery. She seemed more confident now than she had been in the past. Lord Gilchrist contemplated the origin of such change in his sister as they pulled up in front of the vast expanse of the Wintercrest house.

CHAPTER 10

Lady Abigail was not looking forward to tonight's dinner. Though it would be a whole evening with her dearest friends and family, it would also be with Lord Gilchrist. Try as she might, even with her brother's encouraging words, she couldn't bring herself to forgive Lord Gilchrist for his rude behavior.

The whole point of the night was to celebrate his return officially. Lady Abigail imagined Lord Gilchrist would only take the opportunity to offend more people with his grotesque personality.

In the small group were Lady Gilchrist and Lady Louisa, the Marquess of Huntington, his family, and the little trio currently residing in the Wintercrest house.

The duke had also suggested inviting Lord and Lady Cunningham, as they were very close friends of the family. The duchess, however, shot down the idea instantly. Lady Lydia Prescott, their only daughter, had been quite a tormentor of Lady Louisa in their youth and it would not do to have any negativity in tonight's party.

The whole goal of the night for Lady Louisa and the duchess was to ease Lord Gilchrist back into society. They strived to make it a peaceful and comforting environment from the moment Gilchrist entered.

To start, the rooms were much darker than usual, with sparse candles lighting the way. Even the dining room was lit only enough to see the plate in front of you.

Lady Abigail expected that if they wanted the night to be peaceful and calming for the earl, then she would have been better suited to staying in her room. These weeks away from Lord Gilchrist had only spurred on her desire to give the earl a piece of her mind if he attempted to speak to her again.

When the earl entered the house with his party, Lady Abigail was shocked to see his scars anew. Every bit of his body was dressed to perfection in his long, black velvet dinner jacket and charcoal pantaloons. He chose to wear the more fashionable high boots and still carried his very elegant cane.

It was a breathtaking frame of a man until he removed his velvet hat. Then the whole of his face was shown and it was just as shocking as the first time she had seen it.

Lady Abigail did her best to look in the opposite direction of where he was seated while the now completed dinner party sat in the larger of the drawing rooms.

The Earl of Gilchrist was doing his best to be on his most polite behavior for the sake of his mother and sister. The fact that the rooms were barely lit didn't escape his notice. He assumed it was for the benefit of the other guests, who would otherwise be put off from their meals if they saw him in full light.

It was entirely irritating to him. If they didn't want to see his face, then they should not have forced him into this ridiculous dinner.

The look on Lady Abigail's face, when he entered the house and removed his hat, was not missed by him. It was pure disgust and a reminder of the monster he had become.

Though he had made it his mission to win over her

friendship for the sake of his sister's happiness, he couldn't help but be more and more irritated by Lady Abigail's actions.

First was that shocked look at the beginning. Lord Gilchrist thought that a lady with proper breeding, who was already prepared for his disfigurement, should have held herself with a little more decorum.

To make matters worse, she openly went out of her way to avoid him. At first, Gilchrist had tried to join a small group of women including Lady Abigail, Lady Fortuna, and Lady Huntington.

Lady Abigail took one look at his approach and excused herself from the group immediately before his arrival. This event occurred two more times before Colton was assured that she was going out of her way to avoid him.

It was humiliating to be treated like a plague by this lady. All his plans to show her kindness and extend the hand of friendship disappeared from his mind as he sunk in his sour mood yet again.

Finally, the dinner gong rang and all made their way to their seats. Much to Colton's disappointment, he was seated right next to Lady Abigail. It was apparent she too was not aware of this seating arrangement and gave a visible frown as she saw the earl take his place.

A respectable gentleman would have greeted the lady, having not spoken to her thus far, but Colton purposefully did no such thing.

"Lady Abigail, that dress is the perfect shade of pink. I remember you looking at the fabric just the other day on Bond Street. It couldn't possibly have been made so quickly," Lady Fortuna said from across the table.

Lady Abigail was happy for the compliment on her new dress. Very often, her mother would instruct her to buy gowns in any shade other than pink. The Dowager Duchess of Wintercrest believed it clashed too much with the ruby red of Lady Abigail's hair.

Lady Abigail wasn't entirely sure if that was the sole reason why she made an effort to buy dresses in every shade of rose. She did also enjoy the color.

With her mother not in town this season, she happily ordered her first new dress in the latest fashion in this otherwise forbidden color to her.

She was very proud of the garment, because not only had she picked the fabric of soft pink in iridescent silk, but she also had a hand in the design. She had chosen the more fashionable square neckline and, of course, the high waisted bodice. For the inner petticoat, she decided on a rich cream and had a very thin lace trail around all the trims to match the inner skirt.

"It is the same fabric," Lady Abigail informed her cousin. "Mrs. Jenkins' speed, however, was due to the fact that the dress was already made in the shade when we first saw the fabric. I simply had her add the lace trimming."

"And what a smart decision it was. I think it completes the form perfectly," Lady Fortuna continued as she delicately ate her food.

The scoff coming from the seat next to Lady Abigail didn't escape her notice. She turned to the Earl of Gilchrist for the first time that evening.

Lady Abigail was well aware that she was sitting on his good side and no one sat on the other. She suspected this was done deliberately. One, to save him the discomfort of someone on his scarred side. Two, it provided a chance for the earl and herself to get better acquainted.

Since Lady Abigail had made her opinion of Lord Gilchrist known to the duchess, Isabella had made it her mission to change it. It was most likely her doing that Lady Abigail was stuck next to the earl.

Lord Gilchrist was irritated enough that he was stuck at the end of the table right next to Lady Abigail. He was doing his best to eat quickly and just get through the night. He couldn't help but overhear the conversations that Lady Abigail was having with the others.

It was all utter nonsense she jabbered on about. First, the weather as of late with her aunt. Then, her cousin and Lady Abigail spent a whole ten minutes going on incessantly about her dress.

Lord Gilchrist hadn't realized he had made his thoughts verbal until Lady Abigail's eyes turned on him.

From this view of Lord Gilchrist, Lady Abigail only saw a handsome man with a rotten soul. First he had tormented her the whole night through, continually following her from one group to another. Then, in complete duplicitousness, he chose to ignore her from the moment he sat down. To add another insult on top of injury, he had just ridiculed her discussion.

"Is there an opinion on my dress you wish to share, Lord Gilchrist?" she asked with her eyes narrowed.

For a moment, she saw the memory of that handsome, charming man her sister-in-law spoke of. He certainly had a dashing figure, with his perfectly square chin, gorgeous blue eyes, and blonde hair that even shined in this little bit of light.

But then the earl turned his head ever so slightly to give

his response back. It was not because of the scars that his disposition changed, for even with his slight movement Lady Abigail could not see them. It was the look of disgust that transformed him from handsome gentleman to horrible rake.

"Nothing that would be worth my time," Lord Gilchrist replied with a snarky smirk.

"Oh, I am truly sorry that your time has been thus wasted listening in on someone else's conversation. Though it must be hard not to, when you refuse to have one of your own."

It seemed the whole room went silent at their exchange.

Lord Gilchrist couldn't believe the audacity of this little chit. First, she ignored him and blatantly avoided him from the start. Then, when he did the same to her, she had the audacity to call him out on it.

"Forgive me for not engaging you on inquiries of your slippers or hair ribbon," Lord Gilchrist said, looking to the matching pink ribbon that wove in and out of her red hair. He had to admit it was a beautiful contrast. "Next time, I will do better to speak to them before you turn and run the other way."

Lady Abigail's mouth opened wide at his words.

"I only avoided you," Lady Abigail hissed under her breath, "to prevent me from saying something I might later regret. Apparently, you don't hold value in that principle."

"Well, I am not of a very delicate constitution. I can handle anything you wish to say to me," Lord Gilchrist countered.

"Are you suggesting that my constitution is so weak I would faint at any words that come out of your mouth?"

"I merely mean that you may say to me what you wish," Lord Gilchrist responded exasperatedly. Lady Abigail seemed to find fault with every little thing he said.

He wasn't sure he liked this conversation any more than when they were pretending the other didn't exist. It wasn't going in any way how he had planned it.

Lady Abigail was such an infuriating creature. He had to admire her for not wilting away as another lady would, but he also wished she wasn't quite so determined to express her dislike for him in front of a whole wide-eyed table of his only remaining friends and family.

"I'm quite sure there is nothing of a disagreeable nature that Lady Abigail would wish to say to you," the duchess chimed in from her far side of the table.

It was easy to see that Isabella was desperately trying to save the dinner. For Lady Abigail, and even the Earl of Gilchrist, there would be no salvaging a connection between the two of them.

It seemed both their minds were set about the other. There were no foreseeable means for them to come to an agreement from this point on.

The rest of the meal was spent returning to the fact that one didn't see the other. Lord Gilchrist ate quickly and excused himself to the comfort of smoking cigars with the duke, while the ladies took their refreshments back in the drawing room.

Both determined, in their own way, never to be in the presence of the other, if one could help it.

CHAPTER 11

Lady Abigail enjoyed the feeling of the spring breeze as she took a leisurely turn around Hyde Park in Lord Heshing's gig. It was the third time this week, in fact, that the two could be found turning the park together.

Lord Heshing was making a habit of calling on Lady Abigail and, for the first time in her life, she didn't mind this lord's attention to her.

She realized upon opening her eyes that a couple of older ladies were looking her way and whispering. She suddenly felt self-conscious and made sure the parasol was keeping the glorious sun off her face.

"I expect we are starting to cause a stir," Lord Heshing said, tipping his head in the direction of the ladies.

"Whatever for?" Lady Abigail asked, truly confused why anyone would want to gossip about something as silly as carriage ride occurrences in the park. It happened often enough with just about every member of the ton.

Lord Heshing smiled over at her as he eased his horses on. It was a breathtaking moment for Lady Abigail when he did this. He seemed to cause little flutters all over her body.

"Oh," Lord Heshing said, trying to play his words casually, "I am sure for much older ladies who have already had their time in the light, it is great excitement when others seem to have their turn at courtship."

"But we are not courting, Lord Heshing," she said in reply.

"No, I suppose not entirely. Not yet, at least," Heshing answered back, with his eyes ahead of him.

A soft blush rose to Lady Abigail's cheeks. A few moments passed as they rode along in silence.

"Tell me about Wintercrest," Lord Heshing said after a beat.

"What would you like to know?" Lady Abigail replied.

"Well, it must seem very exhausting there, what with your brother's family."

"It is not just Christian's family in the house, but my mother and myself besides. Of course, little Jackie too. Though she probably would rather not be called little Jackie any longer."

"And who is this little Jackie that is much too big to be called little?"

Lady Abigail laughed at herself. She was often one to speak her mind whether the company understood or not.

"She is my eldest brother's daughter. She came to stay at the estate from France when she was around five years old. She is a very dear child to me."

"But perhaps not a child anymore, judging from your comment?"

"No, I suppose not. At least, not for much longer. Jackie is twelve this summer."

Lady Abigail thought of her niece, as well as the twins. Lady Abigail was always sorry to be away from them. She loved her family dearly and hated the idea of being away from them for long.

"Well, it must be quite a busy place at the Wintercrest estates when you are all home."

"Not at all, actually," Lady Abigail said. "You could fit our whole family three times over in the manor and still have plenty of room to spare."

"How very fortunate," Heshing replied.

He paused for a moment and she worried that she sounded prideful in her expression.

"I didn't mean to brag about my brother's estates," she said, trying her best to backtrack.

"Of course not," the earl said, turning his head to her. "I understood your meaning completely. You must enjoy being with your family very much."

Lady Abigail saw the sincerity in his words. She usually didn't care one wit what others thought of her. But the thought that Lord Heshing might think she was prideful had sent a knot to her stomach.

"I confess, it does sound lovely," Heshing continued. "I rarely visit my country seat. It is so lonely in that home all by myself."

"Yes," Lady Abigail said, realizing that the Earl of Heshing was now the last of his family. "I can understand why you must find your London residence more to your liking. I would hate to be in a big country estate all by myself."

Lady Abigail shivered, even with the warmth of the sun. It must be a somber and lonely period Lord Heshing was in. Lady Abigail spent much of her life with other people. She had a hard time imagining what it was like to be completely alone.

For some reason, in that moment, her mind trailed to the Earl of Gilchrist. According to Isabella and Lady Louisa, he had continued to shut himself up for the most part of the days in his office. He only ventured out when it was absolutely necessary for business matters.

She wondered how he managed such a life of solitude. According to Lady Louisa, he scarcely spoke more than a word or two to either her or their mother. Lady Abigail couldn't imagine what it would be like to go days on end without interaction or conversation.

"There are plenty of diversions here to keep me busy," Heshing interrupted her thought. "I have found one in particular that I like this season," he added, winking in Lady Abigail's direction.

"Where is Abigail?" the duke asked of his wife when he

walked into the small drawing room of their London home.

The duchess had been seated by the hearth for some time working on her sewing. It was becoming tedious. She hoped that the duke might stop in so that she could convince him to take a turn around the park with her. She felt in desperate need of fresh air.

"Lord Heshing called for tea. Now they are taking a turn about the park."

"Lord Heshing? Again?"

The duke came up to his wife and gently kissed her on the head before taking a seat opposite her. Grabbing a shortbread still left out on a tray, he popped it in his mouth.

"I believe it's the third time this week," Isabella informed him.

The duke huffed. He wasn't sure he liked the sound of that.

"Perhaps he is taking too much of a liking to her," he said with a furrow of his rose brows.

"I am fairly certain that she is taking an equal liking to him," Isabella replied.

The duke looked at his wife utterly surprised. She shook her head and laughed.

Men knew so little about the few tidbits of affection that women showed. Of course, he was probably even more oblivious since it was his little sister.

"What makes you think that?" he asked as he stretched his long legs out on the rug and settled into his seat.

Isabella had a feeling that his relaxed posture meant he would be less willing to take her out for some fresh air.

"Well, it's fairly obvious, dear," Isabella said, setting aside her sewing. Her delicate fingers needed the break.

"First, Abigail would never let a gentleman take her out three times in one week if she didn't show some interest in him. Such frequent public encounters would catch the attention of the ton and be spoken about."

"Maybe she didn't realize that," the duke said, reaching for another shortbread.

"I highly doubt that," Isabella countered. "Even if that was the case, she talks about Lord Heshing incessantly. She finds him a very worthy suitor, whether she even realizes it or not."

"And what if I don't?" the duke countered.

"She is your little sister—would you ever?" Isabella responded with a soft laugh at her husband.

The duke seemed to think this over for a minute. Isabella worried for little Elisabeth back home. Heaven help her when the Duke of Wintercrest's daughter was finally old enough to make her way into society.

The duke softened into a smile.

"I suppose it would be difficult for me to accept any man catching my little sister's eye. It is not that, however."

"What is it then?" Isabella asked with concern.

"Nothing that is very serious," he said, waving away her worry. "Just some talk at White's. I didn't know much about him and asked around a bit after that day at the races. He seemed to know so much about me…"

The duke trailed off. Isabella did her best to ignore the fact that her husband's inquiry stemmed from the fact that the other gentleman knew more about him.

"So what was it that made you question his worthiness?"

"He seems to be a good chap. Nothing that would be considered ungentlemanly. But some characteristics that would make me hesitate to allow my sister to marry him."

He paused for a moment, and Isabella waited for him to explain more.

"He seems to spend a lot of time at White's, to start."

"Well, he is a single gentleman. It's a reputable place to spend one's time, isn't it?" Isabella asked.

"Yes. Apparently, the Earl of Heshing spends all of that time at the gambling table."

"I see," Isabella said, lowering her eyes to the hands resting on her small lump.

Isabella knew well how excessive gaming could affect a family. Her own father had spent far more than he had in the same fashion. The result left her destitute at his death. It was not a memory that stirred good emotions.

"Is he very irresponsible with it? I know it is common for men to do such things for entertainment. But, of course, there is that line that some men seem to cross, beyond entertainment."

Isabella thought of her sister-in-law. She would not wish her to marry a man who might put her in the same financial situation that Isabella had experienced.

In the few encounters that the duchess had with Lord Heshing, he seemed like a decent man. He was handsome, charming and had a humorous way about his words that brought a smile to anyone.

Her father too had been a natural at hiding his vice. She had never even seen a hint of his problems. Perhaps this Lord Heshing was not so severely taken by gambling as her father, but that didn't mean he wouldn't be.

Isabella did want Abigail to be happy, and she seemed to be so these last few days with Lord Heshing. But a husband that could bring consistent stability would be of more value than a fluttering of heart now.

"Perhaps this is something we should bring to her attention?" Isabella said.

"I have considered that. I would not want to tarnish another gentleman's reputation unwarrantedly. I only have the knowledge that he does frequent White's and that isn't really enough to put him in the same lot as…"

The duke trailed off for a moment.

"As my father," Isabella added for him.

He gave his wife a sorrowful look. It was not her choice that she had been brought into a family with a father that cared more about his cards than his family.

Sometimes it still truly infuriated him that a man would not only leave his financial situation in such a state with a young daughter to look after, but that he also left all he had in the hands of a cruel man upon his death. How had a father, who seemed to care for his daughter, not seen how wrong it was to leave her in the clutches of his business partner?

"It is something we should be aware of, and watch closely for any signs that he might not be a proper choice for her. Only then should we bring it to Abigail's attention."

CHAPTER 12

The Earl of Gilchrist was in an exceptionally temperamental mood this morning. His father had invested in some lands in the Virginia territories, and he needed to make a monthly meeting with the solicitor who oversaw them.

His father had made this a regular meeting at White's. In the time between his death and with Colton unable to leave the hospital, the solicitor had done all the overseeing himself. Now with the earl here in London and a great need to make sure his property was being managed well, Colton had no choice but to meet the man at the pre-arranged appointment.

Lord Gilchrist told himself that he was going to be riding in a carriage and walking into a building where he would have a relatively private meal with a man who knew his family well. There was no need for him to worry about how others treated his scars. Still, he was anxious.

He dressed himself in his most excellent morning jacket. He had never been one to overly care about his clothing, but now he seemed to overcompensate for the disfigurement. He chose a shirt with a high collar and a thick tie to hide as much of his scars as possible.

In truth, they ran down the whole left side of his body to his knee. The little portion that was shown on his face didn't even compare to what was unseen. He could only imagine how people would react if they could actually see the damage done to his body.

He hurried into his carriage, making the distance between the front door and the cover of the vehicle as short as possible. It was not easy to move quickly. Lord Gilchrist's left leg still needed substantial assistance from his cane.

Lord Gilchrist had been assured that, over time, his leg would heal from the garish gashes that cut through his thigh and soon he wouldn't even remember having a slight limp.

Over a year later since the event, he was still in great

pain with every step that put weight on that leg. It was accurate that in the beginning he couldn't walk at all, so comparatively he had improved. Lord Gilchrist could not ever see a future when he wouldn't need his cane, however.

Maybe it was because of the awkward motion of his attempt at a quick walk that he caught the attention of two ladies and their maids walking down the street. Gilchrist tipped his head lower to cover their view. It was late enough in the morning that all the early mist had been burned away, affording him no cover.

"There is the earl I spoke of, the one who is more monster than man," one lady whispered to the other.

The earl may have been missing most of the ear on the side of the ladies, but it still functioned properly, and he heard every word she whispered.

His face burned red with rage as he slipped into his carriage, not even removing his hat before entering.

He would make sure to tell the lawyer that they would be meeting in his residence from now on. He did not need to suffer this type of embarrassment or ridicule.

He arrived at White's and entered the building with little incident. There was a footman at the door who greeted him kindly as he took the earl's hat and outer coat. It was sad to the earl that the paid help was more willing to treat him as they always did than his own kind.

"Mr. Henderson is already here and waiting for you, my lord," the footman informed him.

Gilchrist nodded in understanding. He was about to follow behind him when a commotion caught his attention. He looked just down the hall to see the proprietor speaking with a gentleman. Whatever he was saying was very upsetting, for the gentleman was having trouble keeping his voice at a proper level.

Lord Gilchrist had been a patron of the establishment since he was a young lord and had often come here with his father. He knew the proprietor, James White, very well and found him a most reasonable man.

Instead of following the footman, he forgot his garish face and walked over to aid the disagreement in any way he could.

"Mr. White, is there something I could be of help with here?" Gilchrist said.

He saw, now that he was closer, that the offending gentleman was the Earl of Heshing. He had never actually met the man, though Gilchrist had seen him from time to time.

"It's a private conversation, chap, so if you don't mind—Dear God!" Heshing exclaimed as he turned to smart off to Gilchrist.

It was easy to see that he was teetering out of control with whatever was conspiring between the two of them. Turning to face the Earl of Gilchrist had made him take a visible step back.

"Something wrong, chap?" Gilchrist spat back with a raise of his brow.

Lord Gilchrist had determined at that moment that he didn't care for Heshing and instead thought to turn and walk away.

"No," Heshing said, slowly trying to regain himself. "You must be Lord Gilchrist. Your, um, reputation, precedes you," he said with a slight bow. The scars on Lord Gilchrist's face entranced Heshing.

Gilchrist looked away from the offending earl and, instead, turned to Mr. White.

"Is there something I can assist you with?"

"Thank you, my Lord," Mr. White said with a soft bow. He cared not a whit for Lord Gilchrist's deformed face and looked at him, grateful for the added help.

"I was just telling the Earl of Heshing that it was my

unfortunate task to inform him that he would no longer be welcome in this establishment."

"It's absolutely preposterous," Heshing burst out. "My family have been members here for generations."

"Be that as it may," Mr. White said uncomfortably with this news. "You have built up a significant bill at the tables. Until you pay off a portion of that, I cannot allow you to be a member here."

"This is not something I enjoy doing, but it is part of house policy," Mr. White said by way of explanation to Lord Gilchrist.

"Nothing to worry about, Heshing," Lord Gilchrist said. "Just pay the amount and be on your way."

"This is an insult and I refuse to pay on those grounds," Heshing responded. "My father would never have been treated as such."

"With all due respect, my Lord, your father never had such a significant amount owed."

"It can't be all that bad," Lord Gilchrist said with a laugh.

He too had kept a running balance from time to time when luck was low. So often, gentlemen didn't carry purses of cash on them, and it was custom for the house to foot the bill for a period of time. That being said, Gilchrist always settled his accounts within a short amount of time, never letting it gather.

He knew that not all the lords had the same respect for timely repayment as him. From time to time, Mr. White might need to remind a patron of cost owed. Very rarely did that result in such an outburst.

"Just pay the amount."

"As if I had the funds on me," Heshing spat back.

Gilchrist wasn't at all enjoying his tone. Of course, Heshing had to be embarrassed by this confrontation by Mr. White, but he was only making it worse for himself.

"How much?" Gilchrist asked Mr. White.

He didn't particularly like Heshing at the moment, but it was a typical act for one earl to help out another. Gilchrist did have the means on him at that moment to rectify the situation and proper breeding dictated that he do so.

"One hundred and sixty-two pounds," Mr. White said after a moment of review over his ledger.

Now it was Gilchrist's turn for shock. Over one hundred pounds! It was an offensive amount to owe. No wonder Mr. White was asking him to remove himself from the premises till paid.

"How is it even possible to allow an account to run so high without notice?" Gilchrist asked of the owner.

"Unfortunately, this is just from last night," Mr. White responded.

For a man to gamble away such a vast amount in one night was mind-boggling. Gilchrist looked over at the other earl, full of confusion. His face was red with rage over this uncomfortable conversation.

"I'm afraid, where I would normally help, I don't currently have that amount of funds on me," Gilchrist said.

"As I said, I didn't ask for your help," Heshing spat back, narrowing his eyes on Gilchrist.

Lord Gilchrist couldn't help but be satisfied with the fact that he couldn't help, for honor would have dictated he do so.

Really, Gilchrist could have offered to pay at least a portion to appease the owner, but he didn't particularly want to for this gentleman. He would have sooner taken Heshing in a round of boxing than see even a portion of his bill paid at that moment.

Heshing not only seemed to be a man with no self-control when it came to the cards, but so full of pride as to insult the only person who had come to his aid. He instead deserved what was coming his way in Gilchrist's mind.

"Well then, old *chap*," he said, putting heavy sarcasm on the last word, "nothing left for me to do then, but to see you to the door so that Mr. White can get back to his business."

Gilchrist motioned for Heshing to follow him. Mr. White breathed an air of relief. For Mr. White, there would have been no respectable way to kick an earl out of his building without causing offense.

"You are very welcome to return and will be reinstated upon payment, sir," Mr. White said to lessen the blow.

"Don't count on it," Heshing said before turning to walk out with Gilchrist at his side.

As soon as Gilchrist saw Heshing out, he released the air in his lungs. He was sure horrible, little rakes such as Heshing didn't deserve to be an earl. He thought back to all the men under his charge the last few years. Any one of them deserved Heshing's life over a spoiled brat who threw away money like it mattered not.

Already, Gilchrist could feel his temper rising. Since his

time in the Regulars, it was a constant battle to keep his emotions in check. He smoothed out his jacket front as he calmed himself before turning to the footman still waiting on him.

"I will see Mr. Henderson now," Gilchrist said as calmly as he could muster.

"Very good, my lord. Right this way please, sir."

Gilchrist sat with his solicitor and went over the vast plantations he owned in Virginia. Some of it was a great shock to Gilchrist. It was much more than he had even known about. Not only did his father have the tobacco fields, that he knew well about, but also a sawmill and several hundred acres of land devoted to developing pitch from the pine tree resin.

"Now, your father never set foot on the land, only bought it and managed it through myself and correspondence. I, however, try to make the trip to Virginia at least every other year to make sure I am accurate in the description of its state," Mr. Henderson said after explaining the whole of the investment.

He was a portly man who was well up in age. Gilchrist was a little surprised that he was able to make the journey at all.

"And the last time you visited the site?" Gilchrist asked out of curiosity.

"Just before your father died. I was sorry to hear of his passing upon my return."

Gilchrist nodded in understanding. That meant it would be time to visit the plantation in person again. He wondered if he should do it himself. It would be an adventure to do so. Perhaps, too, he would be more welcome in the wild, new Americas than he was here at home.

"I had waited to make my next journey, to see if that was what you wished. Perhaps you would like to see the land for yourself?"

Mr. Henderson had read the train of Lord Gilchrist's thoughts and Colton smiled, knowing he would enjoy working with such a man over the course of the years.

"Perhaps it might be a good way to procure a wife as well, if you don't mind me being so bold as to say," Mr. Henderson continued.

Gilchrist laughed out loud at the thought. He had known from the first moment he peered at his image in a looking glass that no lady would ever have him now.

"You think a respectable lady would have this," he waved to his face.

"Perhaps women are picky choosers here, but I promise you, in America, women swoon at the mere mention of a title."

"I'm sure my mother would be happy at the idea. I fear she resents me for not only taking my father out of this world, but also preventing a grandchild to carry on our family's estates."

It was the first time that Gilchrist had ever aired his irritations with another. He was just as surprised to speak of such a personal matter with a man he had just met as Mr. Henderson was to hear it.

The gentleman merely brushed the thick mustache that decorated his face with a linen cloth and looked on Gilchrist much like his own father would have.

"I knew your father well and he did deeply worry when you left. We spoke of you and your sister often. He loved both his children dearly. That said, I can promise you that his death was not your fault. It's what happens when old age creeps into ancient bones such as these," he said as he slapped his round belly.

"I appreciate your words," Gilchrist said, not fully agreeing with them. "I will also consider making the trip myself, as I would not want to put your ancient bones on such an arduous journey."

"I am not going to lie; I would be greatly relieved if that were the case. I seem to enjoy the trip less and less every time I go."

Gilchrist shook Mr. Henderson's hand heartily before they parted ways. As he had begun his trip today, he had decided not to meet the man at White's anymore. After speaking with both the proprietor and Mr. Henderson and finding some camaraderie with them both, he decided to keep the monthly appointments in place.

Admittedly, it was a dread for him from the moment he stepped out of the gentlemen's club and back onto the street to his waiting carriage, but he figured it was a small sacrifice to see even just a few moments out of the confines of his home.

CHAPTER 13

Lady Abigail sat in Lady Louisa's drawing room, her meager work in her lap. Though she had promised herself to devote more time to the cause over the last week, it hadn't been the case. The distractions brought by Lord Heshing had veered her off course and now she was very sorry for it.

Each lady had worked hard to make several pinafores. In Lady Abigail's hands were a measly three. She was ridden with guilt that she was not holding up her end of the commitment these ladies had made and children would suffer for it.

"I am happy to announce," Lady Louisa said, as they all took to their luncheon before the trip, "that Lord Gilchrist has been convinced to join us."

"How wonderful to hear," the duchess said with light beaming in her eyes.

"He should be joining us presently," Lady Louisa said.

Just at that moment, the door opened and Lord Gilchrist entered. Lady Abigail couldn't keep her heart from sinking even further down than before at the announcement. She was surprised, however, to see a light of excitement glowing behind his blue eyes. It was a curious sight for Lady Abigail to see.

"I have arrived, ladies," he said with some of his old charm back. "And I promised the duke at our last occasion to speak that, should any ruffians try to harm you, I will scare them off."

The ladies all gave little laughs. All except for Lady Abigail, who was shocked to hear him joke about his scars. Before, he had been so harsh to anyone who merely mentioned them and now here he was joking. It was a curious matter.

He took his spot with his left side facing the fire as he had in the past. He may have tried to make light of his circumstance, but inside he was all turmoil.

Sure, things had gone well at White's earlier, with the exception of any member of the peerage he had come upon. But here, he was going to a house of innocent children. It would either turn out well or even worse than he could possibly imagine.

"Are you to speak with the young boys and tell them all your dashing adventures?" Lady Fortuna asked of the earl.

"Well, I will speak to them. I should much rather tell them to find a better vocation, but I highly doubt that is possible."

"Then you thought poorly of your time in the Regulars?" Lady Fortuna asked, clearly interested in his words.

"No, not at all," the earl replied.

"Well, forgive me, but that seems rather duplicitous," Lady Fortuna added with a little giggle.

He gave a broad smile that seemed to capture Lady Abigail's attention. He could be so charming when he chose to. Having only a view of his right side, with his smart green morning coat and grey pants, made him look very handsome at that moment.

"I suppose it is. My goal is to tell them about some of the grand things of life in a military unit, but also some of the realities that others will often leave out."

"Such as what?" the duchess also asked, keenly interested.

"Well, to start," he said, trying to find the comfort of speaking again as it was not something he had done very regularly, "basic skills they should learn ahead of time. In fact, I wondered if perhaps one of you ladies would accompany me and help with some basic sewing lessons."

Lady Abigail suddenly pricked her finger on the last apron she was finishing. She gave a sharp yelp before putting the offending finger to her lips.

"Oh, Abigail, would you like to join Lord Gilchrist," Lady Fortuna said, mistaking her yelp for some sort of excited volunteering.

The whole party looked at her expectantly. Even Lord Gilchrist had his brows raised in surprise that she might want to take on the task.

"I just pricked my finger," Lady Abigail said by way of explanation.

"But it does seem like a wonderful idea. You must go with Lord Gilchrist," the duchess encouraged.

Apparently, she was still hoping to make a friendship between the two of them.

"But I am surely the worst of us all," Lady Abigail said, panic-stricken indeed over her ability.

"I am confident it will be quiet, simple work," Lady Fortuna said, turning to the earl for confirmation.

"Yes," he bumbled a little. "Just buttons and the simple hem is all. Perhaps darning of socks and mittens."

Lady Abigail could see the thoughts turning in his head. He was wondering if her excuse was genuine or due to him.

She considered refusing again, for truly both reasons were valid. She didn't want to spend any more time with Lord Gilchrist than she needed to and she was very lacking in skills. She could, however, do simple hems, buttons and darning. It would be difficult to say otherwise.

She looked to her sister-in-law who gave a pleading look with her eyes. The duchess was sure that if Lady Abigail spent some time with the man who was like a brother to her, Lady Abigail would see his goodness too.

Lady Abigail felt guilt hit her stomach. She had experienced life when there was a rift in the family. It had been much of her life, in fact. Her father and oldest brother seemed so at odds with her, the duke and their mother.

Even though the Earl of Gilchrist wasn't her family, he was, in a way, a part of it. She would do this to please Isabella. If it took all the strength she could muster, she would be friendly with the Earl of Gilchrist just to prevent yet another rift in her family.

"If you all think I will be up to the task, I will accept," she said, turning back to her work.

Gilchrist was visibly shocked to hear Lady Abigail's reply. He was prepared for some rude comment or slander thrown in his direction. Never in a million years, when he woke after a fitful night of rest this morning, did he think he would be spending the afternoon in the company of Lady Abigail Grant.

The carriage ride to Foundling Hospital was a quiet one. It gave Gilchrist plenty of time to steal glances at Lady Abigail across from him. She seemed racked with nerves. He too was filled with anxiety as he saw all the people passing on the street.

He had kept his whole side towards the inside of the carriage out of respect for the ladies. Now he was receiving shocked glances from anyone who happened to look curiously into their window.

"Colton, would you be a dear and pull the shade," his

sister said from beside him. "the sun is irritating my vision."

It was actually quite a muggy day out. Gilchrist knew his sister's words were only for his benefit and he had to say he was glad for it. With a grateful smile in her direction, he pulled the curtains over the open window, shielding his face from the onlookers.

Entering the hospital, all the women except Lady Abigail peeled to the left of the school to see that the pinafores were distributed amongst the girls. Lady Abigail and Lord Gilchrist, however, would be going to the right, with the headmaster who greeted them upon entering, to see the anxiously awaiting boys.

As was habit, without thinking, Lord Gilchrist extended his arm out to the lady. She hesitated for a moment.

"Oh, I'm sorry," he said, seeing her hesitation. "You don't have to take it if you don't want to."

"It's not that," she said, realizing how he took the offense. "I was just contemplating running back to the carriage. I have no skills that are good enough to teach others."

Lord Gilchrist looked down at her with a new eye. It was a response he never would have expected to receive from her.

"Well, if it makes you feel any better, I wish to run and hide in the carriage as well," Lord Gilchrist said. "But, perhaps together we can keep each other's bravery up."

Lady Abigail smiled at the earl. It was probably the first pleasant thing he had ever said to her.

"I'm actually hoping," Gilchrist said, after Lady Abigail took his arm and they started down the hall together, "the boys will be so mesmerized by your dress that they won't even notice me."

Lady Abigail looked up at him in shock. She was again wearing the pink dress that he had called a silly topic of conversation at their last meeting. Instead of sincerity, however, he looked down at her with a lopsided teasing smile.

"I've gotten many compliments on this dress," she retorted, pretending offense. "In fact, whole conversations have been spoken on it."

"I'm not surprised," Gilchrist countered, "with such a fabulous garment, and made so quickly, I dare say I could speak hours on it," he continued, teasing as if he was a clucking lady.

"You are quite beastly today, aren't you?" Lady Abigail said without stopping to think over her words. As soon as they slipped out, she stuttered, embarrassed. "I mean. Sorry…"

"Don't be," he said, not at all perturbed by her words. He gave her hand a gentle squeeze in the crook of his arm to assure her no offense was taken.

The next hour and a half were spent with the boys looking up at the Earl of Gilchrist like he was the most exciting, incredible, heroic man on the face of the earth. He told them of the realities of military life and the gruesome details, which, though shocking to Lady Abigail, were only the more enticing to the boys.

Finally, at the end, to the surprise of the headmaster, Lord Gilchrist urged each boy to learn necessary skills that were oftentimes deemed the duty of a woman.

"I have brought this very fine lady with me, Lady Abigail Grant, to show you gents the basic skills you will need to keep your uniform in perfect condition. Today, she will be showing you how to sew a button," he looked over at her.

Lady Abigail's eyes went wide with fear. She hadn't anything prepared for such a task. She was a fool not to think to bring scraps of fabric and buttons.

"Headmaster, if you would be so kind as to procure the necessary items for each boy?"

"We don't have that sort of thing. All of that would be kept at the girls' school," the headmaster said, sticking his nose in the air. He was quite above women's work.

"Thankfully, it is only a short walk away. If you would be so kind," the earl said in response.

The headmaster's mouth opened in shock for just a second. He was the one who was supposed to be giving orders, not receiving them. Amidst snickering from the crowd, he turned and left the room to find the necessary items.

Once the items were brought forth, Lady Abigail did her best to show the boys what to do. It was a simple enough task, but she had never taught before. She couldn't help but think that the duchess would have been better suited for the responsibility. Not only had she experience teaching, she was a far superior seamstress.

In the end, most of the boys had successfully added a button to a scrap of fabric. Some took to it quickly and others scoffed at the idea like the headmaster had, but did it anyway.

The whole time Lady Abigail worked, Lord Gilchrist watched her from the comfort of a chair provided for him.

She always seemed so spirited and sure of herself; it was

a shock and curiosity to see her so timid now as she spoke with the boys. As the lesson continued, however, she relaxed a bit, and some of her old fire and spunk appeared now and again.

Once the lesson was over, he thanked her and turned back to take control of the boys. They would have happily followed him into battle. Lord Gilchrist had to admit he had missed this honor that he once had with his own men.

"Next week, the lady and I will return. We will show you how to darn mittens. The military will issue you one pair. Unless you have someone at home who can make you another, this one will not last long without receiving holes. It is important you learn basic darning skills to make yours last the longest," he instructed them.

One small boy raised his hand.

"Yes, Jon," Lord Gilchrist said, already having learned many of the boys' names.

"Sir, we don't have any mittens."

"No mittens?" he said, turning to the headmaster.

"I am afraid funds were not sufficient to get the boys winter mittens."

"Then we shall have some ready for you next week,"

Lord Gilchrist said, motioning between himself and Lady Abigail.

She went pale in the face. Making mittens for twenty-odd boys seemed an impossible task for just one lady over a week's time. It was even more so when that lady was her.

They said their goodbyes to the boys and made their way back down the hall. Gilchrist immediately picked up on Lady Abigail's crestfallen face.

"Whatever is the matter?" he asked once out of the room and alone in the hall.

"I fear you have promised them too much from me. I could never make mittens for all of them in so short a time."

"Oh," he said, a little surprised. He gave a nervous laugh and rubbed his chin with his cane hand. "I actually hadn't meant that you would make them."

"Then, who?" Lady Abigail asked, thoroughly confused.

"I meant me, of course."

"You? You knit mittens?" She spoke laced with shock.

"I'm just full of surprises, aren't I?" Lord Gilchrist replied with another one of those half-sided smiles.

CHAPTER 14

It had been agreed that, over the course of the next week, Lord Gilchrist and Lady Abigail would meet in his drawing room to complete the task set before them.

So, it was with great trepidation that Lady Abigail came to stand in his drawing room.

"Lady Abigail, how good it is to see you," Lady Louisa said, coming in the room. "It's so lovely to have a caller on these muggy days," she added, referring to the drizzle that seemed to never stop outside the window.

"On days such as this, most would rather stay held up in the comfort of their own homes if possible, and surprise visits are less likely."

"I actually came upon a request."

"Request? From whom? Mother?" Lady Louisa inquired as she simultaneously called for tea.

They both sat down by the hearth that was not yet lit. Lady Abigail wasn't exactly sure how to tell Lady Louisa that she had come to call upon the Earl of Gilchrist. It was not at all proper for a lady to call upon a single man.

She also feared that if her reasoning was explained to Lady Louisa she might not entirely believe her. To be honest, Lady Abigail wasn't altogether sure herself that the earl knitting was believable. Perhaps it was all a joke he was hoping to play on her.

"She came to call on me," the Earl of Gilchrist said, entering the room.

He bowed to both his sister and Lady Abigail, who stood from the start of his entrance. Lady Louisa wasn't used to seeing Colton out of his office. In fact, she could confirm that she hadn't seen him at all for the last two days since their visit to the Foundling Hospital.

Lady Abigail was wracked with all sorts of nerves. Part of her was dreading this afternoon and she had almost turned her carriage around on several occasions.

She was still unsure if the invitation had been a joke. If so, she was prepared to give the earl a piece of her mind.

On the other hand, she had been intrigued and a bit confused by this previously unseen side of the earl that revealed itself at the boys' school.

She had seen a light and hopefulness in his eyes that day. It made her curious to see if there was such a man as had been described to her beneath the rough exterior.

"Call on you?" Lady Louisa said with a surprised look on her mousy brow.

"Yes," Lord Gilchrist said, coming to stand before the ladies as they took their seats again.

Lady Abigail couldn't help but notice how smartly dressed he was again. For a man who never seemed to leave the confines of his house, he did still take care to dress the part of an earl.

"I invited Lady Abigail over to complete a little project with me. It's for the benefit of the school children," Lord Gilchrist added when the first explanation seemed even more of a shock to his sister.

"Are you willing to share what that might be, dear brother?" Lady Louisa asked.

"I'm afraid I would rather not."

She nodded, seeming to know something of this

mysterious side of Colton that Lady Abigail couldn't understand.

"Well, I promised to go with Mother to check in on Mrs. Fredrickson today. She has not been at all well as of late and could use the company."

Lady Louisa seemed to look between her brother and Lady Abigail with a twinkle in her eye. She could have no way of knowing that this meeting was strictly a business arrangement for the good of the boys. Lady Louisa seemed to see more in it than Lady Abigail would have liked.

"I will call in Sally to sit with you," she said before bidding her brother and Lady Abigail farewell.

For a few moments, the earl and Lady Abigail shuffled uneasily. Neither one knew quite what to say to the other.

Sally came in with a tray of tea and set it before them. Then, without a word, she took a seat in the far corner where there was a basket of mending which needed to be done.

Sally worked silently, pretending not to notice the goings-on between the two. It seemed to Lady Abigail like a proper chaperone for a meeting with a beau.

She had not intended this at all and wished that Lady Louisa and her mother were present in the room.

"I hope you don't mind," Lord Gilchrist started as Lady Abigail busied herself with serving the tea. "I picked this time purposefully knowing Mother and Louisa would be gone."

Lady Abigail looked at him with pure fear. She couldn't see why he would want to get her so relatively alone.

"Why on earth would you do such a thing?"

He smiled at her shyly, and for the first time, she saw that he was fidgeting nervously. He cleared his throat and adjusted his seating.

"They don't know," he said. When the meaning wasn't clear to Lady Abigail, he corrected, "About the knitting, that is. I would rather they didn't. It's a little embarrassing."

"How did you come by such skills anyway?" Lady Abigail asked, taking the opportunity to retrieve the grey wool yarn and needles that she had brought with her from a small basket.

"I can't imagine an earl would need to learn things like this?"

"No," he said, clearing his throat again. Lady Abigail

could tell he was even more nervous to be here with her than he had been on the carriage ride to the Foundling Hospital.

She noticed he had no tools for himself, so she passed him an extra pair of needles and some yarn.

"Thank you," he said, taking it. "I wasn't sure how I would be able to come by it myself without anyone finding out."

"So, will you share with me the big secrecy behind all of this," she said, motioning between their two hands, "or shall we just work in silence?"

He relaxed a little at her joking words. He began his work and Lady Abigail was surprised to see how fast his hands moved.

"As I said before, many of the younger enlisted men would only have the items issued to them as we travelled across the Channel. My regiment was stationed in Belgium to assist the Prussians there."

Lady Abigail struggled to start her first mitten as she listened to Lord Gilchrist weave his tale. She must admit that she knew little about what had happened to him during his military service. All that she knew for sure was that he had seen hard battles.

"We were there all winter before the battle I am sure you are familiar with."

"Waterloo?" Lady Abigail asked. Its infamy had made it to her ears. It was the ultimate fall of Napoleon.

"Yes, well, winters in Belgium are harsh, to say the least. Many of the men's winter clothes were left in rags. Unlike myself, who was new to the fight, many of them had joined as young as, well, as young as the Foundlings."

"Years in duty and little funds made it difficult for them to replenish what they needed for the cold winter. Some had wives, sisters or mothers back home who would send items when they could. Many of them, however, had to make do without."

"I decided that I would learn how to make these simple items and gift them to the men most in need."

"That was very considerate of you," Lady Abigail said.

It was more than she would expect of any earl, let alone one who seemed so sour in disposition.

"It was less about kindness and more about necessity."

"How so?" Lady Abigail asked, noticing that where he was moving quickly through his first mitten, she was much slower.

"Warm hands reload muskets much faster than frozen ones," he said honestly, concentrating on his work.

"After I gave them to the men, I swore each one to secrecy. I didn't need them telling others that the commanding officer was sitting in his tent doing women's work," he added with a little embarrassment.

"And that is also why you don't want even your mother or Lady Louisa to know. You are too afraid that they will make fun of you?"

"Oh, I know Louisa will," he said with a chuckle. "I have teased her so much during our lives together that she would be happy for the opportunity to repay me."

"I can imagine," Lady Abigail agreed but thinking about her own brother.

"My mother on the other hand, well, I have disappointed her so much already. I would hate to cause her to think even less of me."

"I am sure she doesn't feel disappointed," Lady Abigail said with surprise. She hadn't realized that Lord Gilchrist had thought that.

He opened his mouth to say something, perhaps explain why his mother was ashamed of and disappointed in him. Thinking better of it, Lord

Gilchrist shook his head and motioned to her work instead.

"I can't imagine if I had asked you to do this on your own. At the rate you're going, it would take all year to complete the task."

Lady Abigail put down her needles, exasperated. It was true. She kept making mistakes and having to go back over her work.

"I warned you, I am terrible at this sort of thing," she said, ready to give up.

"No, you're not," he said, coming to sit next to her on the sofa. "It just takes patience. I am guessing that is something you don't have in large supply."

"I just don't see the point of sitting indoors all day long, clinking away with needles. Life is so much more exciting out there," Lady Abigail said, motioning to the dreary weather beyond the window.

"I understand," Lord Gilchrist said. "I was much like you before…" He let his words trail off as they both understood his meaning.

"Here," he said, shaking himself from his memory, "if you hold it this way, you can move a lot faster."

Lord Gilchrist demonstrated with his own hands how to

work the needles with speed. Lady Abigail watched and then tried on her own. She gave a giggle.

"You know," she said, looking over at him, "I never thought, of all people, I would be learning to knit next to you."

At that moment, Lord Gilchrist realized that when he came to sit next to Lady Abigail, he had taken no care of his face. He was seated so that she was looking right at his scars. He was sure it was a ghastly sight.

He moved away back to his usual place with his face towards the hearth. He gave a soft apology.

"It doesn't bother me," Lady Abigail said as she concentrated on her work.

Lord Gilchrist gave her a look like he didn't believe her words.

"I mean, at first it did, but not now. It isn't the scars that are offensive."

"Just myself," Lord Gilchrist said.

Though his words hurt, Lady Abigail could hear the undertone of humor in them.

"You can just be so cross at times," she said, never one to hide her thoughts as she should.

"I know," he said softly. "It is something I am trying to work on."

"Well, I don't see how shutting yourself away from the world will improve anything," Lady Abigail retorted.

"I suppose when I am alone, I am no longer constantly reminded of how I have changed. It is those reminders that often set me off."

"But don't you miss society?" Lady Abigail asked.

Lord Gilchrist thought this over for a few minutes. There were aspects of it that he did miss, such as having conversations with others. Until today, he hadn't realized how much he missed just spending the afternoon in the company of a fine lady.

It also came with less than desirable looks and words spoken about him. That always resulted in him losing his temper. It wasn't worth the risk.

"Perhaps," Lord Gilchrist said, "you will tell me of the things you do when you are not here. In that way, I can still have some connection to society."

Lady Abigail smiled at the idea. She was strangely happy to be of help to the Earl of Gilchrist. Perhaps this was the right way to help him find his place, now that he was out of the service of the Royal Army.

Lady Louisa and Isabella were so bent on getting the earl back out into society, they never stopped to wonder if he sincerely wished to be there. In this way, he could still have the company of others without the anxiety that the peerage seemed to give him.

CHAPTER 15

Lady Abigail enjoyed the rest of the week much more than she had expected to. On two more occasions, she came to sit with Lord Gilchrist as they worked to complete the task for the Foundling boys.

The sideways looks from Lady Louisa and the duchess were not lost on her. Both ladies most likely suspected something beyond the simple task occurring between them.

For Lady Abigail's part, she couldn't say that she wasn't enjoying their afternoons together. He seemed so much more relaxed and easy to talk to in the comfort of his own home. Lady Abigail saw how the stress of others' gossip had weighed on him so much.

It also made her rethink her own love of gossiping. She had always enjoyed finding new tidbits of information and passing them along to others. Now she saw, for the first time, how much words could genuinely hurt another. In a small way, it made Lady Abigail grow more than she even realized she needed to.

She also spent the afternoons sharing with him some of the adventures she would have while not in his company. As she told him of races that she attended or balls and dinners, he too seemed to share in the fun of the events.

For some reason that Lady Abigail couldn't understand herself, she never seemed to find a way to mention Lord Heshing. Though the lord was present for most of the events that Lady Abigail spoke of, she could never seem to bring herself to vocalize his name to Gilchrist.

In fact, as the week went on, she found herself in Heshing's company for most of the time she was not in Lord Gilchrist's. It was such an opposite experience. Where Lord Heshing was charming, flirtatious and bold about his desire to court her in earnest, Lord Gilchrist was instead a good friend that she felt at ease with and comfortable to be herself around.

It was almost as if the time she spent with each earl was

also splitting her person in half. With the Earl of Heshing, she had a fun, spirited adventure. In many ways, it felt freeing and exhilarating. It was often filled with mixed emotions of trepidation, as Heshing seemed always to be pushing the boundaries of society.

With the Earl of Gilchrist, Lady Abigail was eased into the comfort and peace of his tranquil home. After he had shared his secret with her, they had this unspoken bond where they seemed able to share with the other what otherwise couldn't be spoken. It was a kinship she had never felt with another.

There was still so much of Lord Gilchrist she didn't know or understand. He would mention, at times, his inability to control his anger, but could never describe in words what brought such ranging storms within him.

Lady Abigail took solace in her brother's previously expressed views, that the Earl of Gilchrist had seen and experienced much. It would take time for him to sort through these complicated emotions. She was surprised to realize that she wanted to be there to help him through it.

She still had a fear of that deep-seated anger inside him but, at the same time, she wanted to help him let go of it. Lady Abigail, just a short week earlier, would never have dreamed to think on Gilchrist with more than contempt, and was surprised to find that in only this short time her opinion of him had changed so drastically.

"You seem quite lost in thought," Heshing said to Lady Abigail, almost waking her from a dream.

They were seated on a blanket amidst friends, having a lovely afternoon picnic in the park. She had been tasting some delicate, early season strawberries when she had become lost in wondering about the Earl of Gilchrist.

"I was just thinking on a friend of mine," Lady Abigail said, a little embarrassed that she had been so neglectful of her companion.

"And who would that friend be?" Heshing asked, taking his own strawberry from the bowl in front of them.

From his tone, Lady Abigail expected he was hoping she said him. She did care for him genuinely. True, she had begun to feel what Lady Abigail could only assume was affection as she had never experienced it before. But she also was not the type of lady to lie, even if it was to appease a gentleman.

"It is the Earl of Gilchrist. My family has very close connections with his. Do you know him well?" Lady Abigail said.

The Earl of Heshing visibly bristled at the mention of the name. "I met him briefly. He seemed to me a horrid fellow. I can't imagine you being able to stand his garish company long enough to consider him a friend."

"He is not garish at all," Lady Abigail said, not pleased by his description.

It was for these exact words that Lord Gilchrist felt the need to imprison himself.

"I must admit, he was very coarse the first few times I met him. Over time, I have seen he is much more than that," Lady Abigail did her best to explain the feelings she herself didn't quite understand.

"Of course," Lord Heshing said with a soft smile on his lips. "I have only met him one time and very briefly at that. I am sure once I get to know him better, I will think differently."

Lady Abigail felt relief to hear Lord Heshing say such words. She didn't know why, but it was necessary to her that Heshing see the good that she had found in Lord Gilchrist.

"And what would give you cause to meet him on a more regular basis?" Lady Abigail asked, wondering at the meaning of his words.

For surely Heshing wouldn't take it upon himself to call on Gilchrist, and she doubted Gilchrist would ever find himself in Heshing's societal circle.

Where Lord Gilchrist was entombed in his home, Heshing was always out and about with the liveliest lords and ladies. Lady Abigail smiled at the thought that the two could not possibly be more opposite in character.

"Well, you say he has close connections to your family?"

"Yes. Isabella, the duchess I mean, was basically raised inside the Gilchrist household. Her father was often away and she spent many a holiday and social occasion in their company. She has often referred to him as a brother."

"Well then, I expect I will see much of him, as I plan to see much of you," he said, penetrating her with his soft eyes.

Lady Abigail instinctively looked down at her hands as a rosy color came to her cheek. Heshing dipped his head low to keep her gaze.

"Lady Abigail, I mean to ask you," he started in a soft whisper.

"Heshing!" Miss Mary called from across the blanket. "Stop your incessant whispering in Lady Abigail's ear so we may all play a little game."

He gave a huff of frustration at being interrupted when he was, no doubt, about to say something of great importance. Nonetheless, ever the gentleman, he turned to Miss Mary and inquired about the game she had planned for them to play.

"Two truths and one lie," she informed the two interlopers, who were apparently the only ones not already aware of this plan.

Lady Abigail spent the rest of the afternoon enjoying the silly game as each participant took their turn to tell two truths and a lie while the others guessed which one was the falsehood.

She enjoyed the time she spent with Heshing and this little group of acquaintances. It was with sadness, however, that she couldn't call them more than just that. They were all fun to have around for a good game such as this, but there was no depth to any friendship on that blanket they shared.

If there was a moment that Lady Abigail was in great need, she couldn't honestly say that she would turn to any of these lords or ladies. Instead, she would turn to the duke and duchess, her family, like Lady Fortuna, or even, she was surprised to admit, the Earl of Gilchrist and his family.

It made her wonder if her time spent here with these simple diversions was really worth it. It was something she had never thought to ask herself before.

Until that moment, she had planned her life just as any other lady might. She would enjoy her season until the time came that she found a proper suitor, then she would marry and begin to take care of her own household.

It was small diversions like this picnic that she thought would bring her joy. She was realizing, however, that instead she was finding more happiness sitting in Gilchrist's drawing room or with the children of the Foundling Hospital.

Those memories had weight and substance to her, whereas moments like this seemed so fleeting.

"Lady Abigail," Heshing's voice called to her again.

She turned to him, surprised to be off in another place for the second time that afternoon.

"Something must be very distracting for you not to realize it's your turn," Miss Mary said with a giggle. "Perhaps you will share his name with the rest of us," she added.

Lady Abigail looked sideways at Lord Heshing. She could see that he assumed where her thoughts had gone to for the second time that afternoon, and he wasn't happy about it.

She was sorry to offend him so, for she did care about him sincerely. Assuredly, he had more to him than these simple diversions he had shared in just as she did. Perhaps he was only waiting for the invitation to be more, just as she had needed.

Lord Gilchrist had given her the means to see beyond the simple frivolities. She would be happy to share that same knowledge with Heshing. Then, too, she would be able to get to know Heshing on a deeper level. It seemed that her heart was waiting for something of that nature before she could fully accept him as a suitor.

As Lady Abigail retired to her bed that night, she thought over all the new revelations she had experienced over the week. Heshing was a formidable candidate for her hand. Looking through the eyes of society, it was a choice she should not let pass by.

She was never one for caring what was expected of her, however. She did care for Heshing and found him good company. She needed to know, however, that there was more to him than what she had seen thus far on the surface of things.

CHAPTER 16

Lord Gilchrist hated to admit it, but he was actually enjoying his time knitting. It helped pass the time as he sat alone in his quarters. As well as that, as he kept his hands busy, it made it harder for his mind to stray.

So often, when left alone to his thoughts, his mind turned to memories he would rather not remember.

He had done significantly more work than Lady Abigail. He smiled, realizing that this women's work was truly not a strong suit for her. She seemed so confident in everything she did and said, it was nice to know that she was not entirely perfect.

Gilchrist couldn't help but have his mind wander to her on the days she didn't come by and anticipate her arrival on the days she did. He was finding that the more time he spent thinking about her, the less likely he was to snap at a servant or even have nightmares.

Somehow, the simple afternoons they had shared together had brought about a change in him that he honestly didn't think was ever possible.

She had been true to her word that she did not fear his scars. In fact, he was sure the last time she came over, she didn't even so much as notice them.

He never thought a time would come when a lady could look on him and at least not struggle to keep in a recoil. It gave him a flicker of hope.

He realized it meant he was developing feelings for her. It was a stupid notion and if he could have plucked it from his brain, he would have gladly done so.

Lady Abigail was a bright, beautiful, vivacious lady. There was no way that she would settle for being the beauty of such a ghastly monster.

He, after all, was no more whole on the inside than he was on the outside. Though he felt he had improved some, it was not enough to trust himself around others. He feared that one day his outbursts might spiral out of control in Lady Abigail's presence. He would never be able to forgive himself for such an atrocity.

Sadly, once the idea had entered his head, it seemed to take root, and he could think of nothing else. He spent his long days of solitude thinking about what he would say to her next, how he might try to make her slip into one of her soft smiles.

Though he knew she would never care for him in return, he did his best to settle in the fact that, even if it was just for a short while, he could enjoy a friendship with the lady.

A soft knock on the door broke his concentration and he quickly hid his knitting needles in a desk drawer. He bade the visitor enter, expecting it to be a footman.

"Colton, are you busy?" his sister's voice called from the other side of the door as she cracked it open.

"No, not at all. Just doing some paperwork for the plantation," he said as he shuffled random papers on his desk.

"How was your meeting with Mr. Henderson? I feel like we never talk anymore," Lady Louisa said, coming into the room and taking a seat across from her brother's desk.

"It was most edifying. I learned much about the investment that I never knew. In fact," Gilchrist hesitated a moment, "Mr. Henderson suggested I visit the plantation myself."

"He did?" Lady Louisa said with a scared expression.

"And do you think you will go?" she added when she had adequately gauged her reaction.

Lady Louisa did not want her brother traveling far away again any more than she wanted him to stay shut up in his office. What she truly wished for was that things would go back to the way they were before he had left.

She was starting to realize that was never going to be the case, however. Though she would not want Colton to travel such a great distance and be away for another extended period of time, it would be preferable to the life he chose for himself now.

"I'm not entirely sure yet," Gilchrist said, leaning back in his chair.

He scratched the soft golden stubble that had already started to dust the one side of his jawline. It no longer grew on the other side among the torn and healed flesh.

"It seems like an interesting idea. Mr. Henderson also informed me that things are certainly laxer in the budding country. Less pressure and social rules."

"You wouldn't stay, though, would you?" Lady Louisa asked, much in the tone of a fearful little sister.

"I don't even know if I will go," he said softly to ease her worry.

That being said, Gilchrist also didn't want to give his sister a definitive answer. Perhaps he would go and stay. It might be the fresh start he needed to revamp his life and bring some normalcy back to it.

"I am sure this is not the reason you came to see me, though, dear sister. What is it that I can do for you so that I may spare you looking on my garish figure any longer than necessary?"

Though Lady Louisa did better than most in hiding her discomfort, it was still visible there in her soft, brown doe eyes.

"I only fear for the pain you suffer," she said in response to her shortfallings to not see his scars.

"They don't pain me much at all," the earl said, though it was not the truth.

"Well, I came in hopes that you would again join Mother and me for dinner tonight. We don't have any guests. It will just be our small family."

"I really don't feel that to be a good idea, Louisa," Lord

Gilchrist said, leaning forward with each hand on the desk. "I fear it is too upsetting for Mother."

"It is more upsetting for her to have you gone."

The Earl of Gilchrist gave Lady Louisa a look like he highly doubted her words to be the truth.

"It's true," she said with as much earnestness as she had. "She is wracked with guilt that you now avoid leaving this room because of her weak constitution. She feels so awful at the site of your injuries."

"Of course she does," the earl said softly. He instead thought her weak constitution could not bear to look at the outward monster that had ended the life of her husband.

"It is only because she feels the pain you feel," Lady Louisa continued. "She mourns for her child who suffered great pain that she cannot remove from him."

Lord Gilchrist was surprised at Lady Louisa's words. Firstly, it was not at all why he had considered his mother unable to look upon him. Further, he had never contemplated the pain a mother must feel when her child suffered.

It seemed that Lady Louisa's words were wiser beyond her years. For the second time in a short period, he realized how much his little sister had grown in his absence. She had positively been the glue that kept her mother and father together while he was gone.

He didn't want to put any more weight on her shoulders than necessary. If she felt it would bring peace to their mother for him to again join the family for evening meals, he would at least try it once for Lady Louisa's sake.

"If it will make you happy," he said with a huff as he sat back in his high-backed chair.

"It will make both of us happy," Lady Louisa corrected.

She hesitated before getting up to leave. Picking at a ruffle in the cream-colored morning dress she still wore, she looked at her brother as if her eyes might penetrate his thoughts.

"You have spent much time with Lady Abigail this week," she said as casually as possible.

The Earl of Gilchrist huffed air out. Though he wasn't prepared, he had expected his sister to ask as much eventually.

"I've already told you, it is for a project regarding the boys' school."

"I know that is what you say, dear brother, but I wonder if the words are true?"

Lord Gilchrist faked offense.

"Are you impugning my honor?" he asked.

"I would never dream of doing so," Lady Louisa said, hearing his old humor again.

"We used to tell each other everything," she added by way of gleaning more out of him.

"I am afraid I have nothing more to tell you. I am surprised to say that I have enjoyed Lady Abigail's company, but there is nothing beyond that."

"Well, if there was, I might warn you that she has other eyes on her. You might want to make your move soon or miss the chance."

"I will try to keep that in mind in the future. You are a dear for looking out for me, but even if I did have more than just friendship in mind, you forget the lady would need to feel the same."

"Lady Abigail cares not for surface appearance. She is a lady of most pure honor that only sees the heart," Lady Louisa spoke of her best friend's sister-in-law.

Lord Gilchrist reflected on these words as he dressed for

dinner that night. It was correct that of all the people he had been around, he was finding himself most comfortable with Lady Abigail. It was no doubt because she indeed cared about the inward appearance more than the outward.

But he also knew she would deserve better than the life he was destined to lead. He would not subject her to such a path, especially if she had other prospects, as Lady Louisa had mentioned.

CHAPTER 17

When the usual charity party gathered for their weekly delivery, there was a fresh excitement in the air. For the ladies' part, it was no different than the last two weeks they had gone. Each week entailed bringing items to deliver that were most in need.

For Lord Gilchrist and Lady Abigail, there was the added excitement of not only presenting the mittens to the boys who would sorely need them, but also the enjoyment of being in each other's company again.

"Why, Lady Abigail," Lady Louisa said as she watched Abigail walk into the drawing room with her basketful of mittens. "Did you do all of that?"

Lord Gilchrist was already in the sitting room and stood at the entrance of Lady Abigail and the duchess.

"Of course she did," he responded before Lady Abigail could do more than open her mouth. "Why else would she be toting them around if she had not done the work?"

He gave her a sly wink and sat back down.

"They are for the boys. The headmaster said that they had no mittens for this coming winter. Lord Gilchrist told them we would be delivering them so that they can dash them to shreds and darn them up again."

"What a rotten idea for perfectly good gloves," Lady Louisa said, looking at her brother.

"Rotten or not, it is important the boys learn how. Without well-worn gloves of their own, these will make due."

"But all of poor Abigail's hard work," the duchess added.

Lady Abigail wanted to tell her companions that she had not even completed half of the mittens seen here. If the Earl of Gilchrist wanted to cut holes in them, he had every right to do so as he had made most of them.

Instead, she respected his secret and assured the ladies that she was aware of the plan and perfectly fine with it.

It was clear to both Lady Abigail and Lord Gilchrist that both ladies were still teetering on the worry that one might offend the other and end the peace that had happily resided in the families over the past week.

"What else will you be sharing with the young boys today?" Lady Fortuna asked over their light meal, once she joined the party.

Though Lady Fortuna was of a very delicate nature, she not only worked herself beyond what seemed her capability, but also greatly enjoyed stories that she knew she would never have the strength to make on her own.

"I'm not entirely sure. They all were begging for more stories. I am afraid I don't have much. I was gone for only the last two years and then a year in the hospital. I can't imagine rehabilitation to be a fascinating topic for their minds. Though I am sure Lady Abigail could speak for hours on the appalling conditions of patient dressing-gowns in the hospital."

All eyes swiveled to Lady Abigail as the women between Gilchrist and Lady Abigail held their collective breath. Lord Gilchrist spoke the words so calmly and without a look in her direction that the others were sure it was a blatant stab at what he had previously deemed useless conversation.

Instead of being offended at his words and a great outburst ensuing between the two, Lady Abigail crinkled her freckled nose at him.

"I will have you know, Lord Gilchrist," she said with a haughty air, "I know absolutely nothing about hospital gowns and, therefore, could not even comment on the subject."

"How terribly unfortunate that is for you," Lord Gilchrist countered with that wicked twinkle in his blue eyes. "I am sure the discussion of it would have been enthralling."

Isabella let out her air in a burst of hiccupping laughs. It broke the other two ladies from their stares between the two conversing parties.

"I am glad to see you two are on much friendlier terms," the duchess said, putting great emphasis on 'friendlier.'

Lady Abigail immediately looked down at her hands, red with blush. At that moment, she had forgotten the others in the room and continued the same banter that she had shared with the earl on their other occasions in the drawing room.

Now, seeing the faces between them, she realized it most likely teetered towards flirtation. She did her best to ignore the bright smile it brought to her sister-in-law's face as the same assumption came to her mind.

Lady Abigail took a calming breath. She had not woken this morning feeling completely healthy, but she also was not willing to let a little ailment ruin the day that she and the earl had worked so hard for.

Lord Gilchrist wasn't too blind to see that Isabella was insinuating something between them. On the contrary, he was keener to see what Lady Abigail thought of the idea. Much to his surprise, she didn't shrink away in horror as she had done the first night Lady Abigail feared she might dance with him at a ball.

Instead, Lady Abigail looked abashed and, even, dare he think, guilty of knowingly flirting with him. It brought a warm stirring to his heart. For a moment, he forgot all his troubles, the look of his body or even his self-imposed distance from the lady for her sake. For just a split second, he saw what life would be like if he did truly court her and marry Lady Abigail.

The thought seemed to stick in Lord Gilchrist's mind as they made the carriage ride to the Foundling Hospital and school. He was desperate to shake it off, for he was not sure how he could spend the afternoon with her without giving his feelings away.

He stole a look or two in Lady Abigail's direction from across the carriage, but she seemed determined to look out her window in deep concentration. He noticed that she seemed paler since first joining the party and worried that the words had settled in on her and left a sour taste.

She was quiet as they made their way to the hospital and the three other ladies split off in the other direction. Lord Gilchrist reached out his arm to Lady Abigail as he had before and when she gripped it, she leaned on him more heavily than before.

He turned to her then, full of concern. She did look decisively paler and he was sure he could see perspiration beading along the red ringlets that framed her face.

"Lady Abigail, whatever is the matter?" he asked, turning her to face him head-on.

He held both her elbows to steady her.

"I wasn't feeling quite myself this morning. I thought it would pass, but the carriage ride has seemed to make it worse," she said.

Her eyes were deep in concentration, staring straight ahead at the small flower on the earl's lapel.

"Why did you not say something?" he asked increasingly concerned.

"Today was such a special day for all of us. I am sorry to say I was selfish and didn't want to miss it."

"It is not selfish at all to want to see your hard work to its new owner. I cannot let you continue in this state, however. I will take you home right away."

"No, please don't leave on my account. If you would but help me to the carriage, I am sure I will be fine."

"Nonsense," he said, steering Lady Abigail's frame back toward the door. He gripped her hand to turn her and gave a start. "Why, Abigail, you are burning up. That settles it. I am seeing you home right now."

Lady Abigail had to admit she did feel a bit warm. She had done her best to hide her uneasy feeling all morning long, hoping it was going to pass. The jolting of the carriage ride had been too much, in the end.

"What about your sister and the others? You can't just leave them here without an escort or carriage."

"I will have the headmaster go and explain that you are not feeling well. I will ensure that you get home safely and then return for the others," he assured Lady Abigail.

Lord Gilchrist motioned to the headmaster, who was

standing at their side, to go and tell the ladies what he had just said.

The headmaster very much looked like a cat with its hair all ruffled out of place. He had no choice but to do as the earl bid him.

It was not usual for the earl to make demands of those below him, especially when he knew that they would be very displeased with it. This was an emergency situation, however. He was overcome with anxiety and knew he would feel no better until he, himself, saw Lady Abigail safely home.

Though the carriage ride was made as quickly as could be allowed in the streets of London, it felt much too long for the earl. All the jolting and tossing of the ride only seemed to cause Lady Abigail more discomfort.

Finally, they arrived at Lady Abigail's residence. The footman hurried to the door to get proper assistance. Lord Gilchrist, on the other hand, did his best to help Lady Abigail out of the carriage.

Lady Abigail felt quite weakened from the second ride and, between that and her stifling corset, couldn't seem to find enough air. She feared she might faint as the sky seemed to swirl above her.

Without even knowing it, she was caught up in the arms

of the Earl of Gilchrist. He walked as quickly as he could without the help of his cane, a most painful act, while he carried the swooned Lady Abigail through the small front garden and up the front steps.

Just as he felt his hurt leg could take no more, the duke came rushing through the hall and relieved Gilchrist of his burden. He had his sister taken swiftly to her room and a doctor called.

Gilchrist was unsure if he should stay or wait in the hallway for the duke's return. When the man finally descended the stairs again, Gilchrist rushed to meet him.

"Whatever is the matter with her?" Lord Gilchrist asked, full of concern.

"I can't say entirely. Abigail is burning with fever, though," the duke responded.

"I must return. I left the others at the Foundling Hospital," Lord Gilchrist said, torn between staying and going.

"Come with me into my office and tell me what occurred this afternoon," the duke encouraged instead. "Perhaps it will shed some light on Abigail's condition. I have sent for the doctor and he should be here shortly."

"If you would be so kind as to wait for him to convey what you tell me, I will go and retrieve the other ladies. It seems that you too might need a rest."

The two gentlemen walked down the hall and into the duke's office. They both had a good dram of whiskey. The earl's leg was extraordinarily tender and his body exhausted from walking on it, even over that short a distance, without the assistance of his cane.

It didn't matter a whit to him. At the moment that Lady Abigail swooned he thought nothing of the pain in his leg. He only had a resounding urge to get Lady Abigail to the care she would need.

Soon after Lord Gilchrist told the duke all that had transpired, the duke left to collect the others and the doctor arrived. Lord Gilchrist told his story for the second time before the doctor went to look in on his patient.

Upon his return, the doctor informed the earl that Lady Abigail most likely had ague fever from spending too much time out of doors. He doled out his treatments and promised to return tomorrow to check on her condition.

After the doctor left, the duke and ladies arrived. Lord Gilchrist again relayed the details given him, but he was entirely done in. The whole party was invited to stay for a small dinner before returning to their own homes and beds.

The earl would only leave once the duchess promised she would send both he and Lady Louisa any word on a change in Lady Abigail's condition right away. Though it wasn't a happy time, the duchess couldn't have been more thrilled to see this dear gentleman, who was like a brother to her, care so much for the sister-in-law she cherished deeply.

CHAPTER 18

It took Lady Abigail a week before her fever broke and the sickness passed. After that, it was two more weeks before she felt well enough to get out of bed. The illness that had overcome her so suddenly had taken quite a toll on her frame.

The Duke of Wintercrest informed his sister that he was not happy to have his house become a revolving door as, each day, both the Earl of Heshing and the Earl of Gilchrist stopped by to ask on her condition.

As Abigail sat in bed, the duchess, now growing uncomfortably large with child, sat by her side and read or just kept Lady Abigail company while she recovered.

They didn't speak too much about the two gentlemen

who seemed to call each day. Lady Abigail, herself, was too scared to bring the matter up. She was sure that the duchess would favor Lord Gilchrist because of their close connection.

Lady Abigail, for her part, was not of strong enough mind to even consider what it meant to have both gentlemen coming by each day. She knew as she grew in health and strength, she would have to determine which way her heart was leaning, as both men were making an unmistakable gesture.

Soon, Abigail was feeling herself again. She was a little disappointed that the season was soon coming to an end, however, and her small group would be returning to Wintercrest for the duchess's impending birth.

It was her first evening out since her illness. It was a lavish ball, one of the last for the season. She was happy to see all the smiling faces, such as Lady Louisa and Lady Fortuna.

She couldn't help the sting of regret, knowing that Lord Gilchrist wouldn't be in attendance. She had, of course, assumed he wouldn't go, but a small bit of her hoped he would have anyway.

She seemed to forget her regret when the Earl of Heshing appeared and spent much of the evening dancing with her. She was happy to see him again, as well. She had realized that with his devotion to her wellbeing, there must be something deeper to the man than just the superficiality she had seen in the past.

The Earl of Heshing also seemed to want to make his intentions clear to both her and the rest of the crowd that night as he kept to her side. She was happy for the company as he was a charming gentleman.

She told herself that Heshing was a good choice and that if the moment came that he asked for her hand, she wouldn't refuse him. It would be a good choice to make, and her and Gilchrist could remain friends.

Though she spoke the words in her mind, she knew in her heart they couldn't be true. There was a reason that in the time she spent with Gilchrist, she had mentioned everything about her coming and going, except for Heshing. She knew deep down that he would be unhappy to hear it.

If she were truly honest with herself, she cared too much for Gilchrist to share anything with him that might bring him pain. Lady Abigail was sure that the resulting separation of their friendship would bring her pain as well.

As Lady Abigail danced through the night with the Earl

of Heshing, she didn't see the furrowed brow of her disapproving brother or the worried look on her sister-in-law's face. It wasn't until the carriage ride home that Lady Abigail noticed that the other two in her party were filled with concern.

"Whatever is the matter with you two?" she asked on the return carriage ride to their London house.

Both the duke and duchess exchanged looks.

"It's just that you seemed very close to Lord Heshing tonight," the duchess said as delicately as she could muster.

"And what is wrong with that? Is it because I have chosen him over Lord Gilchrist?"

Until the moment that Lady Abigail spoke those words, it had not fully sunk in that her actions that night did reflect a decision of one gentleman over the other. She worried whether she had made the right one, but it was too late to change it now.

"We only want your happiness," the duchess quickly responded. "Of course I was overjoyed to see you and Colton getting close, but if that is not where your heart is, I respect that. It is only…"

"Only what?" Lady Abigail encouraged, unsure of why they would be so hesitant toward Lord Heshing.

"It is only that there have been some concerning things spoken of Lord Heshing," the duke answered for his wife.

"Concerning things? Such as the fact he likes to race horses? You knew this already. You cannot disparage the man for such silly propriety when you yourself did the same," Lady Abigail retorted.

"There were some rumors going about the gentlemen's clubs that he took heavily to gambling."

"He has told me he enjoys the activity. I find no fault with it. It seems he also wins often, so all the better," Lady Abigail defended.

The duke gave a long sigh. He was about to tell his sister something he would rather not.

"When you were ill, Lord Gilchrist came by often. Over the course of time, we discussed a multitude of things. I mentioned that Heshing had also been coming around. He told me a very unnerving tale of the gentleman."

"Go on," Lady Abigail said with her chin held high. She was willing to accept any tale that might be told with courage.

"It seems that, once a month, Gilchrist goes to White's to meet with a solicitor for business. It was on this occasion that he found Heshing arguing with the proprietor. Heshing had racked up a substantial sum of losses in one night and refused to pay the bill the house had footed for him. For this reason, his membership was revoked."

"I am sure it was just a misunderstanding that Lord Gilchrist misheard."

"I suggested the same thing," her brother continued. "But Gilchrist informed me that he was right in the middle of the conversation and had to even make sure that Heshing was removed from the building due to his severe outburst."

Lady Abigail sat back in her chair, truly shocked by this news. Lord Heshing had always made it seem like he had never lost a bet. She would never have considered him to be such a man as to lose and then refuse to pay money owed. She was certain that, somewhere, there had to be a misunderstanding.

He was too kind and light-hearted of a gentleman to picture him giving outbursts and creating scenes in public places. She just couldn't bring herself to reconcile the man she had grown to know with the one her brother was describing.

"I am well aware that Heshing may show up at our door tomorrow asking for your hand after a night like tonight," the duke continued. "I am afraid to say that, after the things I have learned of him, I could not, in good conscience, allow such a match."

"Are you saying that I would need your approval and you would not give it?"

It had been well understood, in years past, that the duke would allow his sister to marry anyone of her choosing.

"I will not deny you on paper, but I will not approve of such a match unless Heshing can vouch for his behavior in a satisfactory manner."

Lady Abigail looked between her brother and the duchess. She hoped that Isabella would come to her aid as she had in times past when the duke was being unreasonable. Instead, Isabella couldn't look her in the eye.

It was then that Lady Abigail realized that the duchess agreed with her husband on the judgment of Lord Heshing. Part of her wanted to accuse them for choosing Gilchrist over Heshing, but in her heart, she could not consider Gilchrist would give false information that would affect the lives of others.

Lord Gilchrist spent the entirety of the season locked

behind doors because of the wrongs others had said about him. Never would a man who had experienced such mistreatment dream of doing the same to another without just cause.

"And if I choose to marry Lord Heshing despite your disapproval?"

No one spoke after Lady Abigail asked this question. Every member of the carriage knew the answer.

The duke and his wife could see no way of accepting a man who seemed to have no honor. If Lady Abigail chose this course that was started that very night in front of the whole town, she would find herself separated from her family.

She thought back to the day that Heshing had taken her in his gig. He had spoken of his lonely existence without another family member to comfort him.

If she chose this path, she would be estranged from at least the duke and duchess, if not the others as well. Was she willing to give up her close connections with her beloved nieces and nephew? To never know the small babe that grew in Isabella's belly?

She partly felt enraged that her brother would ask her to make such a choice. To not even be willing to speak with Heshing and discern for himself the truth of the matter.

She was sure if she asked Heshing, he would clear this misunderstanding.

Lady Abigail thought on the Earl of Gilchrist again. She didn't want to make him out to be a falsifier of information, but in this one instance, he just had to be wrong. She was certain that by morning she would find a reasonable way to resolve the issues between her family, Lord Gilchrist and Lord Heshing.

CHAPTER 19

The next morning, Lady Abigail was wracked with nerves, having not slept well. She paced the drawing room as she hoped that Heshing would call on her. When the butler did come to inform her of a caller, it was Gilchrist instead.

Lady Abigail felt no disappointment in the announcement. Now she could bring her connection to Heshing to his attention and everything would be fixed.

"I'm glad to see you in good health," Lord Gilchrist said as he sat down in the morning room with Lady Abigail.

"I wanted to thank you," Lady Abigail said firstly, "for helping me home. I'm sure I ended up being a great burden, literally, if my brother's telling was correct."

"It was not more than I could bear," Lord Gilchrist said with a humble smile.

"I hope I didn't cause you great pain, though," Lady Abigail added.

Gilchrist shook his head no. In truth, Lady Abigail had no idea the depths of pain that he had felt. None of it had been caused by his leg. It had been weeks of torment, wondering if she would recover.

Even worse was every time he got the courage up to make the short distance to her house to call on her well-being, there always seemed to be an incident.

One day, in fact, he had left the duke's house after calling, only to walk out to a maid taking a child on a daily walk. The child had screamed in terror from one look at him. For several nights after, his dreams had been haunted by the image of crying, fearful children.

"I was grateful to hear that you came so often to check on me. I know that must have been a hardship for you."

"I cannot lie and say that it was easy to do, but…" Lord Gilchrist seemed to take a steadying breath, "it was worth the discomfort to hear that you were mending with each and every visit."

Lady Abigail looked down at her hands. She could hear

the words that Lord Gilchrist was not speaking. He was telling her the affection he felt for her.

"Anyway, it was good to be assured that you were well before I returned to my country estate for good," he said when she gave no response.

Lady Abigail's head shot up in shock at his words.

"For good? What does that mean?"

"It means just that," he said with a nervous chuckle. "Honestly, I can bear the scrutiny of society and the confines of my small London house no longer. I will return to my estates where I will at least have the ease to walk about my own grounds."

The words were like a sinking rock in Lady Abigail's stomach. Was he leaving because she didn't reciprocate his words? She hated the thought that they would be separating on bad terms. It tore through her in a way she had never experienced before.

"Lord Gilchrist," Lady Abigail said softly. "I must ask you something."

"Whatever it is, I will answer the best I can," he replied.

"Last night, after the ball, my brother told me some disturbing news. You see, I have been spending a lot of time with the Earl of Heshing. Christian mentioned that you had seen some ungentlemanly conduct from Lord Heshing."

Lord Gilchrist visibly stiffened at the name. It had been a hard thing to hear that he was not the only one coming to call on Lady Abigail. When he had learned that it was Lord Heshing who was also concerned for her welfare, he had felt no choice but to tell the duke.

Lord Gilchrist often told himself it was for the lady's own well-being that he had done so, but in truth, it was because he was green with jealousy.

"What is your question?" Lord Gilchrist asked, doing his best to hide the icy cold of his tone.

"Well, it's just that. I'm sure you must have been mistaken. I have spent much time with him over the course of the season and I never noticed anything that might suggest he was less than honorable," Lady Abigail quickly rambled on.

"For someone who knows him so well, it is strange that in all our conversations, you never once mentioned him," Gilchrist countered.

He was doing his best to control the emotions threatening to boil over. He couldn't decide what was more hurtful. It certainly couldn't be that Lady Abigail had chosen another over him. Any whole gentleman shined a great light compared to his broken frame.

It was more hurtful that, over their time spent together, he had opened up to her in ways he had done with no one else since arriving back home. It hurt that, in all that time, she had kept something from him.

"I didn't mention him because I didn't want to be rude," Lady Abigail did her best to explain a reason she didn't fully understand herself.

"Perhaps it was for guilt. Maybe you did know that he was not the savory type and knew that I would bring such to your attention had you mentioned him," Lord Gilchrist cut back.

"Those are uncalled for assumptions," Lady Abigail said, now having heat rise in her cheeks.

"Are you calling me the liar, then?" Gilchrist said, coming to stand. "I know what I saw that day at White's and I heard from the wretch's own mouth that he was unwilling to pay a debt he rightfully owed."

"If that is the kind of man you choose to associate yourself with, then I think we have nothing more to say to each other."

"You—" Lady Abigail said, now coming to stand herself.

"You have no right to speak in such a manner. You, who shut yourself up away from the world. How can you possibly judge someone else's character as a gentleman when you don't even have the courage to leave your own house?"

She took a step back, surprised by the words that flowed out of her mouth. She had said too much. Lord Gilchrist was looking at her with rage boiling over.

It was a little bit frightening and Lady Abigail sat back down in her chair. Gilchrist paced the room a few times. He was desperately trying to get control of himself.

In his mind, he was wondering what had ever drawn him to such a woman. Not only had she poor taste in character, but she was maddeningly insulting to boot. Had she been a man under his command, he certainly would have given her a piece of his mind.

Finally, he snatched his cane up and turned to leave the room. There would be no way for him to control his temper in her presence.

"You may do what you like. If you choose to take the rake's word over mine, I can do nothing to stop you. I confess this is where we will have to part ways. I cannot tolerate being in the presence of a woman with so little wits about her."

Lord Gilchrist spoke these words in a soft, defeated tone. It wouldn't have mattered if he had chosen to shout them instead of speaking as he had; they still stung to the very core of Lady Abigail.

In that short declaration, he announced that he had removed all care or feelings for her. Even worse, he had reduced her down to the silly girl who cared for nothing more than to talk about dresses and races.

"If that is how you feel about me, then I agree that we have no more to say to one another. It is a good thing that you will be returning to your country home."

Lady Abigail looked away from the Earl of Gilchrist so that he would not see the tears that stung her eyes. She had grown to see more inside the man than she thought was there. In the end, it seemed that he was truly cruel-hearted deep down to his core.

Without looking her way and without another word spoken between them, Lord Gilchrist took his leave of the room. It was only when he was entirely out of the house that Lady Abigail let herself crumble into the tears that she had held back.

Lady Abigail wasn't entirely sure if she had made the right choice to support Lord Heshing, but one thing she was sure of, she would never forgive Lord

Gilchrist for the hurtful way he had treated her that day.

Lord Gilchrist climbed into his carriage and ordered the driver on to his home with haste. That morning had not gone at all as he had hoped. He had wished to come to her that day to continue to grow a relationship between them.

He had never dared hope that Lady Abigail would come to care for him in the way that he had cared for her. Never in his wildest nightmares, however, would he have considered Lady Abigail accusing him of giving a false statement about another.

Had she honestly thought so little of his character all this time? It was clear that the lady he had thought he was getting close to was not at all the one that was, in fact, Lady Abigail.

He would make plans to leave London immediately. Once proper preparations were made, he would leave his country estates for America. Perhaps in the new world he would also be able to carve out a new life for himself, away from the peerage, the screaming children, shocked ladies, and offending Lady Abigail Grant.

CHAPTER 20

Once Lord Gilchrist had retired to his home, and was calm enough to see clearly, he felt ashamed of his behavior. He should never have raised his voice so, especially at Lady Abigail. It was just further proof to Gilchrist that he no longer had a place in society. He was just as ripped and torn on the inside as he was on the outside.

Over the next few days, his nightly dreams turned much darker than the ones before. It seemed every time he closed his eyes the only image that flashed before him was Lady Abigail's horror-stricken face as he yelled at her and the tears she turned away from his view.

He would never forgive himself for the way he had lost

control of himself. Gilchrist was sure that Lady Abigail would never forgive him either.

The heightened stress of their meeting only seemed to make his emotions more uncontrollable, and he feared another outburst. So, it was with a deep despair that he determined he would never again leave the confines of his house in London, except to take the carriage back to his country seat.

When Gilchrist announced his departure to his mother and sister over dinner that night, they both argued against it. They would not have him run and hide himself away. To Lady Louisa, all her hard work to see her brother return back to his old ways seemed for naught.

Gilchrist listened to their objections quietly. He refused to lose his temper again.

"I appreciate how much you two care for me," he said once they had both said their piece. "I have made up my mind. I will be leaving at the end of the month. I will meet with Mr. Henderson one last time before I go. I need to go over the necessary preparations."

"Preparations? What for?" Lady Gilchrist squeaked, not sure if she could handle more news in one night.

"To see to the needs of our Virginia plantation."

"No, Colton, please don't go again," Lady Louisa pleaded, tears welling in her eyes.

"It will just be for a time. Mr. Henderson is much too old to make the journey anymore."

"So hire another," Lady Louisa encouraged. "Please do not leave."

Gilchrist reached across the table and took his sister's hand.

"I'm sorry, old girl," he said softly. "This is something I just need to do. I can't bear to be here any longer. I fear I will lose all my sense if I am cooped up any longer, and I cannot bear to go out in the community."

"Something you need to do," Lady Louisa said, pulling her hand from her brother's grasp. "That is what you said last time."

Before Gilchrist could say any more to ease his sister, she stood and removed herself from the room. In truth, he couldn't blame her for her anger. He had told her the very same thing the last time he left. That had turned out to be disastrous for all of them.

He knew, however, that this was the right course for him. He needed distance. He needed space between him and an infuriatingly frustrating lady who could never love him as he loved her. He needed to escape the sideways glances and whispered words. More than anything else, he needed to get the image of Lady Abigail from his mind. The only way he could see to do so would be to put the entire length of the ocean between them.

He was sure that, after that dinner, Louisa would go running to Isabella. She would be sure that either Isabella or the Duke could sway his mind. In truth, the only person who could ask him to stay and have it hold weight in his heart would never do so.

He wouldn't even risk the chance of it, however. Lady Abigail could ask him to stay merely upon the request of her sister-in-law and he wouldn't be able to refuse her. Gilchrist knew he surely would go mad if he were to stay, though.

He would not be able to bear the sight of Lady Abigail in company with Heshing. He was sure, after their last conversation, that she would not only include him more in her intimate circle, but most likely marry him.

He would not be able to stand by and watch as she gave her life over to such a horrible man. However, as things stood, she trusted him very little. If Gilchrist were to tell Lady Abigail what he knew to be true of Lord Heshing, she was sure to resent him even more for it.

This was something he couldn't even handle the thought of.

Lady Abigail took quite some time to recover from the events that had transpired with Lord Gilchrist. She had never seen him so out of control of his own feelings, or so hurtful toward her. It affected her for many days after.

Of course, it didn't help that from that moment on, Lord Gilchrist went out of his way to avoid her. Twice, Lady Abigail accompanied the duchess to visit with her dear friends. While she sat and spoke with Lady Louisa and her mother over tea, she secretly hoped that Lord Gilchrist would appear.

He did not leave his office for the entirety of every single one of her visits. It was most disconcerting to her. She desperately wanted to find a way to make amends with Gilchrist. He seemed to be so at odds with Lord Heshing, and the mere fact that she had been developing a relationship with him was offensive to Gilchrist.

What troubled her most was not that there was a rift between her and a friend, but that she feared she might never see Gilchrist again. He certainly made a point to keep them from even looking upon each other, let alone having a conversation.

It was most vexing to Lady Abigail. During the short few months of the season, even when she had disliked him so, Gilchrist had become nevertheless an essential fixture in her life. Now that she had gotten to know him better, she no longer saw the sour exterior that he seemed to turn to as a reflex.

Lady Abigail greatly missed the private conversations they had held in his drawing room while making the mittens for the boys. She had felt so much closer to him than any other lord up until this point in her life. It was as if she had always been secretly holding a small portion of herself back from the opposite sex. With Lord Gilchrist, all her guards had come down and she had felt free to show her whole true self.

"Abigail, is everything alright?" Isabella asked one morning.

The ladies were preparing to leave to visit Lady Louisa's home for the traditional weekly trip to the Foundling Hospital. Abigail hadn't much to show for herself since the last time they had gone to meet with the children. She had been far too weak from her illness.

She still had the basketful of mittens that she hadn't

delivered last time, however. It was Lady Abigail's greatest hope that today would be the day that she finally got a chance to speak with Lord Gilchrist.

"Nothing is bothering me," Lady Abigail said suddenly, shaking herself out of her inner thoughts.

"Are you sure, dear?" Isabella looked on her with worry.

The ladies had just finished breakfast and were gathering in the drawing room before heading over. Isabella laid down the linen she was doing some last-minute fixes to and stared at her sister-in-law intently.

"I'm fine. I have recovered well," Lady Abigail did her best to sound like her usual self.

"I am not entirely speaking of your illness," the duchess responded, a little embarrassed. "I might have overheard the conversation between you and Colton. I never meant to," she added hurriedly, "but these walls are very thin."

"It's alright. I am sure it would have been hard not to hear," Lady Abigail said, shooing away the duchess's worry.

"I so wish there was something I could do to help," Isabella said. "I am afraid I agree with Colton, however."

"So, now you are taking sides?" Lady Abigail said, more exasperated than angry.

"It is not sides. We are just all worried for you, Abigail. I would hate for something bad to happen to you because I didn't voice my concern."

"And I have spent the most time with Lord Heshing over the last few months, far more than any of you. Does that mean you question my judgment? That I am not able to discern when someone is being dishonorable? I can promise you that Heshing has been the perfect gentleman, with no signs of any character folly."

"I do believe you," Isabella said, placing her hand on top of Lady Abigail's. "However, I know that sometimes," she struggled to find the words, "the face a man shows to the ones he cares for is sometimes his best. He keeps the dark parts of himself deeply hidden."

"I wish I could change your mind about him," Lady Abigail said.

She cared for her sister-in-law as much as any other member of her family. She deeply wished she could find a way for them all to come together somehow and find peace again.

"I sincerely hope you can," Isabella said with a soft smile.

CHAPTER 21

The four ladies sat around the comfortable sitting room of the Gilchrist house. In many ways, this room had become a second home for Lady Abigail. This particular day, she sat on the end of her seat, anticipating Lord Gilchrist's entrance through the door.

She wouldn't be able to engage him right away, but he would have no choice but to speak with her when they went to the boys' school together.

Their luncheon was coming to its end, and still, Lord Gilchrist had yet to join them. Lady Abigail didn't want to draw attention to her need to speak with him. She was sure, outside of Isabella, no one else knew the situation that had caused a rift between the two of them.

"Is Lord Gilchrist not joining us today?" Lady Fortuna asked, much to Lady Abigail's relief.

"Unfortunately, he won't be," Lady Louisa said without looking up from her teacup.

The duchess shared a glance with Lady Abigail before asking, "Is he not feeling well?"

"No, he is his same pigheaded boorish self," Lady Louisa said, full of spite.

Realizing she had spoken her irritation aloud, she looked around the room apologetically. The duchess knew that Louisa must be really upset for her to voice her feelings in such a way.

"I'm sorry," Lady Louisa said, setting down her teacup. "Colton won't be joining us today because he is making preparations to return to the country for a short time."

"Returning to the country?" Lady Abigail couldn't help but say, a little louder than she should have. "Not for long, I hope," she added, trying to smooth over her outburst.

"No, not for long," Lady Louisa said, but still with a bitter edge to her tone. "He will be leaving next spring for the Virginias."

All the women in the room sat there with their mouths open.

"We have a plantation there," Lady Louisa explained to the gaping crowd. "He intends to oversee the holdings since our solicitor is getting on in age."

"But, he will not stay?" the duchess asked with concern in her eyes.

Lady Louisa smoothed the skirts of her cotton walking dress to hide the tears welling in her brown eyes.

"He claims that he only plans to go for a short period of time and then return," Lady Louisa finally answered softly.

Isabella reached over and took her friend's hand to give her strength.

"I am sure if he says he will return, he will."

"Yes, but what part of him?" Lady Louisa murmured in despair. "The last time he left, he returned half of who he once was. What will happen this time?"

A tear slipped down Lady Louisa's cheek, and the three women hurried around her like clucking chickens. Lady Abigail did her best to focus on Lady Louisa's pain and not dwell on the lump growing inside of her own heart.

Lord Gilchrist stood outside the drawing room door and listened to the sound of his sister crying yet again since he had told her of his plans.

"Colton is not off to war. Perhaps he will come home better than he has been since his return?" the duchess encouraged.

"You only know the half of it," Lady Louisa said, now overcome with her emotions. She was dabbing at her eyes with a provided silken handkerchief. "He has such awful, violent nightmares at night. He doesn't think I know, but I hear him scream. That is only on the nights he does sleep. Sometimes he will go days without leaving the office."

Lady Abigail was surprised to hear this news. She knew that Lord Gilchrist had struggled with the mental scars that came with battle. She had no idea that it was so devastating as to cause violent nightmares.

Lord Gilchrist was seething now outside the door. He walked away in a fit of rage. It was bad enough that Louisa had been aware of his nightmares. There was no reason for her to go and share his most intimate secret with every lady she sat down to tea with.

Next, there would be a mob outside the door insisting the monster be transferred to Bedlam Asylum. He couldn't stand the betrayal he felt, that his own sister was encouraging others to think him mentally deficit.

He knew that it would only give Lady Abigail more reason to doubt his opinion of the offending lord. She would consider his mind to be totally defective.

Gilchrist paced his office, picturing Lady Abigail and Heshing laughing as they talked about his lost mind. It was worse than any garish stare or pitiful look he might have gotten in the past. The thought of Lady Abigail laughing and continuing to collude with Lord Heshing was more than he could take.

Lady Abigail was wracked with torment as the four ladies took the carriage ride to the Foundling Hospital. It had taken some time to calm Lady Louisa down. The duchess had tried to insist that they cancel the trip for the day, but Lady Louisa wouldn't have it.

It was a toll on her delicate frame to have so much emotion flow out at once. Despite this, she was determined to see this project through for the sake of the children.

"I am sure there is nothing else that can brighten my dark mood other than the smiling faces of the little girls," she had announced when the time came for them to take the carriage.

Now they were inside and traveling down the streets of London. It was far too quiet, giving Lady Abigail plenty of time to consider her own feelings toward Lord Gilchrist's leaving.

She was sure it was all her doing. Gilchrist had only chosen to go after their argument. It was her fault that he would be shutting himself far away and hurting so many whom he loved and cared for.

The weight of guilt was like a stone on her chest, making it hard to breathe. Though she had determined not to cause a rift in her family, it seemed she had done so anyway.

When the ladies walked up the steps to the hospital, they were once again greeted by the headmaster.

"Where is Lord Gilchrist?" the headmaster said when Lady Abigail alone moved to go with him.

"He was indisposed and unable to come today. He sends his deepest apologies. I would be happy to give the boys a small lesson on mending, however."

Lady Abigail did her best to sound upbeat and pleased, though she felt neither. She was also painfully aware that the headmaster had no like for women and little respect for ladies. She shifted the full basket of mittens in her hand, the one that the headmaster apparently hadn't manners enough to take, as she waited for him to lead the way to the boys' school.

"I feel that without your escort, it wouldn't be appropriate to attend to the boys," the headmaster said, looking down his nose at her.

Lady Abigail knew how he felt about her. She couldn't help the thought that slipped past her at that moment. If Lord Gilchrist had been there, the headmaster would never have been allowed such rude treatment of her.

"What about the gloves? The boys will need them this winter, at the very least," she said, motioning to the basket in her hand.

"I will take those now," the headmaster said, removing the basket from Lady Abigail's arms.

His manners were not gracious. Lady Abigail couldn't help but wonder how he expected to get the necessary donations for the children with such an attitude. Without so much as a thank you, the headmaster turned on his heels and disappeared down the hall.

Lady Abigail hesitated for a moment, not sure what she should do next. She could still see the other ladies and hear the soft rustle of their skirts as they moved down the opposite hall. She turned and hurried quickly to catch up with them.

"Abigail, is everything all right?" Lady Fortuna asked when Lady Abigail joined her at the rear of the group.

"Yes, the boys' school headmaster said they had unfortunately made other plans for the day. I thought I might join you ladies instead. If that is alright, of course."

"Yes," Lady Fortuna said with a soft smile on her lips.

"I only wish I had something to give to the girls. The headmaster took the gloves," Lady Abigail said, looking down at her empty hands.

"We will find a use for you, I promise," Lady Fortuna said from her side.

Lady Abigail forgot, or at least placed aside, her worries as she spent the afternoon with the children. With no dresses to fit like the other ladies, Lady Abigail made it her task to entertain the younger children while they waited their turn.

First, she read them a story, then taught them how to play a simple card game. Finally, as the afternoon wound down, Lady Abigail was enthralled in a world of imagination as the girls danced and twirled with little rag dolls.

Lady Abigail was so lost in games with the children that

she forgot where she was for a time. She had so missed playing with her little nieces and nephew, it was a joy to bring a light to small children's eyes again.

It was at this moment she realized how much she missed home. She looked over at the duchess who was very round with child now. It would be only a few more weeks before she would add another babe to the family.

The thought of a new life entering the world filled Lady Abigail with an urgency to resolve the disagreements going on between her and Gilchrist. Lady Abigail was determined that she would resolve the rifts before the newest member joined her family. She would set everything back to how it once had been before their trip to London for the season.

As they walked back to the carriage at the end of the visit, Lady Abigail stayed at the duchess's side.

"I haven't been a very good sister," Lady Abigail said. "I have been so worried about my own life that I didn't even consider how you might be holding up. You must be so troubled, and that can't help your condition."

"Oh, I am a sturdy old thing," Isabella said, swinging her arm into Lady Abigail's. "I am sorry to see Louisa so troubled," the duchess continued with a crestfallen brow, "but short of being there for her, there is not much more I can do."

Lady Abigail put a gentle hand on the duchess's swollen belly.

"The time is getting near now. Perhaps we should return home too," Lady Abigail responded.

"Yes," the duchess said with a deep sigh. "I spoke to Christian about that just today. I think it will probably be only a few more weeks before I really must go. If you wish to stay, I am sure your aunt would be happy to chaperone you."

"I think I might be ready to return home with you," Lady Abigail said honestly.

The duchess raised a brown brow in question. Lady Abigail was always looking forward to the social time of the season. She was never one to want to leave before all the balls and parties were over.

"I miss home, Mother, the children," Lady Abigail explained. "Plus, I fear staying any longer might just cause more trouble."

"I miss them too," the duchess agreed. "You don't have to worry about causing trouble, though. There is nothing you have done or said that could be construed as such.

You spoke from your heart. Your brother and I both respect you for that."

"Yes, well I seem to have caused plenty of trouble with a certain lord," Lady Abigail said under her breath.

"If there is one thing I have learned from my own years of uncertainty," the duchess said with a profound amount of wisdom, "it's that things always find a way to work out. You will get your chance to tell Colton all you want, I am sure of it."

Lady Abigail smiled. Isabella knew her well enough to understand the particular lord was Gilchrist. Lady Abigail couldn't help but feel relieved, knowing that the duchess was in sync with her thoughts. With Isabella's help, she would find a way to make everything right before they had to return to their own country seat.

CHAPTER 22

As Lady Abigail expected, the Duchess of Wintercrest did arrange a way for Lady Abigail to confront Lord Gilchrist. Unlike before, when he had stayed hidden in his office, he had no choice but to join the guests when a dinner party was again thrown at his house in his own honor.

The duchess had used his trip to America as a reason to have one last dinner party before he left. There would be no way that Lord Gilchrist could escape a party held in his honor. It was Lady Abigail's chance to confront him and hopefully mend the bond between them.

Lady Abigail dreaded the thought of Lord Gilchrist traveling far across the sea and all the while holding in his mind the thought that she was nothing more than a silly little girl who had no faith in his judgment.

As Lady Abigail dressed, she took a painstaking amount of time to make sure she looked just right. She had never cared to impress a gentleman with her looks, knowing her natural way was sufficient for her needs. But seeing Lord Gilchrist for the first time in so many weeks made her heart stir with nerves.

She smoothed the folds of her blue velvet dress that contrasted perfectly with the rich, red ringlets she had asked her maid to place in a waterfall effect. She had even taken the time to have a matching blue velvet ribbon woven through her hair along with some pearls.

"Oh, you look lovely," the duchess cooed upon entering Lady Abigail's room. "That dress does wonders for your complexion."

"You don't think it brings out my freckles too much?" Lady Abigail asked, covering the rusty-colored specks along her nose. "Mother always said that dark colors only make one's blemishes pop out more."

"You look enchanting in it," the duchess said with eyes full of truth. "Colton couldn't ignore you, even if he wanted to."

Lady Abigail was about to respond, but just then, the

duchess grabbed the folds of her dress under her swollen belly. Lady Abigail rushed to her side and sat the duchess down in a chair while she took some steadying breaths.

"Nothing to worry about," Isabella said, but she still gratefully accepted the small glass of wine that Lady Abigail poured for her.

"Just this little one reminding me the end is near," the duchess said after a sip. Her tone was very ominous.

Lady Abigail knelt at her sister-in-law's feet. She should have cared how it might wrinkle her gown, but she had no thought for it at the moment.

"Are you scared?" Lady Abigail said, placing a soft hand on the duchess's belly. She giggled when a kick replied.

"No, not really. It was much scarier the first time around. I didn't know what to expect then," the duchess replied, though she was far off in the memory of her twins.

"I would think this would be worse, though, now that you know what is coming?"

"Actually," the duchess replied with a dreamy look in her eyes, "I think I am more excited because I know what is going to happen. At the end of all the discomfort, I will have a beautiful little angel in my arms."

Lady Abigail was so mesmerized by the duchess's words and the impending life that she forgot for a moment what she had planned for the night. Just as the dream began, however, it disappeared, and Lady Abigail was again wakened to her mission.

The dinner party was only the most intimate friends. When Lady Abigail first arrived at Lord Gilchrist's house, he was not in sight, but it was not long before she found him. He was sipping an amber liquid from his glass by the warm hearth, while talking with a portly man with a thick mustache.

Lady Abigail later learned that the man was the Mr. Henderson who facilitated the work for Lord Gilchrist's property in the Americas. He seemed a kind-hearted, jovial man. Lady Abigail, however, had one mission that night and she wouldn't let her mind lose focus of it.

She had to wait, however, until the end of the meal. Lord Gilchrist was seated at one far end of the table, while she was at the other. He seemed to look over the whole crowd with his eyes passing right over her.

No matter how hard Lady Abigail tried to catch his

attention for a moment, Gilchrist was adamantly against it.

Lord Gilchrist would suffer this last night with Lady Abigail. He was reluctant to accept Isabella's idea of yet another dinner party. The last one had turned out so horribly. Why she thought another one would be better was beyond him.

He had to hold onto the hearth when Lady Abigail walked into the room. He was sure he had never seen someone look so stunning as she did that night in her rich, royal blue gown and hair alight in the fire's glow.

Though he could sense she was desperate to get his attention, he couldn't bear it. He would have this night pass as quickly as possible, so he could be on his way and out of her life permanently. Only then was he sure he could release the tension her presence created in him.

As the meal finished and all retired to the drawing room for light entertainment, Lady Abigail was sure that this was her time to confront Lord Gilchrist. It was as the night was drawing to a close and she saw Gilchrist try to slyly make his escape from the room that Lady Abigail blocked his path.

With a sharp intake of breath, Lord Gilchrist found

himself looking down on the lovely face that belonged to such a vexing angel. He had hoped to make his escape before anyone was the wiser, but it had not escaped Lady Abigail's notice.

"Could we please speak for a moment," Lady Abigail said before Lord Gilchrist managed to sidestep her.

"I can't possibly imagine you or I have anything left to say to each other."

"Please, just wait," Lady Abigail pleaded, holding up her hands to stop him. "I cannot bear the thought of you leaving with these feelings between us. There must be a way to make amends."

Lord Gilchrist faltered in his determination to avoid her at all cost.

"Lady Louisa also spoke of some, well, internal struggles you have. I would hate to think that I might have upset you and made things worse."

"I promise my sanity is not based on your value of my character," Lord Gilchrist shot back.

"I am trying to find a way to make this better," Lady Abigail said, sensing Gilchrist's irritation.

"Are you still choosing to take Heshing's supposed

character over my own witness?" Lord Gilchrist asked, cutting straight to the point of their difference.

Lady Abigail opened her mouth, then closed it again. Her situation with Heshing was a very complicated one. When she was alone with Heshing, the world seemed so simple and free to enjoy. When she was away from him, it seemed everything around her was pitted against them.

Perhaps it was for that reason only that she felt so connected to the man. Her mother had always teased her, as a child, for loving the wounded and hopeless. Once, when Lady Abigail was a child, she had found a chick that had fallen out of its nest.

Her mother had insisted she leave it be. Lady Abigail, always determined and stubborn, instead put the chick back in the nest. Again the next day, she found it on the ground. The Dowager Duchess had explained that because Lady Abigail had touched it, the mother had rejected her own babe.

Still, Lady Abigail wouldn't give up on the little thing. She took it into the folds of her gown and brought it home with her. It was Lady Abigail's greatest wish to nurse it to health. Her mother told her it was of no use as the chick would almost surely die.

Lady Abigail was one for impossible causes. She hoped that this need to help others who seemed to have no hope of their own was not the only reason she found herself holding on to her relationship with Heshing so tightly.

"It is only that..." Lady Abigail started. She could see the cool look in Gilchrist's blue eyes. It was not what he wanted to hear. "Please, if you will just let me explain."

"Then explain," he said, waving a hand to two chairs in a small alcove at the side of the drawing room.

They both took their seats in silence. To any onlooker, it would seem like they were mending what was once broken between them. The storm inside Lady Abigail, however, told her that might not be a possibility.

"It is not that I don't trust your judgment or your witness," Lady Abigail started once they were seated. "I just feel that Heshing is seen in an unfair light. He is all alone with no family to support him."

"Choosing to be alone doesn't make one rude, irresponsible and reckless," Lord Gilchrist retorted.

Lady Abigail couldn't help but smile at his words.

"Forgive me," she said when he was taken aback by her look, "but I sometimes picture you like Heshing. All the stories that Isabella and your sister told me. I just see a lot of those same stories in him."

"Well, I am not that man anymore," Lord Gilchrist said, stiffening in his chair.

He didn't want to have this conversation, and he certainly didn't want it to become about who he used to be compared to who he was now.

"Would you tell me?" Lady Abigail asked. When he didn't understand her meaning, she tried again. "Would you tell me what happened to you? We used to tell each other anything. Even the things we said to no one else."

Lord Gilchrist had shared with Lady Abigail what he could never form into words for another. He was surprised that she had done the same. She had seemed so at ease and her normal self with him. How much of herself did she keep hidden from the rest of the world?

Gilchrist thought the request over as he massaged his temples. It was a scene that played in his head over and over again. That alone should have made it easy enough to say. It was a picture forever in his memory but stuck behind an invisible wall.

He hoped bringing it out and sharing it might help relieve the burden, even slightly. If there was one person who he could share this intimate tale with in all his life, it was Lady Abigail. Though they had their differences, they also had a bond of secrecy.

"It was a fire. I was in a tent with a private. He had been injured badly and was seeing the surgeon. I promised to stay by his side. I don't exactly remember how the fire started. It engulfed the tent fairly quickly. I was attempting to get the private out when there was an explosion."

He rubbed his thigh without thinking.

"I am told that some of the chemicals used by the surgeon can be quite flammable. I assume that is what caused the blast. It threw me back and knocked me out. My left side was severely burned, as I'm sure you have noticed," he added with a wry smile, "and several fragments are embedded in my leg. That's why I have the cane."

"And the private?" Lady Abigail asked softly.

"He was just one of the many I couldn't save."

Lord Gilchrist hung his head low. There had been many casualties through his choice to go into battle. He had tried not to dwell on all the men under his command who would not come home to their families, but to be in the same room as one and unable to save him had been too much.

Then, when he had come to in the hospital, burned on half his body and unsure if he would even live, he had been informed that his father too had succumbed to his deadly choice to join the Regulars.

He knew he couldn't prevent all deaths in a war, but maybe, had he stayed home, another would have done a better job in his place. One thing he was sure of, had he not gone, his father would still be alive.

He wasn't feeling better at all for telling his tale. If anything, it only brought it all back to the surface. The feeling of the fire, the inability to breathe in the smoke-filled air, the sizzling crackle of his own flesh. Worst of all were the blank eyes of the private laying on the floor next to him.

Lady Abigail reached across and took Lord Gilchrist's hand. It wasn't entirely proper, but she didn't care. It was easy to see he was wracked with not just the torment of his own injuries but also the weight of all the men who had been in his care.

Gilchrist looked up at Lady Abigail in surprise when she slipped her hand into his. It was as if a window had been opened to let light into a darkened room. In her eyes, he could see her take a portion of his pain and suffering on herself. It was like getting a lungful of air for the first time in years.

CHAPTER 23

Lady Abigail didn't get much sleep the night after Lord Gilchrist shared with her the accident that had led to his permanent disfigurement. Though she had not been there when it happened, she was sure she could see the eyes of the young man in his charge.

It was no wonder that Lord Gilchrist struggled with nightmares and uncontrollable fits of rage. She would feel the same if she had such a weight of guilt on her shoulders. Then to return home with this deep struggle within, only to have the world you once knew reject you.

Lady Abigail was desperate to free Lord Gilchrist from the chains that bound him. She wasn't sure how it would be possible. One thing she knew for certain, however, was that running and hiding would not solve his problems.

It seemed to be all Lord Gilchrist was capable of. He would hide himself away or run to far-off lands when hiding wasn't enough. She knew there had to be a better answer. Lady Abigail was certain she must be the one to find it for him.

"I said, are you having a good time?" Lord Heshing asked.

"I'm sorry," Lady Abigail said, realizing she was being very rude to her caller.

Lord Heshing had arrived just after breakfast to call on her. She had been so occupied with worry over Lord Gilchrist, she was ashamed to say she wasn't the greatest of hosts.

"I feel as if you have been lost in thought quite regularly. Am I that much of a bore?" Heshing asked as he leaned back in his seat.

Lady Abigail looked at his relaxed form. He was only meaning it in teasing, of course. She smiled shyly.

"I only heard some disturbing news last night. It has caused me much distress, is all."

"Well, what was it? I would love to help," Heshing said, coming forward in his seat again.

Lady Abigail would never share with anyone what Lord Gilchrist had told her the night before. It was much too personal for her to speak of, even to Lady Louisa. To tell Heshing, a man who Gilchrist had professed hatred for, was beyond an overstep of bounds.

Instead, Lady Abigail turned to the thought of what Gilchrist had said about Heshing. Perhaps if she shared with him the rumors going around about his behavior, he would be able to clear the air and right all the wrong.

"It is about Lord Gilchrist," Lady Abigail started.

She couldn't help but notice the dark cloud that came over Heshing's normally charming face.

"That old beast," he said, quite proud of his slight.

Lady Abigail didn't like it at all.

"Don't call him that!" she shot out, before she could curtail her tone. "He has overcome much," she added with a soft tone.

She couldn't help but become a little self-conscious when Heshing raised a blonde brow at her outburst. He may have liked her spirited nature when riding in gigs and attending races, but he hadn't seen how strong Lady Abigail could be when it came to defending a friend.

"Plus, it was in regards to you," she added.

Heshing seemed to like that the conversation was turning back to him.

"Yes, and what about me? Does Gilchrist know I beat his time at my last race?" he said rather boastfully.

"No. Lord Gilchrist informed my brother of an incident. It's making the duke very uncomfortable, with me spending so much time in your company, that is."

"Oh really," Heshing said, not with surprise, as Lady Abigail had expected, but with a quiet resolve.

Perhaps he had been expecting this moment to come all along.

"I know the incident that you are speaking of. It was a silly little misunderstanding. I had it all sorted out by that afternoon," Heshing said with a wave of his hand.

Lady Abigail couldn't help but feel a little relief at his words.

"That Gilchrist can be so dramatic at times. It seems he lets his emotions run wild. I am sure he made things out to be a bigger deal than necessary. He certainly did that morning. He was going on and on as if he was some great hero rescuing the poor proprietor from a great evil," Heshing said with a chuckle.

"As you said, though, he has been through a trial. I suppose he is still partly in that military world and sees things as more severe than they should be."

Lady Abigail found sense in Heshing's words. Perhaps this had all been a misunderstanding as she had hoped. Gilchrist could get overly upset very quickly. Maybe he saw more in the situation than there really was.

There would be no point in arguing that fact with her brother. The duke was not very happy with the fact that Lady Abigail still spent much of her time in the presence of the Earl of Heshing.

There would be no way to correct the past misunderstanding, but she could find a way to move forward. If her brother and sister-in-law saw his true character now, they would change their opinion of him.

A wonderful plan was growing inside her mind.

"You do believe me?" Lord Heshing bore into her with his soft eyes.

"Of course," she assured him. "I am sure it is all just a misunderstanding, as I suspected."

"Good," he said with relief as he relaxed his arm on the back of the chair. "Because I would hate if I couldn't call on you anymore."

"Well," Lady Abigail hesitated, "I believe you. I fear the duke and duchess may be a whole different case. I fear that my brother doesn't trust you and would rather I gave my attention elsewhere."

"A simple question could change all of that," Heshing said with that playful gleam in his eyes. "If we were to be, let's say, more formally attached to each other, His Grace would have to accept us."

Lady Abigail felt that flutter in her heart and did her best to swallow it down. She had a feeling that he was very near to asking her to marry him.

"I am afraid, if a question was asked," she said as slowly as possible, "I would have to decline."

"Decline?" Heshing responded with utter shock.

"Not because I would want to. I am sure my brother wouldn't come around if I forced him to in such a way. Both he and the duchess would only push against us harder. It is better to win over their affections first."

Heshing got up from his seat and came to sit by Lady Abigail. The maid in the corner only looked up for an instant before returning to a basket of mending she had at her side. Lady Abigail was keenly aware of their closeness and the masculine smell that seemed to float along the air with Heshing's closeness.

"I think my affection for you has been made quite clear over the last few months," Heshing said in a low voice. "I had thought you felt the same towards me."

"I do," Lady Abigail said.

She did have affection for the man. He was charming and handsome. More than that, she could see herself living a happy life of bringing a family back into his home. A small part of her wondered if she was only trying to save another wounded chick, but she was sure that wasn't the case.

"Then what does it matter what the duke thinks?" Heshing said with a small laugh. "If we both care for each other, then we should agree to marry right now."

It was the first time, after all the months of teasing, that the actual words were spoken. Lady Abigail drew in a sharp breath. She didn't want to hurt Heshing, but at the same time, she could never agree to something that might separate her from her family.

She knew that this was something that Lord Heshing couldn't understand. He had grown up an only child, then spent the last few years alone. So much of what he did was because he desired to, with no regard for how it might affect others. After all, he had no one else to think of.

Lady Abigail wasn't sure how she could make Heshing see that, though she valued her own happiness, she would not seek it when it caused her family unhappiness. There had to be a way, instead, for the two to reconcile.

"I can't do that," Lady Abigail said sorrowfully. "I couldn't bear to choose a life that would separate me from my family. I care for them too much to have hard feelings between us."

Heshing thought this over.

"But, you see, if we married now," he said, as if the idea had just come to him, "they would have no choice but to accept us. We could run away and elope."

"I would never do such a thing," Lady Abigail said. "It is a fearful, spineless move."

"Would your brother truly deny us?" Heshing asked, trying a different tactic now.

"No, he would never do that. He has always said he

wishes happiness for me. He would not deny me if I asked."

"So then, it is settled," Heshing responded, clapping his hands.

Lady Abigail had a strange feeling that this was more of a negotiation than a marriage proposal. It was not at all how she had expected it to go.

"No, it is not," she said firmly. "Christian would agree, but he wouldn't be happy with it. I doubt that taking such a course would help him to see your good character either. We must find a way to resolve the matter first. Only then will we be able to start a life on good terms with my family."

"Is it really that important to you?" Heshing asked, a little exasperated by the idea. "After all, how much would you see any of them? You would come with me to live at my country seat. We would only meet with them occasionally."

Lady Abigail was horrified by the thought. She couldn't bear the idea. Of course, she knew that when the time came for her to marry she would see less of her family. No longer would she live at Wintercrest Manor. She would spend less time with the twins, the new baby, and

Jackie. To have it said so coldly, though, seemed inhuman.

"I understand that I would not see them as much," Lady Abigail said, doing her best to hide her irritation at his words. "However, I would still want to be on affectionate terms with them. If that cannot be done, I see no more reason to discuss the matter."

"I understand," Heshing said, settling back into his good humor. "Then it seems I must not just find a way into your heart, but also into the heart of the duke."

His raised brow at this remark had the desired effect of making Lady Abigail laugh. It was then settled that Heshing would take her on a ride through the park on the morrow, as they had previously planned, but then he would return to have a family dinner with her at the duke's house.

In Lady Abigail's mind, this could be the first of many private audiences with her family that Heshing could use to win them over with his charm. He was so wonderfully humorous and such a likable fellow, she was sure that in no time at all her brother and Isabella would come to feel for him as she, herself, did.

CHAPTER 24

Lady Abigail was happy to walk down her townhouse steps to join Lord Heshing in his carriage. She was surprised to see that instead of the gig they normally rode through the park in, today he had his barouche with the top back.

It seemed a silly thing to bring such an important vehicle when they were only going to turn around the park. Lady Abigail looked up at the sky. Impending bad weather might warrant the use of a coach that could be covered, if needed.

It was, however, a beautiful sunny day. Lady Abigail could only surmise that Lord Heshing had brought such a beautiful carriage with two beautiful chestnut horses pulling it to impress her brother. It touched her heart to know he cared this much about appeasing her wish for him to make friends with her family.

She sat down in the seat next to him at the front of the carriage where he controlled the steeds. It was a bit tighter quarters than she was used to, but she felt it silly to sit in the back when he sat up front.

"I have a surprise for you," he said, hitching the horses and starting on his way.

Lady Abigail could tell by the way he hadn't looked her way yet that he had to be nervous. Her eyes didn't miss the tight grip his gloved hands had on the reins.

She wasn't dressed for anything outside of a trip around the park in her soft cotton walking dress in a shade of dark cream.

"What is it?" Lady Abigail asked when he explained no further.

"If I told you, it wouldn't be a surprise anymore," Heshing replied with a wicked slant to his eyes.

They sat in silence as he drove down the street. She watched as they passed all the entrances to Hyde Park. She wondered if he was perhaps taking her somewhere else. Soon, the whole of the city seemed to be passing her by. She began to grow worried when they finally stopped at an establishment.

"Is this where the surprise is?" Lady Abigail asked.

She looked up and down the building. It was a tavern of some sort and not a very reputable one, if she judged correctly. Not only the building, but this whole part of London seemed to be coated in a thick layer of grime. It was not at all where she had hoped to take her journey today.

Heshing stepped out of the front seat, hooking the leather leads to the seat for safe keeping. He reached up to take her hand as well. Lady Abigail hesitated.

"It is only a stop, not the final destination," he said, waiting for her hand.

Lady Abigail sighed softly in relief. She placed her hand in his and he helped her down. He walked her to the back of the carriage and motioned for her to take her place there.

"Heshing, whatever is going on?" Lady Abigail asked, full of confusion.

"All will be explained shortly, my dear," he said as she got in.

Instead of seating himself beside her, he instead flipped up the retractable hood and entered the establishment.

Lady Abigail sat nervously inside the small compartment. She was full of worry, unsure what exactly Heshing had arranged. He did tend to have a spontaneous personality, but this seemed like much more than even she had expected from him.

Finally, she caught a glimpse of Heshing's brown velvet hat as he emerged from the tavern. In his company were two other men. One seemed to be a coachman, as he promptly sat at the front of the carriage.

The other man, who appeared to be a servant, stood and spoke with Heshing for a moment. Finally, Lady Abigail made out a note being passed from Heshing to his man before the latter turned and walked away.

She leaned forward in her seat as Heshing came to join her. All the warmth of the sun seemed to vanish under the dark cover of the carriage. When Heshing entered, a cold wind blew in with him.

Heshing tightened his riding jacket a little closer around himself and blew warm air into his gloved hands.

"It's getting beastly cold out there," he said by way of conversation.

Lady Abigail was stunned. He was speaking to her as if this whole occasion was utterly ordinary. It was anything but that in Lady Abigail's mind.

"Heshing, you must tell me what is going on. I am becoming a bit concerned," Lady Abigail said as coolly as she could muster once the carriage started again.

"Do not worry, my dear. All will be explained in due time."

It was the second time he had called her such. It was an endearment meant for two attached. Though they had spoken of the possibility, she didn't think that warranted the use of the intimate term.

She sat silently as the journey continued. They passed through the city and began to enter the outlying lands.

"I wish you would have told me that we were to leave town. My brother is expecting us for dinner. I would have brought a maid along, as well," Lady Abigail added.

She was never one for propriety, but there was a difference between taking an open gig ride in the park with a gentleman and driving a carriage to an unknown place out of town. They were dangerously close to causing much gossip after this matter.

Though she rarely cared what others gossiped about her, it would make it that much more difficult to win her brother over to Lord Heshing. This was a bold move which bordered on that recklessness that the duke had worried about.

"I sent a note along with my man. They are aware that we won't be returning tonight," he replied coolly as he looked out at the passing landscape.

"Not tonight? What does that mean? Really, Heshing, this is too much for me. I think you should tell me right now what is going on or take me home," Lady Abigail said, mustering all her will to control the frustration inside her.

He smiled softly at her. Heshing had a dull, calming look to his eyes that instilled fear in Lady Abigail. Removing his gloves one by one he began to get himself comfortable in the carriage for a long ride.

"You see, I couldn't wait for your brother to come around," he said, stretching his legs as much as the tight confines allowed. He was sitting with his back to the driver and across from Lady Abigail.

"We are on our way to Gretna Green to be married."

"What?"

It was the only word that Lady Abigail could manage to procure from her mouth. He had stated the fact so naturally, like it was apparent.

"I knew once you were in the carriage with me, you would see reason. Your brother is dear to you, this I understand, but it shouldn't impede our happiness."

"Happiness? Heshing, you have kidnapped me! I want this coach turned around this instant!" Lady Abigail said in a full rage.

"Yesterday, you said yourself that you agreed to us being married. I am merely speeding up the process."

"This is not how I would want it to be done. I would want my family around and happy for the marriage. I thought you understood that?"

"Unfortunately, I don't have time to wait for that," Heshing said with a tilt of his head.

"What does that mean?"

"You see, I have been growing a rather increasing amount of debt over the last few years. I came to London to find a wife and rectify the situation. You seemed all too happy to fill that role. Now, we are to be wed and my financial situation will be fixed. Isn't it a bit of luck that we also find each other agreeable company?"

He spoke his words as if all of this was perfectly logical. To Lady Abigail, he would have been clearer speaking a different language.

"I don't find you at all agreeable at this moment. You will take me home this instant!"

"My dear, I have already sent a note on, as I said, explaining to the duke where you will be. What other concern might possibly warrant you wanting to turn around? I know you are sorry to not have your family with you, but they will come around in time," Heshing said as if he was speaking to an errant child.

"How about that I refuse to marry you! I was mistaken in thinking I know you at all. I will not marry you, Lord Heshing, and I demand you take me home at once," Lady Abigail said, fully aware that her face was puffing with rage.

She leaned forward in her seat to catch the attention of the driver. Lord Heshing tilted to the side to block her way.

"You have two choices. You may return to London as the Countess of Heshing or be ruined. It is already well known that we are taking a carriage ride together. Not to mention the fact that many have already begun to talk about our intimate connection. If it were known that you left town with me this day in a closed carriage and returned unmarried…"

Heshing made a tisking sound as he allowed Lady Abigail's mind to finish what his words did not.

"Then I shall risk being ruined and just hope no one saw," Lady Abigail replied.

She was desperately hoping a fragment of the charming man she had known remained yet in the man seated across from her.

"I made sure they saw, my dear," he said, looking down at her pitifully. "Not to mention the note I sent on to your brother."

"I will tell him we had a misunderstanding. That I didn't explain myself well last night and you took my words a different way."

"Yes, but the note was in your hand," he said while he rubbed his own hands together in front of him.

"That is not possible," Lady Abigail said in a breathy whisper.

"It doesn't take much to pay a woman to write a note. He will see the feminine handwriting signed with your name and assume that it is, in fact, you. It would only make sense that you, a lady full of spunk and adventure, when told by her brother that he didn't approve of her choice, would run and marry anyway."

"Christian will know it's not me," Lady Abigail said, trying to convince herself as much as Heshing.

"The point is moot," Heshing said, growing irritated with this argument. "You are here in this carriage now. You will marry me or be ruined for the rest of your days. Is that what you want for yourself? For whispers to be spoken about the other members of your family on your account?"

Lady Abigail did waver at this. It seemed there would be no choice for her now but to marry Heshing. How could she have been so wrong about this man in front of her? At that moment, she thought of her family.

How much hurt she had caused this day, without even knowing it. She worried over the duchess who was already in a fragile state. How would her mother react when she learned that her daughter was dishonored, had run away, and was married to a dishonest man?

Her mind turned to Lord Gilchrist. He had tried so hard to put distance between Heshing and herself and she had ignored all his warnings. She couldn't help but wonder if she would return to see his gloating face, as he was right and she was so wrong.

The thought caused her heart to sink even lower than she thought possible. Gilchrist wouldn't even have the chance to show her how right he was, as he was sure to be already gone. It seemed the only friend she had outside her family was now gone from her.

She was alone now. She had made her choice when she made friends with Heshing. It would be her downfall. Lady Abigail, however, was not one to go down without her chin held high.

CHAPTER 25

The Duchess of Wintercrest read over the note her husband had handed to her for the third time. The words were easy enough to see, but the meaning behind them was harder to understand.

"I can't believe this is true," she finally said, releasing the note back to her husband.

She sat down in the leather chair in his office. She rubbed her swollen belly lovingly while she took *steadying* breaths.

"I am not sure what you don't believe," the duke said, taking his own chair in the cozy office. "It is in her own hand, explaining they were not going to be taking their usual turn of the park. There is nothing more that can be done. It's clear she chose to marry him, despite our thoughts on the gentleman."

"Abigail would never do that," the duchess stated with conviction.

"She would if she felt she loved him," the duke retorted.

"I agree, Abigail did have feelings for the gentleman. She also cares deeply about your opinion, Christian. She wouldn't run away."

"Perhaps Heshing convinced her," the duke said with an exasperated wave of his hand.

Isabella seemed to think this over. As much as she wanted to resolve herself to this fact, she couldn't believe it. Finally, she stood and faced her husband.

"I'm sorry, but Abigail would never do such a thing. We need to go after her," the duchess declared.

At that very moment, she had to sit back in her seat with a sharp pain. In an instant, the duke was at her side.

"I promised I would allow Abigail to marry who she wanted. If this is her choice, I won't stop her. Besides, you are in no condition to go anywhere but to your own bed."

"I know in my heart this isn't what Abigail would want.

Even if she cared so much for Heshing that she would marry him despite your suggestion otherwise, she wouldn't do it this way. She wouldn't bring this added stress upon your mother."

Isabella looked at her husband with pleading eyes. The duchess was sure that Abigail would never take this course. If she could only help her husband see the truth of that, they could overtake the couple and stop a terrible mistake.

"If she didn't want it, why did she go with him? Why write this note?" the duke asked, waving his hand towards the parchment on his desk.

"I don't know, but we must go," Isabella urged her husband.

"Whether it is to save her from a terrible mistake or be the family by her side, we must go."

"I am afraid you cannot go anywhere. However, I do agree with you. Perhaps Abigail made the decision in haste. Someone should go. I can't leave you in such a state."

"Colton," Isabella said suddenly. "Colton will go and bring her home or be the family at her side. If there is anyone I would trust, it is him."

The Duke of Wintercrest stood and paced the room as he thought this over.

"I agree that he would be the best choice. I would say of all the others I could ask to do this task, I know he would do it swiftly. I worry about what might happen when Heshing and Gilchrist meet again."

"I know you mean Colton's temper," Isabella said as she continued to soothe her round belly. "I know that he will be able to control himself. He may have trouble mastering his anger, but when it counts, he will do what it takes to ensure her safety."

The duke seemed to consider this.

"My concern is if he comes upon them and Abigail is in truth set in her ways, will he allow her to do so?"

"He cares for Abigail. He would respect her choice either way. Truly, Christian, this doesn't sit right with me. I don't think this is what Abigail would want. Something in that letter doesn't fit with Abigail."

"I will make a call on Gilchrist. I am sure he is still here in town. However, we also do have to worry if he will be willing."

"He will," Isabella said, more trying to convince herself than her husband.

The Duke of Wintercrest moved with haste as he made his way to Gilchrist's house. Time was of the essence in these situations, and he knew they were already far behind.

"I hate to barge in on you like this," the duke said upon being shown into Gilchrist's office. "I have a rather urgent favor I need to ask of you."

"Of course," Gilchrist said, standing from his seat behind the desk and motioning for the duke to join him. "Whatever you need, Your Grace."

"Are you leaving shortly, or will you be in town for a bit? I don't want to interfere with your plans?" the duke asked as he did his best to sidestep around the matter.

He would need Gilchrist in his best mood. Blundering this delicate situation wouldn't help. The duke was quite sure that Gilchrist had some feelings for Abigail and coming out and saying she had run off with a man he despised wouldn't do.

"I don't suppose till the end of the week. Why? What is it you need?" Gilchrist asked casually.

He made his way over to the table of spirits and poured a small glass of sherry for the both of them.

"It's about Abigail," the duke said with a huff.

Already he could see Gilchrist stiffening against his words.

"She might have gotten herself into a situation. I would take care of it myself, but the stress on Isabella has been too much. I fear to leave her alone in such a state."

"I will help if I can, but I don't see how that is possible. Lady Abigail doesn't seem to listen to me on most matters. Very stubborn, that one."

"I couldn't agree more," the duke concurred. "She left this afternoon for a ride around the park with Heshing. She does it quite often, and I don't see any harm in it. That was until about an hour later when we received a note from Heshing's man."

"Well, out with it. What did it say? Is she alright? Did the rogue take her in a race and injure her?" Gilchrist was already spiraling with worry.

"No, according to the note, it was from Abigail claiming they have decided to elope."

The room went still for a pregnant pause. Gilchrist seemed to weigh this in his head.

"It would seem you don't believe it by way of your explanation," Gilchrist finally said.

The duke slumped in his chair, visibly stressed from this whole matter.

"I don't know. Isabella seems to think it might be a forgery of some sort. She believes Abigail would never do such a thing."

"And you don't agree? You would know Lady Abigail best of all, wouldn't you?"

The duke thought the matter through for what seemed the millionth time that day. He had gone back and forth both ways.

"Part of me knows Abigail to be a bit hasty when she makes a decision. Another part of me agrees with my wife. She knew that Isabella was delicate and that we would be returning to Wintercrest shortly because of it. There would have been no reason to do it now when it would affect Isabella so, and she would know that."

"So, you think it is some kind of a lie then. If so, where is Lady Abigail?"

"Isabella fears that she is with Heshing somewhere and perhaps in danger. Either she meant the trip and will go through with it, or she didn't and needs rescuing. I am not entirely sure, but my wife will find no peace until the matter is resolved before it is too late."

"And how can I help with this?" Gilchrist asked with a weary expression.

"I can't leave my wife, and she will only be soothed if someone overtakes the pair and determines if this is truly Abigail's wish."

"And you want me to go after them?" Gilchrist said, pointing to his chest with a scoff.

"You are the only one the duchess trusts with the task."

The Earl of Gilchrist seemed to think this matter over carefully. He did care for Abigail, and if the fiend had kidnapped her, he would be the first to run to her aid. But he wasn't entirely sure he would be willing to stand by if she, in fact, had set out to marry the man.

"You know even if she doesn't wish to marry Heshing, she will be ruined all the same."

"I am aware. I didn't bring it up with Isabella for fear of upsetting her more, but I know it to be true. There will be no way to overcome such a travesty for her. Perhaps she will choose to marry Heshing solely for that reason. There won't be any other suitors or trips to London for the season after this. Marrying the man could quite possibly be the only way she can salvage her reputation at this point."

"I could give her another way," the earl said softly.

"How so?" the duke asked, intrigued by an alternative means of saving his sister's reputation without marriage to the foul Lord Heshing.

"I could offer her marriage to me instead. Of course, with your permission," Gilchrist added quickly.

The duke was stunned by his offer.

"I know you had an interest in her, but truly do you think that is a wise decision?"

"I know I am grotesque to look at, but it would be the difference between horrid on the outside or horrid on the inside. I would make sure she was protected and well taken care of," Gilchrist was spilling the words out of his mouth.

The duke gave a soft laugh, "I didn't mean it would be an unwise decision for Abigail. She would be lucky that a substantial gentleman such as yourself would be willing to take her on after such an event. I meant for you?"

Lord Gilchrist wasn't quite sure how marrying the beautifully enchanting Lady Abigail Grant would ever be a wrong choice for him if she would be willing to accept.

"I mean, you would be giving up your chance to find a proper match."

"What woman would be willing to match with this," the earl said, motioning to his face. "Giving Lady Abigail a marriage outside of Heshing is about the closest I will ever be to convincing a woman to be my wife."

"I see far more to you than what is on the surface. You would be giving up a chance for a woman to see the same," the duke responded.

"I enjoy Lady Abigail's company, and sometimes the same can be said of her with me. I can't say that I expect more than that from a lady I hope to wed."

"Whether she needs rescuing or not, I will take on this task for you," Gilchrist said, coming to stand before the duke. "It will take them at least two days to get to the Scottish border. Most likely he will go at a slower pace after the first night, as from that point on there will seem to be no hope in reclaiming her reputation so she will have to go through with the wedding."

"If I journey by horseback, with luck, I may overtake them before that point," Gilchrist added, though he highly doubted the possibility.

"Either way, would you see her home safely?" the duke

asked, rising to face Gilchrist directly. "We would be greatly in your debt."

"Of course," the earl said before showing the duke out.

He knew there were a great many preparations to be made and in haste. If he rode his steed at breakneck speed, he would have to change it every few hours. This would give him an opportunity to check all the inns and taverns along the way.

He groaned inwardly as he thought about this. That would mean stopping every couple of hours, walking into full establishments of shocked faces and horrified looks to ask around for two interlopers.

He highly doubted anyone would give up such information without a hefty price. It wasn't only his coin bag that would suffer on this trip, but also his ego. Was he really willing to step outside the safety of the cage he had built for himself all for Lady Abigail's sake?

CHAPTER 26

The Earl of Gilchrist had answered the question in his mind before he even finished asking it. He would have done anything for Lady Abigail. Try as he might to hide himself away and put as much distance as he could between them, Lady Abigail would always be tethered to his heart.

His most significant fear was making the journey only to stand witness to her marriage to the horrible Earl of Heshing. He wasn't entirely sure if that was possible or would be the last straw to send his mind spiraling beyond recovery. It was a risk he would just have to be willing to take.

He collected any items he would need, dressed as

warmly as possible, and prepared his fastest steed to begin his journey.

Though he made good time between the taverns he passed along the main road, Gilchrist lost much time with each stop he had to make. There was no way of knowing which one Heshing might stop at to rest his horses, and therefore Gilchrist had to check them all.

It became more difficult to convince the proprietors of the establishments to give up information as the night drew on. Now he was not just a beastly creature who pursued others, but one who stalked in the night.

He couldn't risk halting his pursuit. Taking on the night was his only chance of interception.

Gilchrist's anxiety worsened as stop after stop resulted in no answers or leads. It was entirely possible that Heshing had taken a longer but harder to track side route. If that were the case, his only chance of catching them would be right at the Scottish border.

Finally, as midnight set in, Gilchrist got his first good news. The owner of a moderately dingy inn, after a large sum of money, confirmed that a couple matching their description had in fact stopped and dined in his establishment.

From the estimated time given, it put Gilchrist only a

few hours behind his target. He would be able to overtake them by dawn if they had decided to stay the night instead of continuing to drive.

From the innkeeper, it seemed that they ate at a relaxed pace while their own horses rested and were watered instead of changing them out for another pair. That told Gilchrist they were in no hurry, and Heshing had no idea that he was being chased down.

Gilchrist did his best not to think about what he would come upon if Lady Abigail was, in fact, complicit in all of this. Especially if he was to come upon them in the middle of the night.

Over and over the Earl of Gilchrist repeated the mantra that he wouldn't lose his temper. He had done it once in front of Lady Abigail; he would not do so again.

He would tell himself he would not concern himself with his own happiness but only the comfort of the lady, whatever that might entail. He would be there to support her either way for the sake of Isabella.

"I don't care who yer lookin' for sir; I want you o'my place this instant!" a fat woman bellowed across the almost empty room.

"Madame, if you will allow me to explain," Gilchrist said, doing his best to keep his cool.

The woman, who had been cleaning the tables and preparing for the morning meal, screamed when he first entered.

"A man such as yer'self has only one ting on his mind when he be asking about a couple headed north. I won't be lettin' a hired thug like you stop some poor lovers!"

She waved the rag in her hand at him like he was a rat.

"Shoo now! Out wit' ya!"

"I will have you know that I am Lord Colton Frasier, Earl of Gilchrist, that you are so rudely denying information to. I am here to capture a rake that has quite possibly stolen a lady against her will. If you have any information on the matter, I suggest you speak it now before I have you arrested for impertinence."

The woman opened and closed her mouth a few times like a fish gasping for water. She seemed to look the earl up and down. Though his face was ghastly and his clothes covered in mud, he did have the stance and clothes of a fine gentleman.

"Pardon me, m'lord," she said humbly, still with an eye to his face.

He was sure the lady was wondering how a lord could possibly have such a disgusting face. In her mind accidents that caused such markings were undoubtedly reserved for the lower class.

"Well?" Gilchrist asked again, now shouting.

The lady jumped at the resounding echo of his word.

"They did stay here but left early this mornin', m'lord. No more than an hour before you walked in yer'self."

"They stayed the night then?" he asked in a low tone, hiding his own disgust as much as possible at the thought.

"But respectfully," she added quickly. "He seemed a handsome enough 'gent. Got her a separate room an' all."

"Looks don't always match the man inside," Gilchrist spat back at the woman. "And what of the lady? Did she look willing?"

"Hard to say," the woman responded now, scratching her mop head with the dirty rag hand. "She was so quiet. Din' say much at'tal. I figured she was just one u'those blushin' brides."

It wasn't the answer that Gilchrist was hoping for, but it also wasn't definite proof that Lady Abigail was going along with the elopement. The separate bedrooms for the night was not only a relief but also further evidence that she may not be willing.

Lady Abigail shifted in her seat for the third time that morning. Though they had been traveling at a leisurely pace, it did nothing to prevent the jolts and bumps from the well-worn road.

Though Lord Heshing had tried to spend the night sharing her bed, Lady Abigail had refused, threatening to scream if he so much as dared.

She may have been forced to marry this man she knew no better than the others sitting in the taverns they passed, but she would not allow him such liberties before their wedding day.

Heshing had not been happy with her refusal. No doubt he saw it as one more way to secure herself, and dowry, to him. He had woken her with a loud banging on her door and insisted they leave at once.

She hadn't even had a proper breakfast before they set out on their route again. Heshing seemed to drive the coachman harder this time around. She wondered if he was becoming nervous that they were being followed.

As much as Lady Abigail wished her brother would come after them and stop this sham from happening, she couldn't see how that was possible. With a note written explaining her false desire to marry the man, there would be no cause for the Duke of Wintercrest to come after them.

"Why can't you just sit still, it is very distracting, you know?" Heshing muttered as he again seemed to focus on the road behind them.

Though at their speed it was uncomfortably chilly to have the top down, Heshing insisted upon it so that he might get a good view of anyone approaching.

"Why can't you just take me home," Lady Abigail spat back.

"My dear," he replied, looking at her with that oily smile. "It doesn't matter that we spent the night in separate beds. A day has passed, and you are as good as my wife."

"Well for someone who is practically a husband, you would think you would do better to see to your falsely taken wife's comfort. It is dreadfully freezing," she added.

"I could have you sit next to me for warmth," Heshing said with a raised brow.

"I would rather not," Lady Abigail retorted with her head held high. "I don't enjoy close contact with strangers."

"How could you possibly call me so. I am the same man you have spent your last few months with."

"I am sorry, Lord Heshing, but you are not at all the man I thought I spent my days with. In fact, you are worse than a different creature. You are the one I was warned of and didn't believe the truth about. Had I only listened," she added in a softer tone.

"Ah yes, your dear Gilchrist pet. Such an ugly pet if you ask me. I am sure he did his best to blather on about me to anyone who would listen. It will make no difference, though. With your money in hand, I will pay off any debts I have incurred. The ton will be none the wiser to any unsavory business and Gilchrist will go back to being a raving beast."

"You are the most horrible rake I have ever laid eyes on. To speak of an honorable gentleman in such a way," she shook her head in disgust. "You will never be half the man Gilchrist is."

"Hm," Heshing said, reaching forward and taking Lady Abigail by the arm. It was quite tight, and Lady Abigail did everything not to show the pain on her face.

"Perhaps he was more than just a pet to you. Are you in love with Gilchrist?" Heshing asked as if the idea was laughable.

Heshing glared into Lady Abigail's eyes for an answer. When she wouldn't give it, he finally released her.

"Sorry to say, my dear, but I will be severing that tie first thing. You can wave your little pet goodbye for he will never be welcome in my house."

Lady Abigail glared across the carriage at her intended as he went back to searching the roads behind them. She would have much liked to scratch his eyes out at that moment. She saw no point, however.

Her only hope was to pray that her brother was on his way and would find them in time. She cared not a whit that it would mean a life of solitude. At this point, she would gladly be put away instead of being attached to Heshing the rest of her days.

Finally, just after noon, they stopped to rest the horses for the first time that day. Lady Abigail was beginning to recognize the land. She knew that meant she was close to Wintercrest. Just beyond her brother's lands was Scotland.

They were seated quietly in an establishment that was at least the cleanest that she had seen as of yet and were waiting for their humble meal to be brought to them. So close to the end, Lord Heshing seemed to give up his anxiety of the morning finally.

He relaxed into rambling conversations of what he had planned for their future. Lady Abigail would not listen to any of it. Instead, she chose to stare into the fire and do her best to tune out his voice.

It was then that the inn's door opened, and a lady seated just next to it gave out a scream of fear.

Lady Abigail turned from gazing at the leaping flames, to see the scarred Lord Colton Frasier, Earl of Gilchrist, standing in the doorframe. His eyes seemed to scan the room for only a second before they fell on her. In that instant Lady Abigail gave a great sigh of relief.

CHAPTER 27

Lord Gilchrist strolled with determination, ignoring the stares and startled screams from the rest of the guests in the busy inn. It didn't take long for Heshing to notice him either.

Heshing turned to Lady Abigail and hissed, "Remember, you marry me, or you can kiss your and your younger family members' reputations goodbye."

Heshing stood, putting space between Gilchrist and Lady Abigail. For a moment Lady Abigail thought Lord Gilchrist might just barrel right through him. However, he stopped abruptly before Heshing and looked down on him.

Until this moment Lady Abigail had never realized how

much taller Gilchrist was than most other men. He seemed to glare down at Lord Heshing with all the hate she had ever seen in a man's eyes.

"Gilchrist, old boy, what a surprise to see you here," Heshing said casually.

"I have come to take Lady Abigail home, on behalf of her family," Gilchrist said directly.

He spoke so calmly and at a steady pace that Lady Abigail suspected he had practiced saying it just so a few times. Heshing made a big deal of looking around Gilchrist.

"I don't see the duke? How am I to know you are not here on your own delusional course. Lady Abigail and I are in love and have decided to marry against the lies you have poisoned her family with."

Lady Abigail watched Lord Gilchrist's fists ball at his side. She knew Lord Heshing was only trying to get a rise out of him. If Heshing could get him to lose his temper and create a scene, he would be removed from the establishment. It would give Heshing the chance to escape.

As Lady Abigail sat there, she could only keep her mind on her nieces. It was for their sake she would continue with this charade. If they had an irrational aunt who eloped, they still would have a chance at happiness themselves. A ruined aunt, on the other hand, would seal their fate along with hers.

Luckily Lord Gilchrist didn't take the bait. It was a control that Lady Abigail had yet to see in him until now.

He leaned towards Lady Abigail instead, "His grace wanted to come, but the duchess took the news very hard. He felt the need to stay at her side."

"Oh Isabella," Lady Abigail spoke for the first time. "Is she alright?"

Heshing didn't wait for an answer. Instead, he grabbed Lady Abigail's arm to pull her to stand.

"I am sure she is just causing a scene to force you home. You, however, know the consequences of such," Lord Heshing added under his breath. "I believe we should be on our way, having nothing more to say to the gentleman."

Lord Gilchrist looked into her eyes for any hint that she had changed her mind. Up until this moment, Lady Abigail had said next to nothing. For all he could see of the two, it would seem that Heshing was right.

Lord Gilchrist couldn't believe that Lady Abigail had

been tricked so easily by this man. How could she not see him as the fiend that he indeed was?

Heshing's tight grip on her arm and the confusing warning he spoke didn't go unnoticed by Gilchrist. He took a step forward, catching Lady Abigail's eyes wholly for the first time.

"If you don't wish this, I can take you home now. Just say the word," he encouraged.

"She has nothing to say to you," Heshing replied, trying to get between the two again.

"Actually, I do," Lady Abigail said.

She would be sorry to sacrifice her nieces' reputations, but her brother had clearly seen fault in this sham to send Gilchrist. He had to know that it wasn't what she wished and that it was the work of an evil mind. Perhaps that alone would be hope yet for her nieces.

"I didn't write the letter sent to my brother. Nor did I have any idea when I stepped into Heshing's carriage yesterday that he planned to take me outside of town, and certainly not to a marriage."

"Then you are not willing in this?" Gilchrist asked, showing a light of hope for the first time.

"Of course she is," Heshing said, staring daggers at her.

"No," Lady Abigail said firmly. "Heshing recently confessed to me that he was in severe need of replenishing funds, and when I refused to marry him against my family's wishes, he devised this plan to force me instead."

"Well then, I believe that settles the matter," Gilchrist said, turning to Heshing. "You will remove yourself from Lady Abigail and your person from this establishment before I do it forcibly."

Heshing hesitated. The cold but fierce look in Gilchrist's eyes was not only calculatingly dangerous but also ready to act within an instant. For that reason, Heshing decided to do as he was told.

Lady Abigail melted back down into her seat. She gave a great exhale she hadn't realized she was holding since yesterday afternoon. She knew this was only the beginning to unraveling this disaster, but at least it was a start.

Lord Gilchrist sat down too, once he was assured that Heshing had fully left the premises. He called over a maid to bring him some refreshment, having not eaten since the day before.

He was weary in body and spirit. At the same time, he was relieved that Lady Abigail was now safe and in his care. It was enough to make him collapse with exhaustion right there at the table.

"Are you truly alright? Did he hurt you..." Gilchrist hesitated for a moment before adding, "in any way?"

"No," Lady Abigail said quietly. She looked down at her hands, embarrassed not only by her situation but the fact that it was Gilchrist whom she first had to stand before. "Nothing beyond my pride and reputation, that is."

"I believe we will stay here for the rest of the day," Lord Gilchrist said, satisfied with her answer to her physical health.

"I only came on horseback. I will need time to procure a coach. We are near Wintercrest. If you would like I could take you there instead to save you any unnecessary..."

Gilchrist seemed to trail off in his words, unsure how to say the next part.

"Gossip? Downcast looks? Or perhaps outright shameful things spoken of me? I believe all things you yourself have been forced to suffer and for far nobler a cause than me."

Lady Abigail took a deep sigh.

"I would like to make sure Isabella is alright. I will hate if this causes her or the babe any stress."

"I will send a letter to them today. They will receive it quicker than we could possibly reach them."

"I appreciate that," Lady Abigail said softly. "In fact, thank you for all you did for me. I'm sure it wasn't easy for you."

At that moment, both looked around the room. There were still eyes glancing their way and a few downright nasty stares.

"I hope you don't mind me asking," Lady Abigail said after looking back towards the earl. "Why did you come? Trust me, I'm glad you did. But why would you agree to help me?"

"Your brother asked me to," Gilchrist responded, much shyer than usual.

"And you just said yes?" Lady Abigail asked, unable to let the subject die.

"I care for your family very much. Isabella is like a sister to me. I would do just as much to help her as any other family member."

Lord Gilchrist also wanted to tell Lady Abigail that he would do anything for her as well. That he hoped once her nerves were again settled, she would consent to marriage with such a beast as himself.

Lady Abigail was still reeling with the events of the last hour. She had gone from a desperate need to escape, to finding her rescuer before her. She had hoped her brother would come to her aid, but honestly, she felt no disappointment to see the Earl of Gilchrist instead.

Though the earl looked essentially dead on his feet, his hair was a frazzled blonde mess with sticks and leaves still stuck in it, and his clothes were caked in a thick layer of mud from the road, Lady Abigail had never seen a better sight.

"You will probably want to rest," Lady Abigail finally said.

The conversation between them was thick and tentative. It was a raw situation for both parties.

"Perhaps we should get some rooms?" she suggested further.

"Yes, of course. I am sure I am extra frightening in my state," he responded, waving a maid over.

"It's not that," Lady Abigail replied, not wanting him to think she saw any less than a knight in shining armor. "I mean you do look a fright," she added with a giggle, "but only because you are still wearing most of the travel on your person."

The earl relaxed into a smile at her words. It was the ice breaker they needed. He reached up into his hair and fingered out a stick before tossing it in her direction.

After a hearty meal was consumed by the earl, the maid showed the two up to their own separate rooms to freshen up and rest. Lady Abigail was just as grateful for the time out of the carriage. She would have rather dreaded having to turn back around that instant and spend several more days without reprieve from the rocking and bumping.

The Earl of Gilchrist had meant to wash himself, freshen up his clothes and make preparations. Instead, he collapsed onto his bed, without even removing his boots, and slept more soundly than he could remember ever doing in the past.

Lady Abigail sat anxiously on the bed in her room. She wasn't entirely sure what she was supposed to do now. She was grateful to be free of Heshing but at the same time didn't know what consequences were in store for the rest of the single ladies in her family.

Her biggest worry was for Jackie. She was just the age to be entering society in the next few years. Jackie would have a hard enough time as it was making a good place in society with her unique parentage. Lady Abigail hated that she might have made things all the harder for her, as the ton would be slow to forget untoward behavior associated with her aunt.

She thought perhaps it would be best to have the earl return her to Wintercrest. It would be better for Jackie if Lady Abigail was never seen in society again. Maybe in that small way she could improve her niece's chances in society.

It would mean setting aside her pride and hiding from those who would speak ill of her. She didn't like the idea of shrinking away and hiding but saw no other alternative.

Gilchrist woke just as dusk was starting to make its presence known. He quickly washed in his now cold basin of water and saw to a carriage for their return trip the next day. It wasn't until after he had found the proper transportation that he stood before Lady Abigail's door to inquire if she would take dinner with him.

They sat at the same table Gilchrist had found her at

earlier that day as they ate their meal. It was just a spreading of ale, meat pie, and some boiled potatoes. It was humble but still served its purpose.

"I have procured a coach and driver. We can leave first thing in the morning," Gilchrist informed his companion.

"I was thinking," Lady Abigail replied. "If it's not too much trouble, I think I would rather return to Wintercrest Manor?"

"Of course," Lord Gilchrist said, doing his best to discern her reasoning. "It would actually be more convenient for me anyway. My country estate is only a day's ride west of it."

"Really?" Lady Abigail was surprised to hear this. She had no idea that it was quite that close.

"Yes. Generally speaking though, we have stayed at the house for quite some years. My father always enjoyed staying in town. The estate is called Cumberton Park. I haven't been there since I was a child and don't remember it much."

"Will it be ready for you then?" Lady Abigail asked.

Indeed, it was the only reason he had stayed in London so long after deciding to leave. A house out of use for so many years would take time to get ready and accumulate staff.

"As ready as can be needed for just one person," Gilchrist responded. "I don't think Louisa or my mother plan on stopping in anytime soon," he added with a hint of humor.

"I just mean you are welcome at Wintercrest as long as needed. I am sure my brother would gladly have you stay. He planned to also return early from the season due to the duchess's condition. Though now I do hope she can travel. I would hate to think I had kept her away from the twins longer," Lady Abigail said to herself.

Without much thought, Lord Gilchrist reached over the table and laid his hand on top of Lady Abigail's. Though it was from the damaged side of his body, it was not as scarred as the rest of him. He rested it gently on the top of Lady Abigail's hand and cherished the warm comfort of a touch. It was something he hadn't experienced for some time.

"I am sure Isabella is fine. She is a tough girl."

Lady Abigail didn't pull away from his touch. In fact, she was just as comforted by it as his words. Though she would have thought to recoil at the roughness of the scar tissue, it was in fact actually very tender and delicate.

CHAPTER 28

The following day the road-worn and rumpled pair made their way into the back of a coach. Lady Abigail was happy to see that Gilchrist had produced a proper vehicle for long-distance travel with a sturdy roof and much plusher cushioning to the seats.

It wasn't until they got into the carriage that Lady Abigail realized for the first time that Lord Gilchrist was not using his usual walking cane.

"Forgive me for asking, but has your leg healed? I just noticed you are walking without assistance."

"Oh," Lord Gilchrist said, unconsciously rubbing his left thigh as if he too had just realized for himself that he was doing well without the help.

"I actually didn't bring it because it would have been hard to keep at such a speed on horseback. Honestly, though, until just now I had forgotten all about the pain."

"How interesting. You walk as if you never needed it," Lady Abigail continued.

She was happy that at least for the remainder of this carriage ride up north she would now have a companion worth conversing with.

"Perhaps it was just all up in my head," Gilchrist said with a chuckle to himself. "I suppose much goes on up there that I am not entirely aware of," he added, then instantly regretted giving up such information so freely.

Lord Gilchrist always seemed to find himself sharing with Lady Abigail more than he wanted or had ever done with another. There was something about her, most likely the way he felt about her, that made him willing to share all of what he had with her.

"You know Christian told me a story once of a man on his ship. He had been holding on to some rigging during a storm. A giant wave had crashed the vessel, and in the process, he was whipped from his spot while his arm was still tangled in the rigging. The force of the wave… well," Lady Abigail seemed to blush knowing that what she was about to say was not exactly proper conversation to come out of a lady's mouth.

"Well, it removed his arm completely. The point of the story is," she added hastily when Gilchrist sported that smile ready to tease her for her unladylike story, "that the sailor claimed he could still feel his arm. Even though he knew full well it wasn't there, he said it still held a constant grip to the rigging in his mind."

"So you think my mind was holding on to the pain until something came along that forced me to forget it," he said to follow his own line of thought.

Gilchrist considered this for a minute. It certainly was true that his mind was holding on to a great deal of pain that he would have otherwise rather let go off. It brought logical sense to his words.

"Then I suppose I should thank you," he said after a beat.

"Whatever for?" Lady Abigail asked with her eyes open wide in confusion.

"Had you not been taken by Heshing I might have always needed the cane. You have saved me a great deal of pain for the rest of my life."

"I am quite sure you did the same for me," Lady Abigail

responded.

They rode the way to Wintercrest, arriving on the estate well into the night. It was a relief to Lady Abigail when her sleepy eyes beheld the long gravel road with towering trees on either side that led to her home.

She wasn't sure if there would be any reception for them as they were not expected and came in the dead of night. There was, however, a footman who must have been alerted to their approach as well as the head housekeeper waiting once they pulled up to the main door.

"Lady Abigail," Mrs. Smith, the housekeeper, said with a curtsy. "Forgive the disorganization; we didn't know you were expected."

"Nonsense," Lady Abigail waved the lady off. "I didn't know either until just yesterday. Please let me introduce Lord Colton Frasier, the Earl of Gilchrist. He was kind enough to see me safely home."

"And it's just the two of you," Mrs. Smith asked, looking around for perhaps a maid that might have accompanied her.

"Yes," Lady Abigail said, not wanting to answer the unasked question of why she was alone on a trip spanning several days, traveling exclusively with a man.

"Would you please see that Lord Gilchrist is made comfortable for the night?"

"Yes, of course, my lady," Mrs. Smith said, coming back to her senses.

Lady Abigail knew the woman to be kind and not the prying type. She was an immense step up from their last housekeeper, Mrs. Peterson, who had been altogether too prudish and strict. However, with two of the servants already aware that she had arrived unaccompanied with a man, it would not take long for the rest of the household to whisper over the cause.

It really didn't make much difference anyway. Heshing had seemed to make a point of taking Lady Abigail away from her London home in the most public way. It was inevitable that the whole ton had already spread the news of their disappearance.

Even if Heshing had the gall to return to town without her and spoke nothing on the matter, she would still be damaged goods. The chances of Heshing keeping his mouth shut and not spreading his own telling of their adventure was a minuscule chance.

The following morning she was woken by three bouncing bodies jostling her bed. It took Lady Abigail only a second to realize that Jackie had helped the twins escape the nursery to come find their aunt upon news of her late night arrival.

"Auntie Abigail!" the twins seemed to shout over and over again. "Where is Mummy? Did she and Daddy come home with you too? Nursie only told us you were home," they barraged Lady Abigail with question after question.

Finally, Lady Abigail managed to sit up in her bed and wake up properly while the twins bounced in place, eager for answers.

"Your mother wasn't feeling well and will be coming home not far behind me."

"Not that I'm not happy to see you, but then why are you here without them?" Jackie asked as she sat much calmer at the edge of Lady Abigail's bed.

"Oh," Lady Abigail said with a huff of air. "It is a very long story. I must tell it to your grandmother first. I promise to visit you all in the nursery later, though," Lady Abigail responded.

Jackie got the two small twins to reluctantly leave their aunt's side as the lady's maid came in to help her get ready for the day. It was so lovely for Lady Abigail to be home again, she was rather preferring the idea of never returning to town.

Lady Abigail found her mother seated alone in the breakfast room. She couldn't help but feel guilty for leaving her mother so alone these last few months.

Her mother walked over and embraced her silently. She didn't have to know what happened to see that something devastating had brought her daughter back home. In an instant Lady Abigail began to shed tears she had not known she was holding back.

They held each other silently in the breakfast room while Lady Abigail released all her fear, sorrow, and anxiety of the previous few days in her mother's arms.

Finally, the two came to sit, and in the peace of the early morning light that streamed through the window, Lady Abigail told her mother all that had happened since leaving Wintercrest. By the end, both ladies were yet again dabbing at their eyes with handkerchiefs.

"I am so sorry, Mother, I have ruined us all," Lady Abigail said, meaning her nieces along with herself.

"Of course not, my dear. Elisabeth is much too young for this to matter to her standing. Jackie…" the dowager duchess hesitated, knowing that this would affect her oldest grandchild.

"Is tainted by being my relation," Lady Abigail finished. "I feel so awful about it."

"We will find a way to make it right, not just for Jackie, but for you also."

"I'm afraid the only way to do that would have been to marry the man. I couldn't bring myself to do so when my rescuer came to my aid."

"And I am glad he did. I would not wish you to marry such a man. The minute I see Lord Gilchrist I will kiss him on the cheek for all the good he has done for you."

She paused for a minute, and Lady Abigail smiled to herself. She had described Gilchrist's scars to her mother, but she wondered if she would really go as far as to kiss him on the cheek when she did finally set eyes on him.

"If we simply procure a suitable husband for you, and quickly, it will fix all of this mess that the horrible Lord Heshing caused," the dowager duchess said, as she reached back to the recesses of her mind for just such a candidate.

Before Lady Abigail could respond to her mother's wish list, the doors to the breakfast room opened, and both ladies turned to see Gilchrist enter.

"Forgive me, Your Grace," he said with a bow to Lady Abigail's mother. "I didn't mean to interrupt. I was instructed here for breakfast, but I can come back later."

He was prepared for a ghastly look of fear from the lady or at the very least an indication that she was taken aback. It must be admitted that the dowager duchess did open her mouth in shock for an instant.

She needed no introduction, however, to know that this man before her was Lord Colton Frasier, hero of her daughter's virtue and the Earl of Gilchrist. She promptly stood and, walking over to the confused gentleman, landed a kiss right on the side of his right cheek.

CHAPTER 29

Lord Gilchrist stood in stunned silence. He was sure that was the very first time he had received such a reaction when meeting a lady for the first time. Lady Abigail, however, burst out in tears, this time from laughter.

It took a good minute before Lady Abigail regained her composure, so comical was the sight that had transpired before her. Finally, when she did, she made the proper but probably not necessary introductions between her mother and Lord Gilchrist.

"I am so grateful to you, Lord Gilchrist," the dowager duchess said with every fiber of her being.

"It was an honor, Your Grace," Gilchrist said with another embarrassed bow. He still hadn't quite overcome their first sudden meeting and was pink in the ear.

He shuffled his way over to take a seat at the breakfast table after the dowager duchess encouraged him to do so. He couldn't bear to raise his eyes to meet Lady Abigail.

Normally he would have jabbed her good for laughing at his expense. However, he had heard the words the dowager duchess spoke before they were drawn to his entrance. It reminded him of the promise he made to the duke to offer Lady Abigail marriage.

It has seemed like a logical idea at the time. That seemed a million years ago now and not just a few days and a couple of hundred miles. It would have been a reasonable idea for Lady Abigail to save herself the embarrassment of an elopement gone wrong.

At the same time, it would have given him a wife to produce an heir to the Gilchrist name. This was something he was sure he would never have gotten otherwise, even in the wilds of the new Americas.

The logical agreement had been all business. However, Gilchrist couldn't deny the feelings he had for Lady

Abigail that made the whole thing far less of a contract of convenience for him.

Lord Gilchrist, however, knew the longer he waited to bring up the matter the harder it would be. Soon the duke would arrive at his home and ask his sister what her answer had been to Gilchrist. What would happen when he learned no question had been asked?

"Lady Abigail," he finally said midway through his morning meal. "I was wondering if perhaps this afternoon you might take me around the grounds a bit. I wouldn't mind seeing some of it before I am on my way, if you don't mind?"

Both ladies' red brows were peaked at this question. He couldn't help but notice how much Lady Abigail was a younger version of her mother. Yes, the dowager duchess had more years worn on her face, and the vibrant red of her hair was dulled with silver, but she was still a very fine-looking woman.

His heart beat fast at the thought that it could quite possibly be the face of Lady Abigail he would see in the future, should she accept his proposal.

"Of course, I would be happy to," Lady Abigail responded.

"You are welcome to stay as long as you would like, Lord

Gilchrist," the dowager duchess chimed in. "I am sure my son won't be far behind your own arrival. You must promise to stay till they both are here at least?"

Lord Gilchrist thought that all rather depended on the answer that Lady Abigail would give him this afternoon. That was if he had the courage actually to ask. Nonetheless, he promised to do so for the sake of the dowager duchess.

For the first few minutes, Lady Abigail took Lord Gilchrist around the gardens just behind the manor house. She could tell there was something weighing intensely on his mind.

"When your brother came to see me," Gilchrist finally said, "and told me about what happened, I told him I would be happy to take his place in searching you out."

Gilchrist seemed to fidget with his hands as a nervous habit. Lady Abigail wasn't sure if she had ever seen him nervous like this before.

"You see, we weren't sure if you had truly gone willingly with Heshing, though your brother suspected otherwise. I promised that no matter the reason for your departure, I would make sure you were seen safe and securely settled."

"And so you have," Lady Abigail said, still unsure where he was going with this speech.

She looked up at him, squinting against the rare rays of sunshine they got so far up north. As always, he had made sure to keep her on his right side, though she was sure he knew that she was not bothered by his deformity. In this light, however, looking on his perfect side, she imagined it was what a Greek god from old mythology might have looked like.

"Your brother was very concerned about the repercussions of retaking you from the unwanted elopement."

"For my nieces," Lady Abigail, said filled with a massive guilt.

"Not just them, but yourself as well. I also couldn't help but overhear your mother's last few words before I came into the breakfast room this morning."

It seemed to be an embarrassing way to ask a woman to marry him, but Gilchrist couldn't seem to manage any other way. The charming man he once was had long since died in the fire. The man that was left was ultimately not up to the task of enticing a woman to marry him.

"I am not quite sure what you are trying to say," Lady Abigail said, shielding her eyes with a gloved hand against her face as she looked up at Lord Gilchrist.

She had been happy to free herself of parasols and hats now back at her own home and away from the judgmental eyes of the ton. At this moment, while she had to look up to see Gilchrist's meaning on his face, she rather wished she had suffered one.

"What I am trying to say," Gilchrist took a deep breath before stopping and turning to face the lady head-on. "I suggested to the duke that a marriage contract be procured between the two of us," he said in a quick succession of words.

Once it was out, he gave a deep sigh. He had done his part. If the lady refused him, he would inevitably break into a million pieces, so much did he care for her. But that being said, he would also respect her wishes to live a life of her choosing. He would not force himself upon the lady.

Lady Abigail seemed to look up at him for some moments. In that time Gilchrist studied the curves of her face, the delicate speckles along her nose, and even the soft strands of hair that let loose and blew in the wind.

He would accept her answer whatever it would be. However, he would not stay long if she did not wish to attach herself to him. It would be too much. In his mind, he prepared for this to be the very last time that he looked on the face of Lady Abigail Grant.

"Are you asking me to marry you?" Lady Abigail finally formed the words.

"Yes," he said with an embarrassed laugh before rubbing the unscarred side of his chin, "that is what I meant."

"But why? Why on earth would you want to do that? There is no benefit to you. I could never do such a thing to save my own dignity. I would never ask such a thing of you."

"I know, I'm asking you," Gilchrist said with a little tease, not precisely happy with the answer he got.

"But you would be stuck with me. I thought you rather didn't like me much?" she said, looking back at him.

"I agree we have had our differences, but I find you a good friend. I can share with you things I have never put into words for another. I would give you my name for protection; my home would be your own. You would not be so far from your family. I know that you also find my sister and mother good company. It wouldn't be so terrible for you," he seemed to try to convince her of the benefit of this union.

"I am well aware why accepting your marriage proposal would be a good and logical choice for myself. You have done so much for me. However, I don't know that I could ever wish to lock you in such a situation."

"Why ever not?" Gilchrist said, trying to hold in his laugh. This woman honestly had no idea how much he wished that she would not only marry him but perhaps even find a way to care for him over the years.

"Well don't you want to, you know, find a match of your own choosing?"

"I can't imagine many will be lining up to be the Countess of Gilchrist. My mother quite hates me for that fact, I am sure."

"You mean for lack of an heir," Lady Abigail said with a deep swallow.

Gilchrist imagined it was the first time that the realization of the results of their marriage had come to her mind. He was sure at that moment she could not stomach the idea of having his child. He would not require such of her if she didn't wish it.

"That is her reasoning, yes. I would be happy just to

appease her with a wife. It would also be nice to have a companion in life, if that was something you also wished for," Gilchrist added tentatively.

She turned from him at this point and walked forward a few paces as she thought the matter over. For all reason, this was a very good choice for her, and in reality, the only one. Could she find herself living with Gilchrist's unpredictable nature though? They were on good terms now, but that seemed to shift and change so much between them.

Her greatest fear was that though he was now doing what he thought was gentlemanly and right, he would later come to resent her for it. She wasn't entirely sure if she would be willing to marry a man solely for her own benefit.

"If I said yes," Lady Abigail said and then paused to see if Gilchrist would follow. He gave a soft smile and began again to meet her step for step.

"If I said yes," she repeated, "you must promise to never hate me?"

Gilchrist stopped her again and turned her to face him. He looked down at her with all the love and affection of his heart. This woman would give her life to the beast before her to save her family's reputation and good name, and all her concern was that he didn't resent her later for it.

He reached up and gently cupped both her elbows, gently drawing her just a step closer to him. He looked down at her; he would have liked to kiss her, but knew she wouldn't want it.

"I promise that no matter what, I will never hate you."

CHAPTER 30

With the decision made, quick arrangements were compiled for Lady Abigail's quiet wedding to the Earl of Gilchrist. A few short weeks passed with the necessity of banns being read at Lady Abigail's country parish.

It gave time for both the Duke and Duchess of Wintercrest, as well as Lord Gilchrist's sister and mother to make the journey to Wintercrest Manor for the event. Lady Abigail was just as relieved to have her sister-in-law safely home without further health complications, as the duchess was to be reunited with her children.

Lady Abigail hoped that the extra weeks would also give her a chance to settle into her new life as wife to the Earl of Gilchrist. This seemed to be a much harder task as he appeared to seclude himself more and more with every family member who arrived at the house. She noticed it the most when his mother came.

She suspected there were still some deep unresolved issues between the two of them. It saddened her deeply that Gilchrist seemed to stay far away from her, not to mention the pain and discomfort that Lady Gilchrist visibly felt in her son's presence.

The twins, however, seemed to seek out Gilchrist just as much as Lady Abigail. They were fascinated by the man. Lady Abigail wasn't entirely sure if Gilchrist was bothered by the children's attention or not.

Gilchrist was always polite to them and did his best to answer their barrage of questions when they did seek him out, but at the same time, he didn't seem very happy and somewhat uncomfortable at their big eyes studying his every feature.

Isabella looked to have just barely made it home in time. The guilt that Lady Abigail felt in knowing that she may have caused the early arrival of the baby was eating her alive. She did everything she could imagine to help the duchess in the household duties and see to her comfort.

Between the happy preparations and the work needed to keep the house running while Isabella rested and prepared for the arrival of her new child, Lady Abigail had little time to hunt down Gilchrist as the twins seemed to have.

Before she even realized it the day of her wedding came, and she had not spoken more than a handful of words to her intended. She was still trying to reconcile with the idea that she was to be married and that the man who would be her husband was Colton Frasier, Earl of Gilchrist.

The culmination of all her interactions with the earl made Lady Abigail wonder if she should be happy and excited or dreading the day. Either way, however, she had no choice in it. The matter was set, she had agreed to the terms, and was determined to do her best to see the consequences through.

She dressed that morning with the help of her lady's maid in a simple cream dress and decorated her hair with dried pink roses. Her mother was of course against this since she was sure that pink strongly clashed with her rust-colored hair, but she cared not. She loved the smell that the dried flowers gave and thought it might give her some courage with every deep breath.

She was taken to the small county chapel sponsored by her brother in the family carriage. She wondered if this would be the last time she would ride in the familiar vehicle. Through her future mother-in-law, Lady Abigail was informed that Cumberton Park was now suited to the arrival of its master and new bride. They would be leaving the day after the wedding for what would be Lady Abigail's new home.

She took solace in the knowledge that the country seat of her betrothed was only one day's carriage ride from her own. She reminded herself often if things went sour between herself and the earl, she could always return home. Her family would certainly welcome her back, at least she hoped so.

And then there was also the information that Gilchrist had given her previously about traveling to America. Was he still making preparations to do so? She shuddered at the thought of being left all alone in a new land so far from any connections she had.

Her carriage stopped with a hard jolt. She rode along with her brother. No words had yet passed between the pair. Isabella, who had greatly wished to come, was forced to stay in bed by her well-meaning husband. Lady Abigail couldn't blame him for the loss of her comfort, though. Isabella was in considerable discomfort and soon to have the child, quite possibly before Lady Abigail left the manor house.

"I know you might not have wished this," the duke said

nervously, "but I promise you I wouldn't have recommended such a situation if I wasn't completely assured that Gilchrist would be a good husband to you."

"I know," Lady Abigail said softly. She was such a jumble of emotions at that moment, it was hard to explain let alone comfort the duke.

He patted her hand gently as they made their way into the chapel.

"Lord Gilchrist is making a great sacrifice of his own happiness on my behalf. I could not be more grateful to him," Lady Abigail finally said softly.

"It is a great sacrifice to you both," he replied.

The gravity of his words hung in the air as they made their way into the chapel. Lady Abigail still had not yet decided if she would make the sacrifice that her brother spoke of and the soon to be Dowager Countess Gilchrist hoped for.

She did her best to focus on the room alone as they made their way to the man and reverend waiting at the front of the pews. She had attended this chapel her whole life, and was even baptized in its font as a baby.

She noticed that small bunches of wildflowers decorated the edges of each pew. The fragrance mixed with her own dried roses, sending a sweet perfume into the air. She was grateful for its relaxing effect. She studied the stone walk in front of her and listened to the sound of her feet clicking.

She could feel Gilchrist's eyes on her though she refused to look back. The duke's words hung heavy in her mind, and she feared her thoughts would betray her if she met his gaze.

Finally, she found herself standing across from the earl. He had positioned himself so that he was slightly turned, showing his good side for the most part to both her and the reverend. The preacher was the same man whom she had listened to for as long as she could remember.

He was a quiet, rather dull man. She supposed it was how all vicars meant to behave but that didn't mean she had ever particularly liked him. She did her best to keep her eyes focused on the preacher however as vows were exchanged.

Lady Abigail's heart thumped with nerves at the encroaching end of the service. Would she be told to kiss her now husband? Was she willing to do so? She didn't so much fear Gilchrist or feel disgusted by his deformity, but more worried about her own abilities.

It was right that she did care for him, and indeed cherished the friendship they shared when they were on good terms. At the same time, she couldn't say she loved him, nor thought she would have ever been resolved in marrying a man she didn't have such passionate emotions for.

"You may now kiss your bride," the reverend said in a very droll manner.

For the first time Lady Abigail, now the Countess of Gilchrist, lifted her eyes to meet her husband's. He was watching her intently, and she wondered if he had been trying to catch her eyes this whole time.

His blue eyes seemed to show much darker at that moment as they filled with pity on her. She hesitated to take that small step forward to close the gap between the two of them. The small space was packed full of words unspoken between the two.

Finally, Gilchrist let his eyes drift down to her hands placed at her side. Reaching over, he took one with his right hand. She could feel the weight of the moment shoot through their touch. Raising her hand to his lips, he kissed it ever so gently.

Barely, she could make out the subtle difference between the right side of his mouth and left. Strangely, the left's scar tissue that crept in on his lips seemed soft and almost delicate. Lady Abigail had expected it to be coarse and dried.

Instead of releasing her hand, he turned to face the small group in the pews and placed her arm snugly in the crook of his own. Reverent cheers and congratulations came through the crowd.

Abigail stopped at each guest to receive their words of kindness.

"I am so happy to have you as a sister now," Lady Louisa said as they embraced. "I do wish you would return with us to London," she added.

"They will need some time alone to get to know each other better," the Dowager Countess responded quickly.

Abigail wanted to correct her mother-in-law. She was sure that the Earl of Gilchrist's decision to return to his country seat had little to do with getting to know his new bride and more to do with his removal from the ton.

CHAPTER 31

Abigail sat before the mirror brushing her already untangled hair for the third time. She didn't know what else to do. Was her new husband going to come to her room? Did she even want him to do so?

Her lady's maid had insisted she wear the new nightgown that her mother had requested be made for her. It was made of the lightest sheen material she had ever seen in her life. Though she had accepted the garment from her mother, she had never actually thought she would be wearing it.

A soft knock on her door distracted her from the thought that plagued her mind. She did her best to smooth out the fabric out of habit, then decided to add a silken cover over her shoulders to at least downplay the nightgown.

"Come in," she said, standing.

She was not a shy type, but at that moment she was feeling very demure. Gilchrist entered the room and closed the door softly behind him. He was still fully dressed in his exquisite black jacket and matching pantaloons from earlier at the church.

Neither had spoken much to the other since that moment next to each other in the chapel. Abigail had barely been able to meet his gaze, though she was sure that his eyes had never left hers.

He came to sit on the bed without speaking a word as Abigail stood and waited. She supposed at that moment he intended on making this marriage as valid as any other. He took one long boot off and then the other. She could hear the strain as he worked the boot on his left side.

Though Gilchrist hadn't used his cane for some time, the pressure of a whole day on his weakened limb came with a toll. Though he had tried to gauge his new wife's feelings on the entire situation, she seemed to avoid even the meeting of his eyes at every turn.

"I thought we might talk a little," Gilchrist said, patting the spot on the bed next to him.

"Talk?" Lady Abigail's eyebrows rose in question.

"Yes," he said with a soft laugh. "I already promised I wouldn't ask more of you than you are willing to give. I'm afraid that to ensure the validity of the union we must spend this night together."

"I assure you, I will be a gentleman about it, however, and take my place by the hearth," he added, motioning to the small fire already crackling away.

Lady Abigail hesitated a moment longer before taking the few steps across the room and sitting next to her husband.

"You know," he said with a playful tone, "I think this is the quietest I have ever seen you. You scarcely spoke more than five words at dinner."

"It was only that I couldn't seem to get a word in with the twins there," she retorted.

Usually, the twins took their meals with the governess and nanny before joining the family in the evening when guests weren't present. As a special treat, however, they were welcome to join the family that evening for the wedding dinner.

"Yes, they did have quite a lot to say," he responded a bit absentmindedly.

Lady Abigail didn't have to ask to know that he was not

fond of the attention they gave to him. She feared he saw it as a gross mortification, but it was only innocent interest on their part.

"They were just excited that they could now call you uncle," she tried to explain.

She was at least satisfied in knowing that her choice of a husband had been heartily accepted by every single member of her family. She was sure that would have never been the case if Heshing's plans had come to fruition. She shuddered involuntarily at the thought that she could have been spending her wedding night in his company instead of Gilchrist's.

She looked over at him with new eyes at that moment. Of course, there had been reasons on his part for agreeing to the union, but she found a whole new reason to be happy with it.

"Do you think you will mind coming to Cumberton Park? I didn't think about it till Louisa said as much. Perhaps you would rather return to London with them?"

For some reason, Abigail didn't like the thought of her husband staying in his country estate all alone. She felt it was a duty of hers to at least accompany him for the first portion of his time there.

"I don't mind it at all. In fact, I am curious to see the place."

"I must confess I am a little curious myself. Hopefully, it will be to your liking. Of course, as lady of the house, you are free to change things as you see fit," Gilchrist seemed to ramble off.

She smiled at her husband; perhaps he was just as uncomfortable with this night's situation as she was.

"Lady of the house," she said out loud. "It seems a little strange to think of myself as such."

"Well, you are," he responded without hesitation. "The Countess of Gilchrist and with that title comes my protection and home. It is yours now as it is mine."

"But you always knew such a thing would be yours," Lady Gilchrist said, finding comfort in their conversation.

"Yes," he responded, leaning back on his arms. "I suppose so. Didn't you also always assume you would be the lady of some house?"

"No," Lady Gilchrist said in honesty. "I enjoyed the season and what came with it as a young lady. But that being said, I never made a marriage, or even marriage to a peer, a priority for myself."

"Then what was your priority?" he asked, stretching his long legs out in front of him.

"I suppose, just to have happiness in life. If that meant a husband, then all the better. If not, I was content with being a sister and aunt."

He seemed to think this over for a few minutes.

"And now?" Gilchrist said softly, looking her over as he absentmindedly fiddled with the bed cover.

"Now," Lady Gilchrist seemed to think it over as if it was the first time the thought had come to her, though she had contemplated it plenty in the last few weeks. "Now, I just want to take things one day at a time, I guess."

He seemed satisfied with her answer. Lady Gilchrist was sure it was not the one he probably wanted to hear but it was honest, and she supposed that was enough for him.

"Well, I best make my bed. It's getting late, and we will have an early start."

Gilchrist stood and moved to the head of the bed to remove a pillow. She watched him work, still unsure of what to say. As he made his way back across her and towards the hearth, she stopped him.

"Lord Gilchrist, it seems a silly thing for you to sleep on the hard floor. The bed is certainly big enough for the two of us. I would not be offended at all if you laid next to me in it."

She blushed furiously as she spoke the words. Though she hoped that her message was clear that she wanted nothing more than sleep, Lady Gilchrist still couldn't believe she was inviting a man to her bed. It mattered little that the man was her husband.

"If you're sure," Gilchrist said with a slight hesitation.

He certainly wasn't looking forward to a night on the floor. He had slept on much harsher and colder ground in his time in the service, but that still didn't make the prospect of a makeshift bed on the hard wooden planks any more appetizing.

"Yes, of course," Lady Gilchrist encouraged.

She stood and made her way to the opposite side of the bed. She slipped out of her shawl and into the sheets as fast as she could manage. Gilchrist made his way back over to his side of the bed and gently set the pillow back in place.

"Perhaps, then, if you didn't mind terribly since we will

be sharing sleeping arrangements, you would call me Colton and allow me to call you Abigail," he asked as he slipped out of his coat and threw it across a chair next to the bed.

"Alright," Abigail said softly.

She hesitated for a moment in watching him as his hands went to the knot at his neck. The light was dim with darkness outside, the fire burning, and a simple candle on either side of the bed.

Abigail's eyes lingered on the long fingers as they worked out the knot before they raised to meet his. Seeing Colton's eyes watching her with an inquisitive expression made her blush all over again.

She turned away and blew out the candle on her side. Snuggling down into the plush mattress, Abigail turned away from her husband to give him privacy in his undressing.

She felt the movement of the bed as he slipped into the covers next to her. He lay there for just a moment before rising and blowing out his own candle. In silence, they kept to their own sides of the bed as the sound of the fire helped them find sleep.

The following morning they were up early. In fact, it was before either the sun or the rest of the house had risen. Of course, the staff was awake and already milling about their duties. Abigail was grateful for this fact so that her lady's maid could help her dress and get ready for the long trip. She was satisfied in knowing at least for this long carriage ride she could prepare for it.

It wasn't as extended a trip as to London, only lasting the one day, but she still had a sour taste in her mouth from her last long trip. Today she was in a comfortable brown traveling dress and had her hair set in a relaxed braid at her side.

They climbed into the cabin of the vehicle, and Abigail prepared for a long journey with her husband at her side. Every moment now seemed so much more pregnant between the two of them since their union, and Abigail was struggling to find once again that comfort they once had with the other.

For the majority of their journey, they studied the countryside in silence. As they drew closer to Colton's estates, he began to point out various things he remembered from his time spent here in his youth.

"Are we very near the coast then?" Abigail asked as she found their carriage riding along a road mirrored by water.

"Yes, we have been traveling southwest I suppose,"

Colton told her for bearing purposes. "We are just below the Lake District. This is Morecambe Bay here. We will go along it for the remainder of the trip. Cumberton Park is just south of it. Liverpool is only about a day's ride south of us," he added as an afterthought.

"Liverpool?" Abigail queried.

"Yes, it is a rather large port city," he replied.

"I am familiar with it. I just wasn't sure why you used it in your mapping of the area."

"Well," he responded awkwardly, rubbing his chin. "I hoped you would know it and have an idea of the place for one. Also, I suppose because it is where I plan to procure passage to America."

Abigail said no more on the matter, but couldn't help the abstruse knot that sunk into the pit of her stomach. So it was true then. Colton was still determined to make the journey and quite possibly very soon if he planned to go before summer's end.

She looked out her window, seeing nothing but the strange land that she would now have to call home, and likely do so all alone.

CHAPTER 32

They arrived at their new home just as dusk was settling in the warm summer air. Abigail had to admit the place was breathtaking. It seemed much older than her own home at Wintercrest. The massive structure was made up of large stones intricately placed together and decorated with impressive stone angels on every corner. In fact, it seemed impossible in her mind that such a large and magnificent place could have been made by man.

The whole estate was one long majestic-looking castle. It was raised slightly higher, causing the horses to strain to make the last leg of their trip. Abigail wondered if perhaps a moat once surrounded the four-turret structure.

Finally, the carriage leveled out after a few switchbacks taking the ride up the steep incline. She was sure that the household had watched them take the long back and forth path up to the main gate, as they were all standing on the other side.

"So many," Abigail said more to herself.

Colton had made it seem that the place would be barely suitable for living. From the look of the gardens on the outside and the large staff, Abigail would guess they had the house fully functional.

"Well, it is ancient. With that means a lot of people needed to keep it up and running. Perhaps that is why my father chose to stay in London. He preferred not to deal with all the work of it."

"I am just surprised that you found the people necessary. I feel as if I've seen nothing but countryside for the last several hours."

"Yes, that is true. To the north of us is mostly just open land. There is a village not far to the east, however. Maybe two miles at the most. This area is not very conducive to farming, so there were plenty of people in need of employment."

"What employment can people seek here, if you don't mind me asking?"

He smiled softly at Abigail. In truth he was happy to see the light of interest in her eyes. He partly feared she would take one look at this rocky marshland and beg to be returned home.

"A great many live in small fishing villages along the bay. I would say that is the predominant occupation. For some time there were tenant farms here, but they rarely produced enough for their own needs. My grandfather decided to combine the plots and give them to sheep herds instead."

"And what happened to the families that lived on the land?" Abigail asked with concern.

She thought of the tenant farmers she had known well back home. What would happen if their livelihood was removed from them?

"My grandfather wasn't the kindest of men, and he left many to return to the local village where they again took their place as fishermen. Sadly, I can't say my father changed much. There were some hired on to tend to the sheep and deal with the preparation and transportation of the wool down south."

"But your father was so kind and had such a happy disposition. I can't imagine he would treat others so cruelly."

Colton shrugged.

"I don't think he found it cruel, in his mind it was just good business. Wool is much more profitable than tenant farmers. That helped him, all of my family, keep the lifestyle we were accustomed to. I knew he would also pay anyone's voyage to Virginia if they wanted to go. In return, they worked my father's land for an allotted amount of years."

Colton could tell by Abigail's furrowed brows she was not happy with this story. It had never sat well with him either, to be honest, and became increasingly more the case as he joined the Regulars and saw first-hand how much those below his station had to struggle just to survive.

In a way, his return to Cumberton Park was more to help the surrounding community than anything else. He really didn't need to return to the country; he could have left Abigail in London and taken a ship straight from Liverpool.

He felt in this small way he might have helped ease the economical struggles of some of the people of the land. It most definitely took a small army of his own to keep the estate house up and running. Even after he left for his New World adventure, he planned to keep the house fully staffed.

Finally the carriage stopped before the front of the house and all the staff stood a little taller expecting their new lord's appearance. Colton exited first and then turned to help Abigail down. They both felt stiff after the long ride.

When Colton turned to greet the staff, shocked expressions overcame them. He was sure that they had all been warned by Mr. Johnson, the head butler, of his appearance. The warning must have not done justice to the deformed figure before them.

He bowed his head, letting the brim of his hat cover as much as possible. Mr. Johnson, however, did his best to show no emotion at all and merely stepped forward to introduce the earl and countess to the vital members of staff.

Abigail was happy to place eyes on her new lady's maid, a girl who seemed the same age as herself named Mildred. Abigail could see a long list of questions unraveling in the girl's mind as she looked between the scarred face of the earl and Abigail.

They found the house to be not only prepared but adequately warmed and inviting. They were given a quick tour around the main floor, as neither had knowledge of its layout. There was an office that also opened into a vast library, a morning room, sitting room, breakfast room, and the vast dining room where they ended the tour.

Already a beautiful setting for two was placed at the far end of the table and trays of ham and warm meat pies were being placed down. Both Abigail and Colton were grateful for the warm meal prepared for their arrival and took their places.

"It's so quiet," Abigail said halfway through the meal.

Colton looked up from a pile of notes that had accumulated here since the time he took leave of his London house. He seemed to look around the room as if noticing it for the first time. In truth, silence had been his companion all these years since his injury, and he was very content with it.

"I am just so used to having the twins and Jackie. They bring so much happy noise into the house," she added when he didn't respond.

"Yes, I dare say it will be a while before I forget the continuous speech that seemed to flow from those two. I actually was rather enjoying not having to answer so many questions while I ate," Colton said with a lopsided smile on his lips.

"Did they bother you terribly then?" Abigail asked,

wondering if her new husband was averse to just his niece and nephew or perhaps all children.

"No," he said with a heavy sigh. "Well, a little actually. I just wasn't used to that kind of attention."

"You were very dear to them these last few weeks," Abigail encouraged.

"I think I was more like the attraction of Astley's Circus."

"Not at all," Abigail said with deep sincerity.

Over the next few days, Abigail settled into making a routine in her new house and new position. Most of her time was spent with the housekeeper, Mrs. Hanse. However, soon there was little left that Abigail needed to instruct her on. This left Abigail endless hours of the day to wander alone.

Colton, on the other hand, went right back into the same routine he held back in town. He spent most of his days in his office reading books from the library before the fire. From time to time there was work to be done, though his father and grandfather had made sure the estate was fairly self-sufficient.

He enjoyed the seclusion of his new library. It was much larger than the small cramped office of his London home. It also had its own sitting area with plush couches and chairs. It was perfect as he read up on the country he was about to visit.

He wondered about Abigail, whom he saw so little of. Would she stay here in this big house alone after he left? Perhaps she would return to London and to the society that she seemed to thrive in.

Unquestionably she could return now. In fact, she could expect to now be welcomed with open arms as a permanent member of the peerage. It seemed like it would be a logical choice for her.

Rarely did Colton see her during the day. In fact, other than their evening meals together, he almost didn't see her at all. He assumed that she kept herself busy, though he wasn't entirely sure how.

Most of Colton's focus was now on his preparation for travel and avoiding as much of the staff as possible. Though all had been polite to his face, he knew what it was like in a small country village. He was sure he was the talk of every pub and tavern for miles around.

CHAPTER 33

After two weeks had passed in her new home, Abigail was sure that she had wandered around every room in the house as well as the pebbled path gardens around the estates. Her life was becoming very dull and she was desperate for any distraction. For this reason, she started to seek her husband out.

It wasn't an easy task at first as the estate was so vast. Finally, Abigail remembered that Colton had often retreated to his office and she should expect to find him there again. She did so.

She looked at Colton as she quietly slipped into the room. There was no sound outside the flip of his book page and the soft swishing of her cotton morning dress.

When Abigail took a few soft steps into the room, Colton raised his head to the sound. It was easy to see that he wasn't expecting her. Abigail came to sit on the couch across from Colton as he set his book to the side.

He watched her movements and seemed to wait for her to speak first. She didn't really know what to say. All she was sure of was that she didn't want to be left alone in such a big house any longer.

"I got a letter from Isabella," Abigail finally started after a few moments of silence.

"Oh," Colton said, now seeing perhaps she was here to share the news with him. "And how is she?"

"Fine. She had her baby. It was a little girl, and both babe and mother are healthy."

"That is a relief. I must admit I was a tad worried about her health at the end. But she has always been so strong…" he trailed off.

"Yes, I suppose that worry was my doing," Abigail said, looking at her hands with guilt.

"Completely," Colton agreed.

Abigail's eyes shot up from her hands to meet his cool gaze. It was not a proper sort of response. She relaxed a bit when he gave that soft teasing smile he wore from time to time.

Abigail was happy to hear him tease her again. Her relationship with Colton seemed like she was traveling over a mountain range continually going up and down. The last weeks since their marriage had been full of apprehension and unease. She hoped that perhaps now they were turning the bend for another upswing.

"What did she name the baby?" Colton asked, actually enjoying keeping a conversation up for the first time in a very long time.

He couldn't help but recognize that any time he had enjoyed conversation was in fact with Abigail. Any other person, even those under his employment, he rather dreaded speaking with. With Abigail, however, it was like a ray of sunshine in what was otherwise a dreary world.

"Um," Abigail hesitated with a rosy blush to her pale cheeks. "They named her Abigail actually."

"A splendid choice, if I do say so myself," Colton responded, thoroughly enjoying the embarrassment Abigail was experiencing from the knowledge that her niece was named in her honor.

"Do you really think so?" Abigail asked with an upturned brow.

She seemed to show no genuine belief in his words.

"Well," Colton responded, relaxing back in his seat and rubbing his chin in thought, "I mean I can't speak for anyone else, but in my opinion ladies named Abigail tend to be quite unique."

"Unique how?" Abigail encouraged his flirtation.

"Stubborn, to start."

Abigail opened her jaw in shock. She wasn't truly offended by his words for she was a stubborn creature.

"They also tend to have a wild spirit, an aversion to keeping their thoughts to themselves," he narrowed his eyes at her, "even unpleasant ones that shouldn't be spoken. More than this, I have found them to be quite enchanting and without a doubt a rare gem."

Abigail looked away, blushing at his last words. Now that they were joined together in matrimony, his teasing seemed to press heavier on her heart. Unquestionably, he didn't mean any more of it than he did before.

"So was it the letter then that brought you to seek me out," he asked after a few more seconds of silence.

"No," Abigail responded. "I wanted to seek out the library for a book."

She looked to the shelves behind him. It was partly right, but she was also looking for someone to talk with. She wasn't used to going so long without having someone to speak with.

"I never really took you for someone who enjoyed reading extensively," Colton retorted.

"No, I suppose not. I prefer to be outdoors. I know that won't be possible soon, however, so I guess I am looking for alternative uses of my time. I'm not used to being alone for such long periods."

Colton felt a stab of guilt at her words. Abigail wasn't the type to be shut away in a country estate all alone. Perhaps he would suggest that she return to London and stay with his sister and mother, as he thought she might have wanted to have done already.

"Do you think I could join you here from time to time?" Abigail asked before he had time to suggest another alternative to her loneliness.

"If that is what you wish," he hesitated for a moment, "but why?"

"I can't bear the silence any longer," she said, always full of honesty.

"I am sorry things haven't been to your liking here," Colton replied.

It was an intriguing thought to Colton that, where he had relished the privacy the country home had afforded him these last weeks, it was probably miserable for Abigail.

"It's not that. The place is beautiful. I am settling in very well actually. I just…" Abigail hesitated a minute, not sure how to put into words what seemed missing from her life now. "I suppose I need someone to talk with from time to time. I know you must be very busy, and I don't want to interfere with that, but perhaps if we could set aside time just to visit…"

Abigail seemed to trail off in her words. She wasn't exactly sure how to express her feelings these days as she regularly felt a jumble of emotions as of late.

"I think that might be nice," Colton said before she could finish her thought. "The town is also not that far away. You are welcome to go anytime you wish."

"Would you come with me?" Abigail asked, watching him hesitantly.

He opened his mouth to respond but knew it wouldn't be the answer she was looking for. He had no desire to leave the safety of his home. He couldn't even imagine how these country villagers would treat him. His own kind had been nothing but disappointing, how could he expect any better from those here?

"I'm not sure that is a wise decision for me," Colton said, turning his scarred face away from Abigail. "But you are welcome to take Mildred and go on your own. I can assure you it is very safe here."

"Yes, of course," Abigail said, not wanting to push the subject.

Unlike Lady Louisa and the Duchess of Wintercrest, Abigail had never seen the need to push Colton out of this fortress he built around himself. She much believed that she should let others do as they wished, within reason of course. She hoped for the same courtesy and it would be hypocritical of her not to allow the same in others.

Now that she found herself completely alone and miles away from any connection or relative, she discovered her husband's protective shell was very cumbersome. If they were to stay here together, he would need to open up more, at least to her.

"What are you reading there?" Abigail asked with a nod to change the subject.

"It is a narrative on an explorer's experiences in the new America."

"So, you are still planning on going then?" Abigail asked, doing her best to hide her disappointment in the fact. She would be left here completely and utterly alone.

"Yes," Colton responded, having no idea of her reservations.

In fact, in many ways, Colton thought he was doing his new wife a favor by removing himself. She would be free to attend society with his name as protection and without the necessity of his presence.

It would seem gossip-worthy for a new wife to attend events while her husband stayed back in his country estate. If he was, however, adventuring and seeing to property in other lands, it was entirely within reason that she would attend without his presence.

He thought he was restoring to her the freedom and happiness she once had. It seemed to be the only way he could provide pleasure to his bride in their new marriage.

"Would you tell me what it is about?" Abigail asked, not

ready to end the conversation. "I have heard only a little bit about the separation of the territory from the Crown and what it is like there."

"If you wish," Colton hesitated for a second, "Abigail," he finished, trying her name on his lips.

He relaxed into his seat as he spent the rest of the afternoon explaining to his bride all the dangers, perils, and excitements said to be found in the New World. As he spoke of all he had thus learned, he couldn't help but feel more excited about the prospect.

The war may have changed him vastly inwardly and outwardly, but he still had that small spark of adventure within him. He wondered how his father would feel about him taking on yet another long voyage to an unforgiving front. A pang of guilt struck a chord at the thought. He would never know the answer to such a question, and it was all his fault.

"But surely you will not be where the natives are or criminals you speak of?"

"Well, not entirely. The plantation is very close to Williamsburg, which is a well-established colony. Of course, many of the people on the plantation are goodly folks as they have come from here as I said earlier. But there are a great many in Virginia who were deported from the debtors' prisons."

"I suppose it will be very exciting then," Abigail said with a longing look in her eye.

She couldn't help but feel that her husband was about to embark on what seemed to be a fantastic adventure while she would be left alone in this oversized, empty castle.

CHAPTER 34

The following morning, Abigail did take Colton's advice and asked Mildred to accompany her to the local village. Mildred had suggested they take the carriage for her ladyship's comfort, but it was still a warm summer day, and Abigail rather liked the prospect of walking.

As they took the pebble and dirt road that led to the small fishing town, Mildred filled Abigail in with information on the inhabitants. Other than the fishing along the bay, and the few who were employed as part of the wool trade, there was also a large copper mine a few miles to the north of town that supplied most of the livings for the villagers.

It hadn't been there in the past, but with the late Earl of Gilchrist, two generations ago, deciding to remove all tenant farms, a wealthy man, Sir Edward Blanchard, had come and provided the jobs necessary. Though Mildred spoke of gratitude for the mine, her own father worked it; it didn't seem to Abigail that the conditions were more desirable judging by Mildred's tone of voice.

Abigail had seen her fair share of country villages both small and large over the course of her life. She couldn't help but gasp when she finally found this one coming around the bend. It was nothing more than a few little shacks all stacked near each other.

Mildred informed her that the fields surrounding the small town on three sides were communal. The barley growing there was the main source of sustenance for the residents outside of what was caught in the bay. Abigail knew little about farming but she could easily see by the sickly-looking crops that this land was in fact very poor for growing.

In a way, Abigail understood why Colton's grandfather had removed the farmland and given it to pasture. It was certainly a better use of it. She couldn't, however, understand how he could have left these people so destitute.

"I know there is not much here, m'lady," Mildred said, seeing Abigail's crestfallen face. "But we do have a small general store that has some supplies that might interest your fancy. And the big village is only a half day's walk away. I suspect, in m'lady's carriage, it would take not but a half hour. We could inquire of a cart here and continue on if this doesn't suit you, ma'am?"

"I think this will do for now," Abigail said, doing her best to hide her shock for the sad state of the town.

She wondered if Colton had any idea. She was sure he didn't. He may have been shut up into himself, but that didn't affect his charity. Her thoughts were confirmed when Mildred continued her chatter as they walked.

"You wouldn't believe how grateful we all were to have his lordship return to the big house. You wouldn't believe how much things have already improved in the short time your ladyship has been here."

"What of the local parish? It seems that there is much work needed to be done here. Perhaps I should contact him to help."

"Unfortunately, the nearest parish is in the other village I spoke of," Mildred replied. "In times past, I've been told, the Earl would have patronage at the estate parish and allow all the townspeople to attend it. I believe it was one of the things done away with when the Earl's grandfather made his changes."

Abigail felt bitter about her house and comforts. It

seemed that it had all been bought at the expense of these people here. She would bring this first to Colton's attention and make sure that patronage was found again.

They made their way into the small shop that connected to what seemed to be the only tavern. They both sat on the main strip of road that ran straight through the town. It appeared any and all other shacks and homes stemmed from this main road.

Already there was a small crowd of people standing in front of their houses to watch them come into town. The children looked overly thin and sickly, though their eyes were lit with excitement.

Abigail donned the sunbonnet that she had been holding in her hand as they walked. She detested wearing such a thing when the warm sun could shine freely on her skin, but she knew for the next several hours she was really the Countess of Gilchrist and would have to present herself as such.

A small blonde girl ran up to her with a small handful of forget-me-nots in her hand. She handed them up to Abigail with a scared smile.

"For you, your ladyship," the little girl said.

Abigail knelt down to the girl's level, not caring if the

hem of her dress was ruined in the dust and dirt. She took the small token out of the child's hand.

"Thank you," Abigail said. "What is your name?"

"This is Ester, my little sister, m'lady," Mildred responded for her.

"Well, it is very nice to make your acquaintance, Ester," Abigail said to the little girl who looked away shyly.

They made their way into the small general store. For the most part, the humble shelves were neatly stacked with the necessities of life. Abigail's eyes, however, fell immediately on the jar of peppermint sticks at the front table. She would make sure to buy them all with the small bag of coins in her gown pocket. The children would be so thrilled for the treat.

She walked the shelves as Mr. Smith, the proprietor introduced to her upon entrance, stood tall and proud. She found a few things here and there like some small sewing notions. She thought she might start right away to make some simple items for those most in need.

She suddenly wished the ladies of her small charity group from London were here with her. They would certainly do a much better job at the work. She was determined to take whatever time was needed to see that needs were quickly met in this little fishing town. She certainly had no shortage of time to give.

"What is this?" Abigail asked the proprietor.

She was pointing to a shelf of some small mismatched items in jars. They seemed to be all sorts of concoctions.

"Why that is the small medicine cabinet, m'lady," Mr. Smith responded. "It is just some cough drams, for a cough is very prevalent amongst the miners, and some various salves."

"Perhaps do you have anything for pain from an injury?" Abigail asked, thinking of Colton.

He had not used his cane for some time, but she could still see the injury to his left leg hurt him. Perhaps he didn't know that she noticed in the few moments they were together, but he would seem to massage it more in the evening and even begin to walk with a limp as the day wore on.

The merchant looked over his shelf before settling on a small round-shaped jar that seemed to be filled with thickened cream. The paper that sealed the top crinkled when he removed it from its place.

"You're in luck, your ladyship. This is Mrs. Smith's own making. Scarce can keep it in stock. Many of the menfolk use it to massage out the pain in their muscles after a hard day's work. I'm afraid it is the only type of pain treatment I have. I don't know if it will work well on any other ailment other than stiffness and sore muscles."

He looked her over, not ever imagining that a lady such as herself would have need of a salve made for hard-working men.

"That is actually exactly what I am looking for. You say that Mrs. Smith makes it? Your wife, I would assume."

"Yes, your ladyship," he responded with a proud nod.

"How regularly do you get the product? I would love to buy more. It is for his lordship, you see," Abigail finished by way of explanation.

She wondered if he would, in fact, know her meaning. Certainly, Mr. Smith had never met or even laid eyes on Colton. Perhaps it was just as curious to him that a gentleman of the peerage would need a working man's treatment.

He nodded his head in understanding, however. Perhaps the talk of Colton's injury had already traveled to town.

"I will speak to Mrs. Smith today. I can ensure that she

will deliver regular amounts as needed if it would suit you."

"Yes, that would be very fine," she said, taking the precious jar presented to her.

She was excited to have found something to bring back to Colton other than the news of the sad state of living here.

Before leaving the shop with her parcels in hand, she made sure to buy the gentleman out of peppermint sticks to hand out to all the children before returning home.

As she passed out the candy to the happy and grateful children, she replayed over and over in her head the list of things that would need to be done first to see these people settled right. Of utmost importance would be to discuss matters with Colton tonight over dinner and ensure that a vicar was procured for the estate parish.

When she had woken that morning, she had felt the same despair and loneliness that had prevailed in her heart since arriving. Now she seemed to have found her purpose here at Cumberton Park.

CHAPTER 35

"How was your trip into the village?" Colton asked over dinner that night.

Abigail was glad that he brought the subject up as she wasn't sure how to do so herself without sounding as if she wanted to critique him.

"It was very eye-opening," Abigail responded over their meal of roast pheasant.

"In what way?" the earl asked as he casually sipped his glass of wine.

Abigail spent the next thirty minutes of their meal explaining all that she had seen and experienced that day in the village. With each sentence she spoke, she saw the earl's face become more and more grave. It was clear he had no idea of such things.

"I am aware of a Sir Edward Blanchard. He came to call on me shortly after our arrival. He seemed an honorable gentleman. I am sorry to hear that he has not treated his employees as well as it would seem. Though I suppose I must be equally ashamed of my family's own treatment of these people."

"I am sure your father was not aware of such matters. I couldn't imagine he would allow such poor living circumstances to continue if he had known," Abigail responded.

Colton wasn't sure if this was true, however. His father, like himself, had become accustomed to a certain standard of living. He may have been a kind man for the most part, but Colton wasn't entirely sure his father would have been willing to give up his own comforts.

"I suppose the first thing to do," Colton said as his mind worked, "would be to acquire a vicar. I wasn't going to originally since I plan to leave soon and assumed you would do the same. I can see now that having one on the premises is of the utmost importance."

"Why would I leave too?" Abigail asked, surprised by his words.

For just a moment she had an idea that he planned to take her to America as well. It wasn't one she had considered until this second, but now that it came into her mind it was a little bit of an exciting prospect.

"To return to London, of course. I assumed you would return to the society you are used to once I left for the New World."

"Oh, yes. Of course, that makes sense," Abigail said softly.

It was strange the hurt and disappointment his words created in her. She had known that this marriage was nothing more than convenience for the both of them. Even with that knowledge, she had hoped that they would not spend their whole lives separate from one another.

If Colton planned to send her back to London, she knew that would be the case. She was sure there was no reason on earth that would cause Colton to return to town and the ton.

"Perhaps I might stay though," Abigail said, surprised at her own words. "There is much help that is needed here. The village and people in it have not recovered from the changes. I feel it is my duty to stay and help create the change needed."

Colton looked his wife over. He felt great admiration for her at that moment. She was not the type to idle away while painting fans; she meant to use her title and influence gained to help those less fortunate.

"I had planned to leave before the winter storms, but now knowing about the condition of this area, I cannot leave in good conscience. I will plan to leave next year instead."

"What about your land in Virginia?"

"It has kept these last two years without a visitation. I am sure it is fairly self-sufficient. It will keep well enough until I can make plans to get there."

"So you will stay here with me?" Abigail asked, an unsure tone in her voice.

His wall softened just slightly at her words. Perhaps it wasn't such a bad thing to have Abigail here with him. By his side, Abigail could do the things that he was not able to on his own. In fact, without her presence, he would have never known how much the area was in need of recovery.

Things had indeed been better for him mentally. Though he still had regular nightmares replaying the events leading up to his injury, and a constant smell of burning flesh was never far from him, at least he had calmed in personality.

His uncontrollable fits of rage had lessened since leaving the city. He was sure the peace and tranquility of the country was just the medicine he needed to restore his mind.

"I would be most honored to stay here with you, Abigail," he replied.

A small tingle ran up and down Abigail's spine at the sound of her name on his lips. She had a secret hope that maybe as they lived together here over the next year, she might convince him to stay by her side permanently. If that meant here at Cumberton Park or in Virginia, she cared not.

They spent the next few weeks side by side each day as they acquired and then began to work in conjunction with the new vicar to see the needs of the community met.

The vicar was a Mr. Fitzwilliams. He was on the younger side. Abigail was happy with it. His youth seemed to give him the energy needed to accomplish the many tasks before them. Abigail spent much of her time now walking the village with Mr. Fitzwilliams and meeting with the various community members in need.

She so wished that Colton would accompany them to the village, but he always refused her requests. She understood why Colton didn't want to leave the safety of their home. It was clear that the members of the village had a morbid curiosity over him. She feared that his unwillingness to show his face would only let their fears and superstitions take over them.

Colton wasn't entirely happy to see the new vicar was a youthful, handsome gentleman. He felt even less pleased about the prospect of his wife spending so much time in his charming company. He had to continually remind himself that theirs was a marriage of practicality and nothing more in Abigail's eyes.

"I'd forgotten something," Abigail said one night as they sat together in the library after dinner.

Colton was going over plans for new cottages to replace some of the most dilapidated. Abigail for her part was planning a dinner party to host Sir Blanchard.

Colton didn't relish the idea of having the man back in his home, especially after hearing how he treated his workers, but a good relationship would be needed between the two men if Colton had any hope of improving the workers' standard of living.

Abigail reached down into a small basket at her side. She pulled out a glass jar and passed it across to him.

"I got it that first time I went to the village. Mr. Smith, the man at the general store, explained that it is used for pain and soreness. I thought you might like it for your leg," Abigail added.

"I completely forgot about it once we started making plans for the village. But today, Mrs. Smith, his wife who makes the cream, gave me a second jar thinking I had finished with the first."

Colton reached across the small space between their two chairs and took the item from her. He let his fingers linger for just a second on top of hers.

"Thank you. I didn't realize you noticed," Colton said softly.

"Of course I did, why wouldn't I?" Abigail asked, surprised at his words.

Over the last few weeks as Abigail had worked closely with her husband it was as if they were working on mittens all over again. She had enjoyed his company and friendship so much in these last weeks. More than that, she began to feel for him more than just affection and friendship.

With every teasing word that slipped from Colton's lips she found herself secretly hoping he meant them. Every touch he gave to her, no matter how short or subtle, would send a euphoric chill up and down her body. She secretly wanted to be closer to him.

He still had that hard wall up around him. Abigail understood he had gone through a traumatic experience, but she had a feeling that his need to keep all others out had less to do with the act of scarring his face or even the scars he now was burdened with. She knew there was still more to this story that he had yet to open up to her about.

She was determined to not only find a way into his heart but also through that impenetrable barrier that he kept so tightly guarded around himself. Though she was happy that he had decided to stay the year and help restore Cumberton Park to its former glory, she was more pleased with the fact that it would mean a whole year together before he would leave her. Perhaps in that time, she would convince him to do otherwise.

CHAPTER 36

The weeks were going wonderfully in Abigail's eyes. Not only was she getting along with Colton, she felt they were also already making a big difference to many lives. Tonight was the night that she had been preparing for.

Sir Blanchard and his wife had accepted their invitation and would be joining them and the Reverend Mr. Fitzwilliams for dinner tonight. It was their wish that conversations could turn to making working conditions better for all those involved.

"Lady Gilchrist, it is wonderful to make your acquaintance finally," Sir Blanchard said in greeting as he came into the drawing room that night.

She took the briefest of moments to size up the gentleman as well as his wife. They were most likely her mother's age, and Sir Blanchard was almost entirely gray of hair. He surprisingly wore no wig, which was common among the young portion of society but not for someone of his age.

His silk words and the fact that he seemed to stay up to date in the fashion of his clothes and style immediately told Abigail that society was essential to the man.

Mrs. Blanchard didn't say any words but merely looked around the house with a downcast look on her face.

"I must confess," Sir Blanchard continued, "that Mrs. Blanchard has wondered for some time what the inside of this estate looked like. We quite thought we would never see the place open again."

"My father was never one for country life," Colton said in response, "But I find it to be very relaxing."

"Something I am sure you are in great need of after your time serving the King. You certainly gave more than I would ever be willing to do," he added with a wink.

Though it was said in a joking fashion, there was no laughter in the room behind it. Colton's condition resulting from the war was not a laughing matter to him.

Instead, Colton quietly cleared his throat and turned to greet Mrs. Blanchard. Abigail decided in that instant that, where she might have held back judgment before, she now had her verdict on the man.

The dinner was a tedious affair. Regularly Mr. Fitzwilliams found opportunities to bring up the livings of Sir Blanchard's employees and again and again Blanchard found reasons to wave them off.

"Yes, it is most unfortunate that I cannot give more," Sir Blanchard said as if he ran a charity. "But the copper trade is not what it used to be. I have seven mines dotting these lands. Each one seems to produce less and less as the years go by. Now that relations are beginning to be reformed between the Crown and the colonies I fear we will lose a great handle on the market."

"Surely that doesn't prevent you from showing Christian goodwill to your fellow men?" Mr. Fitzwilliams retorted.

Abigail was seated on the sofa in the large drawing room next to her husband. Mrs. Blanchard hadn't said more than a handful of words and those spoken were so quiet Abigail wasn't sure she had even heard them right.

She had given up all hope of finding a connection with the lady and settled instead on listening to the gentlemen's strained but adequately spoken discussion. Colton for his part interjected and mediated between the other two between sips of his glass of sherry.

"I promise you, vicar," Sir Blanchard said, now feeling rather exasperated by the constant barrage from the preacher, "I do my Christian duty by providing these people with means to support their families."

"And what of the twenty-six men removed from their jobs over the last year alone? Have you done your Christian duty by them?"

"As I said there have been many setbacks as of recently and sadly my employment may reflect that. It is strange you claim to be such an authority on my business when you, yourself, have been here such a short while?" Sir Blanchard spat back.

Abigail feared that things were starting to get out of control. She looked over at Colton who smiled down at her assuringly before standing to intercede yet again.

Abigail couldn't help but feel some pride in watching Colton come to stand and walk so smoothly. Usually this late at night it was a struggle for him to do either. She was sure it was the salve she had given him.

Colton had already requested the second jar, having finished off the first. Not only did he seem to move more smoothly, but she was also sure it improved his spirits as well.

"I think what Mr. Fitzwilliams is trying to explain is that people in your employment find themselves unsure if they will have secure employment in the future. Perhaps if there was a way to reassure them they would be more efficient at their work."

"I thank you for your advice, Lord Gilchrist. You will forgive me, but I believe I know my business better than you do."

"Of course, Sir Blanchard. I only mean to give suggestions to see to the needs of those in my district seat. I would not fulfill my duty if I did otherwise."

Though no agreements had been made that night, Colton was hopeful that over time, with the knowledge that Colton would be there to oversee how Sir Blanchard treated the people of the area, things would improve.

Abigail was less convinced. She made her distaste for the man known once all the guests had retired to their own homes for the night.

"Fitzwilliams was trying so hard to give him gentle counsel, and Sir Blanchard seemed to just walk all over him. I fear we may have just made things worse and not better."

"I don't think that is true," Colton said, happy to see Abigail return to her seat next to him on the sofa instead of the one across from him, as she usually did.

"Sir. Blanchard knows that I am here now and that I will keep an eye on him. I can influence his dying trade in ways he will not like if he doesn't adhere to my request."

"Such as what?" Abigail asked, surprised.

"Regulations on trade to start. The House of Lords doesn't take much convincing when it comes to adding regulating taxation," he added.

"And you think that would help?"

"I think the knowledge that I am here and displeased with his actions is enough for him to reform before I take those drastic measures."

"You seem to be well versed in politics like this. I find it all to be slightly slimy," Abigail said with a little shiver.

"I took my commission to seek adventure. Instead, I got a proper education in the politics of our world. Though my father may not have wished me to go, I am sure that my time spent in military service prepared me to be the

Earl of Gilchrist more than anything else in the world could have."

"He was not happy you went then? I remember Isabella saying he supported the decision."

"Well, he did for the sake of my mother. She can have such a weak constitution at times. He did his best to talk me out of it, though. If only I had listened," Colton added with a scoff.

Abigail thought he was referring to his pain and scarring. She had no way of knowing the guilt that dug deep into the core of him. He was sure if he had just listened to his father, his father would still be alive.

"I can see it has changed you much from the man that I once heard stories of. That being said," Abigail continued, "I am sure I much prefer the person you are now to the ghost of the one you used to be."

Colton raised a blonde brow to his wife as he looked down at her. He couldn't believe that she would actually prefer the scarred mess he was now to the possibility of being married to a regular peer of the realm.

"Yes, well I suppose if I was not the man I am now," he said waving at the left side of his face, "then we would have never come to Cumberton Park, and you would have never had the acquaintance of the charming vicar."

Abigail stared at him, surprised at his words.

"Mr. Fitzwilliams?" she stammered out.

"Yes. You two seem to be very good friends," Colton said, trying but failing to hide his jealousy.

"Colton, do you think there is something between the preacher and myself? How could you possibly think that?"

"You are a young and attractive girl; he is a charming man, why wouldn't you?"

"Because I am married to you, and he is a preacher!" Abigail said, still holding on to the fact that he had called her attractive and was clearly jealous.

She took a steadying breath to hide her racing heart at the thought of his jealousy. "You have nothing to fear. I made my promise to be devoted to you."

Abigail hesitated for just a second before reaching her hand out to him. Colton thought so little of himself that he actually thought that she was willing to look elsewhere for happiness. She slipped her hand into his.

Colton looked over at Abigail, surprised by her initiation of the touch. He could tell she was nervous but also saw something else in her movement. He couldn't believe she might actually feel something for him.

"Abigail, I have no illusions about how this marriage was formed."

Abigail nodded her head, "I know we both had our own reasons for why we chose to marry. Even before that, I can't really say we always got along," she added with a smile. "But I can promise you there is no one else I would rather be with."

Colton looked down at their intertwined hands, relishing the feeling of her touch. She was risking everything at that moment to tell him how she felt about him. He could see from her nervous eyes; she had no idea that his feelings for her had run more profound and much longer than their union.

"I have cared for you," he said in honesty as he turned her hand in his, "since long before I asked you to marry me."

"You have?" Abigail asked, surprised and relieved at the same time.

Colton gave a soft laugh as he turned in his seat to face her head-on. He reached his hand up to brush along Abigail's cheek. He had wanted to touch her for so long.

"I never thought you would feel for me anything remotely close to what I feel for you. I was happy just to have your companionship as long as you were willing to stay by my side."

Abigail tilted her head up to look deeply into his blue eyes.

"What if I want to stay by your side for the rest of forever?"

"I think I would like that," Colton said, dipping his head low and kissing Abigail softly on the lips.

CHAPTER 37

Abigail lay contentedly next to her husband for the first time since they married. She was happy and comfortable in his arms. She never thought she could have felt so right in all her life.

Slipping an arm around her husband, she snuggled against him before drifting back to sleep.

Colton was struggling to see through the fog. No, it wasn't fog but smoke. It was thick black choking smoke. He could scarcely breathe. He was wandering in the dark heat not really knowing why. All he knew was that he was searching for someone, though he had no idea who.

Finally, he could see a clearing in the smoke before him.

Colton made his way forward, desperate for the fresh air it would bring. His body felt like it was searing inside and out. Through the smoke, he saw the outline of a figure in the clearing.

His eyes burned and blurred with tears. It was hard to make the person out. He called out a few times. Whoever it was, maybe they needed help to escape. He hoped that making his way to the clearing and figure would also lead to his way out of this dark, hot place.

Colton froze in his tracks when he finally reached the small pocket of fresh air and saw the person standing before him.

It was his father, only not how Colton had ever seen him before. His eyes were sunken in and surrounded by dark circles. His once light-filled face was now drawn and dull. He reached a hand out that looked more skeletal than human.

"Colton," a hollow voice called out to him.

In the blink of an eye, the figure was now standing a hair's breadth away from him. His father's arm, previously reaching, now wrapped around him and gripped him tight. Colton struggled against the unearthly strength of his father.

"Why?" his father said, completely calm though Colton struggled against him. "Why did you do this to me?"

Colton summoned all the strength he had and burst from his father's grip, sending him soaring away and back into the smoke. Colton woke to the sound of his own voice screaming as he sat bolt upright in bed.

He was drenched in sweat and disoriented. He realized it was not just his voice alone that had screamed. He looked around, remembering what had transpired that night.

He leaned over the bed, not daring to look at what he was sure he would find there. Sure enough, a stunned Abigail who had been thrown from the bed struggled to untangle herself from the blankets that had followed her.

"Colton! What happened?" she asked, both shocked and still not fully awake.

Colton slid from the bed to help Abigail up. He felt so ashamed. Not only had Abigail heard his embarrassing, childish nightmare, but she had also been physically harmed by his actions in it.

"Abigail, are you alright?" he asked, still breathless from it all. "I am so sorry. I never meant to...I promise I won't ever let this happen to you again," Colton struggled to say as he helped unwind her from the fabric.

"It's alright, Colton," she said, coming to a standstill before him.

Though he was mortified to touch her again, it was plain to see that Abigail was weak at the knees still, so he wrapped a steadying hand around her waist.

"I should go. I should have never done this," he waved to the room around him.

"Go? What are you talking about?" Abigail responded.

Neither one could see much, and both seemed to be feeling the other in the darkness to check for injuries.

"Let us return to bed, my love," she continued. "It was just a bad dream. No harm was done."

"No harm?" Colton spat back, pulling her away from him to arm's length. "I could have hurt you. I never wished you to see how broken I truly am. I am so sorry for that. I won't let the dangers of my splintered mind endanger you."

She tugged on his hand now and tried to ease him back to the bed. Colton wouldn't move from his place. This was truly his greatest fear and why he kept himself so far removed from anyone else.

"Come," Abigail cooed again as if she were calming a skittish animal. "Lay down, and we will both catch our breath. Please, don't shut me out again," Abigail added in a pleading tone.

Colton softened at her words. The adrenaline that was pumping through his veins had finally begun to lessen and he felt like the sting in his lungs from the dream was dissipating.

He sat down on the bed, still keeping a hold on her two hands. He took a deep breath and let it all out again.

Abigail came and sat down next to him. She gave him a few moments as he collected himself.

"Perhaps," Abigail said, "it might help if you told me. Whatever is bothering you is too much of a burden to bear alone. Share it with me and together we can find a way through it."

He looked over at his wife in the darkness. They had yet to light a candle, and for the most part, he could see nothing but an outline of her frame. Reaching up, he grabbed one of the long locks of her hair that had spread around her shoulders. He didn't have to see it to picture the copper shine that glittered in the light with every movement.

Colton had no desire to burden her with the guilt that

was bursting to come out of him and the nightmares that plagued him constantly.

Abigail was patient as she waited for Colton to speak. She remembered the advice of her brother all those months ago. She knew that there was no fast way to help Colton overcome his demons as Isabella and Louisa had hoped for. Instead, he needed time, and he needed someone to share his burden with.

She was ready to be that one if he was prepared to share. However, Abigail was preparing herself that he might not be ready for this step. If that was the case, she only hoped that he would not again shut her out and away from him.

"Remember I told you my father was against my commission," Colton finally said softly as he continued to feel the silky smooth lock in his hand.

"Yes," Abigail encouraged just as softly.

"He wasn't just unhappy about my choice, but actively against it. I more or less blackmailed him into putting on a front of support."

"You wouldn't do that," Abigail retorted.

"I did. I told Father that it was in my mother's best interest that he go along for her sake. My mother was always his weakness. He cared for her so dearly. And so he did as I asked."

Colton released another long sigh and removed his hand from Abigail's hair to rub his chin. Abigail could hear the sound of his palm against the rough stubble already growing along his square jaw.

"When I was injured, at first they didn't think I was going to make it. In all honesty, I probably shouldn't have. The stress of it all, well it killed my father. I killed my father."

"Why would you think that?" Abigail said, shocked with the revelation. "No one else believes the same."

"My mother does."

"She would never say such a thing. She was so excited to have you home. I can't imagine she would ever put such irrational blame on you for your father's death."

"She may not have said the words, but she didn't have to. I can see it clearly in her eyes. She holds me to blame for the loss of her husband."

"I lost so many over the years I was fighting. Men under my command. The boy whom I was meant to see safely from the surgeon. That guilt I think I can manage, but the added knowledge that I have taken my own father's life is too much. It was the last life I took and the one that broke me."

"You are not broken, first of all," Abigail replied with a determined tone.

"Abigail," he said with a huff of disappointment in himself. "Look at what I just did. If that is not the mind of a man destined for Bedlam, then I am not sure I know what is."

Abigail scooted closer to her husband so that they were right next to each other on the bed. She lifted his left hand, not caring a whit for the scars, and kissed it softly.

"I promise you, you are not broken," she repeated, this time softer.

Abigail laid her head gently on her husband's shoulder and sighed in contentment. Her heart was breaking for the turmoil inside of Colton, but at the same time, she was relieved that he had in fact opened up to her instead of running away as he so often did.

"Your mother loves you and doesn't hold you responsible. But I fear it is your own heart that needs to let go of guilt for the situations you couldn't control."

"And if I can't? What if I am this way forever? Are you sure you can bear to be around such a monster?"

Abigail smiled against her husband's shoulder. After the night she had shared with him, she was confident she would die if she were ever to be separated from him.

"You may call yourself a monster if you wish, but I don't see you that way. You are my husband and my love. I will stay by your side always whether you want me there or not."

Colton smiled down at the tenacious lady at his side. He lowered his lips and kissed her softly on top of her head.

"I will never know how I got so lucky as to trick you into marrying me," Colton whispered against her hair.

EPILOGUE

"Abigail, I am beginning to think this is not a very wise decision," Colton said as he watched his wife go over the list of supplies and luggage one last time.

"What isn't a good idea?" she asked, not removing her eyes from her page. "Oh, I must tell Mildred only to pack my cotton dresses. I am told that Virginia can be quite stifling in the heat of summer."

"That is the decision I am speaking of."

"Cotton dresses?" Abigail retorted, knowing full well that wasn't what Colton meant.

Colton gave a heavy sigh. It was probably his own fault that such a teasing nature was rubbing off on his wife.

"I don't know it is wise for you to make the journey. It will not be an easy one."

"Plenty of others have sailed the Atlantic, why not I? Plus don't you think it is a little late to be having these second thoughts? We leave for Liverpool in the morning, my love," Abigail expounded quickly and waved him off.

"You are not just anyone," Colton replied, reaching to wrap his arms around his wife. "You are the most important person in the world to me, and I couldn't bear it if something were to happen to you."

"If you haven't noticed, Colton, I am not a very dainty and delicate lady. You will not stop me from going, not now," Abigail said, wrapping her arms lovingly around her husband's shoulders.

Colton smiled down at his wife. Try as he might, she was as stubborn as a wild horse. He doubted he could force her to stay even if that was what he wanted. In honesty, however, he was sure he couldn't bear the time away from her.

"What if those natives pick you up and take you away?" Colton retorted with narrowed teasing eyes. "What if they chop you up and turn you into stew?"

"Well I fully intend on you rescuing me before that happens, or you will feel the wrath of my words."

"I shan't want that to happen; you can be so fierce when you want to. Like poor Sir Blanchard. If you do to the natives as you did to that man, I fear they would run at the mere sight of the color red," he added with a flick of a copper lock that dangled down her neck.

"I wasn't that horrible to the man. I simply told him the truth that no one else had the courage to say."

"You called him a disgrace to society and that you would be sure to inform every person you met of that fact until he was willing to treat his employees better."

"Well, it was true," Abigail retorted like an errant child. "Something had to be done. The vicar's words did nothing to move the man."

"Yes, and you found his weakness. He had a desperate need to get in with societal connections," Colton said with pride in his wife's abilities.

"And so I threatened to rob him of it, is that so wrong?" Abigail asked, looking at her husband innocently.

"For you, my love," Colton said with a great big grin, "absolutely not."

"And now I am happy to report," Colton continued,

"that Sir Blanchard has increased the pay of all his workers and made conditions much safer for them. They all have you to thank for it too."

He leaned down and gave his wife a soft kiss. He removed his lips from his wife's to look her over again.

"Now that I think about it," he said with his wicked teasing grin, "it might be best if you come with me. That sharp tongue of yours can protect me from any native or scoundrel I might encounter."

"You rescued me once," Abigail retorted, "so it only seems fair that I return the favor."

"I promise you," Colton said, placing a soft kiss now on the tip of her nose. All humor was removed from his face, and he spoke with deep sincerity. "You have already saved me from the misery I was trapped in. You are the light that helped me through my darkness."

Epilogue 2

"Mildred, will you bring me the wash bin," Abigail called to her lady's maid when she entered the large suite of the bedroom.

Mildred, who had insisted on taking the trip along with her mistress, did as she was bade before returning to her tasks for the day. First Mildred went about opening the long wall of doors that opened out onto a veranda.

In her mind, Lady Gilchrist did seem a bit pale that morning in bed, and a fresh breeze might do her some good. Before she was even able to push back the sheen curtain of the first set of doors she heard the sound of Abigail being sick in the basin.

Mildred turned to the lady with concern.

"Are you alright, m'lady? Should I send for a doctor?"

"No, thank you," Abigail said as the wave of nausea finally subsided.

"Let me have someone bring up Lord Gilchrist in the least, ma'am. I don't believe he has left the house yet," Mildred said as she went back to letting in some air for her mistress's sake.

Abigail could already hear the sound of insects singing on the warm breeze that blew in. The sun had scarcely risen and already the day was hot and sticky.

"No, please don't bother him. I assure you I am fine."

"Well you don't seem fine to me," Mildred said, placing her hands on her hips. "Why on earth would you be trying to empty your already barren stomach if you were fine?"

"Because," Abigail said, realizing her lady's maid was much too young to have any idea what was actually happening, "I am not *barren*."

She waited for her meaning to sink in with the maid. It did take a few seconds of thinking before Mildred's face lit up and she squealed with joy.

"Oh, how wonderful, m'lady. Does Lord Gilchrist know? I bet he was just beaming with pride."

"I haven't told him yet," Abigail confessed. "I only realized myself halfway through the voyage. I didn't want to tell him then. Plus it was easy enough to hide with seasickness."

Abigail placed a hand on the small round bump at the base of her torso. It was barely there at all really. They had only just settled into their new lodgings on the plantation. She was planning on telling Colton, but just waiting for the right moment.

That moment came two nights later. Colton had finally finished his tour of all the property and buildings on it. They were sitting on the porch drinking a warm spiced wine as the sun was slowly sinking over the fields before them.

"It is quite beautiful here," Abigail remarked.

"Terribly uncomfortable heat, however," Colton retorted casually.

"How long do you think we will stay?" Abigail asked slyly.

"Not long at all. I am hoping to organize a boat back to England before the end of summer. We should be home in time for the holidays," he said looking to her.

"Unless that is not what you want?" Colton questioned, seeing a different look in Abigail's eyes.

"I do agree, it would be nice to be home for the holidays. I am afraid that we may not be able to leave quite so early though."

"And why would that be, my love?" Colton asked with affection in his voice.

He would have been happy to stay if Abigail wanted it. He didn't particularly like the heat or the chafing way his sweat-soaked clothes rubbed against his scarred body, but he would stay as long as his wife wanted.

"I have found myself in a condition that won't allow for traveling for some time," Abigail said, looking over her husband's face.

Mildred might have thought that Colton would be

happy at the news, but Abigail wasn't entirely in agreement with that assumption.

"A condition?" Colton asked, looking his wife over.

As far as he could tell she looked to be in good health. She had been very sick on the voyage over and because of it lost a significant amount of weight. He wondered if perhaps she wanted more time to recover before stepping back onto a boat.

"I'm going to have a baby, Colton," Abigail said softly when he didn't catch her meaning.

Colton sat stunned next to his wife for a few moments. He wasn't sure he had heard her right. She was going to have a child, his child.

"You're going to have…we are going to have…here?" Colton managed to stammer out.

"Well yes. Apparently this little one doesn't have any qualms about heat."

"I hope you won't mind terribly," Abigail added timidly.

"Mind," Colton said with a hearty laugh before standing to pull his wife into his arms.

"I promise you, I don't mind at all. In fact, quite the contrary, I couldn't be more excited."

He leaned his head down and kissed his wife wholly on the lips. He cared not for the servants who passed by after the day's work. Let them see. Colton loved this woman with all his heart and he would be damned if he didn't make sure the whole world knew it.

THE EXTENDED EPILOGUE
SAVING LADY ABIGAIL

I am humbled you finished reading my novel **Saving Lady Abigail**, till the end!

Are you aching to know what happens to our lovebirds?

Click on the image or one of the links below to connect to a more personal level and as a BONUS, **I will send you the Extended Epilogue of this Book!**

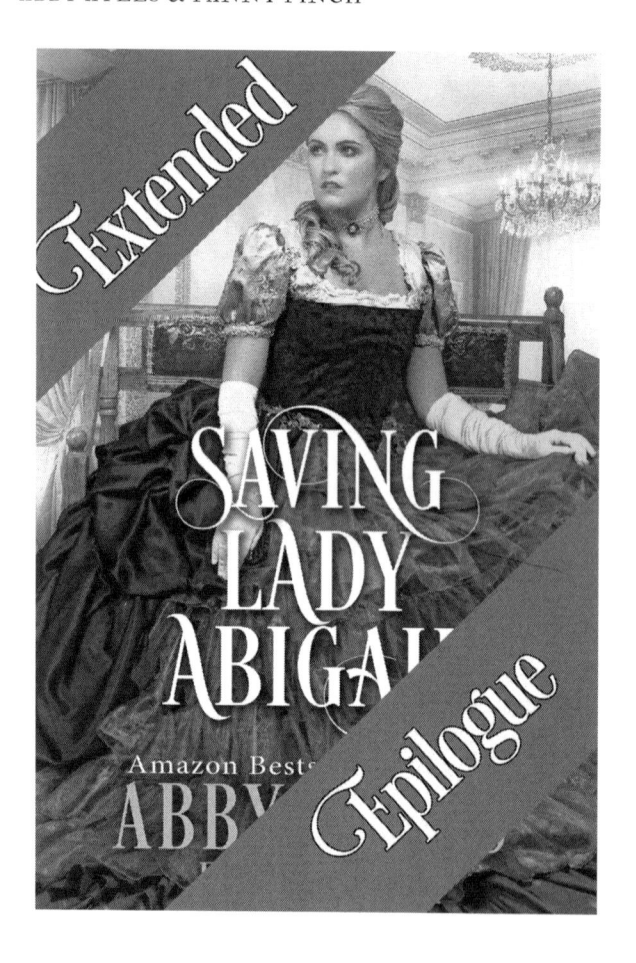

or click here
BookHip.com/CVTHPB

If you loved the story I would love to see your review!
Click here to post your awesome review
Link

With Love

Historical Romance Author

DO YOU WANT MORE
HISTORICAL ROMANCE?

Turn on the next page to read the first chapters of my best-selling novels: **The Lady's Patient** & **The Lady's Gamble**!

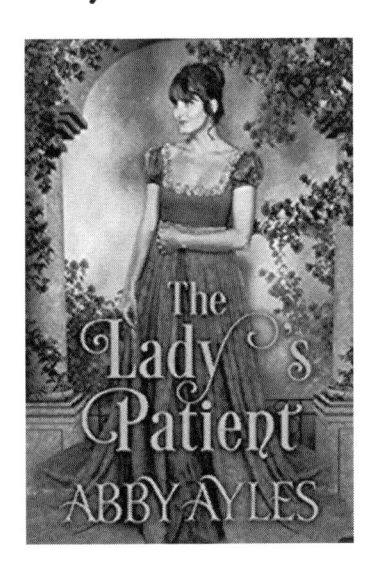

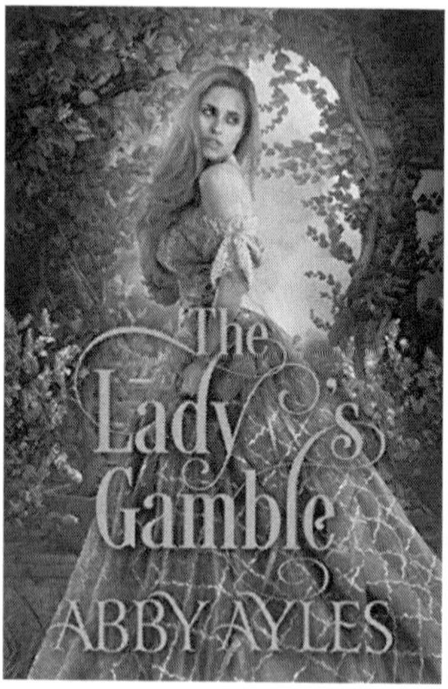
The Lady's Gamble
ABBY AYLES

THE LADY'S PATIENT

CHAPTER 1

Kitty looked at the pile of suitcases on her bed and smiled in relief. It was time to return home. *At last!*

It had been a pleasant stay at the resort. She had enjoyed her usual week, plus an extra two days when, during a massage session, her elbow had become too loose and almost came out of its socket. But now everything seemed to be in place again.

Suffering from rheumatism, even only a mild case, was not easy. Kitty knew she was blessed to be as strong as she was and to have the money for proper care.

The doctor knocked on the door and walked in looking pleased. He smiled warmly. "How are you feeling, Miss Langley?"

She smiled back. "Very well, thank you. I feel revitalized and prepared for my journey."

"We have not yet had news about your coach, but no doubt it shall arrive soon," the doctor reassured her. "How is your elbow?"

"No complaints, doctor," she replied.

"And everything else is as it should be?" he asked.

She nodded. "A thousand times better than when I first arrived."

The doctor smiled and scribbled some notes into his journal. "You have done very well, very well indeed, Miss Langley," he said. "I am sure that Dr. Allen will be able to pick up from where we're leaving it off."

Dr. Allen was the family doctor. He had cared for Kitty ever since she was a little girl, for her mother when she became ill. And now, he tended to her father as well ever since a terrible bout of pneumonia left him with a painful cough.

Dr. Allen would have appreciated his three-week long holiday, but would no doubt be home several days before her coach arrived, and her room would be perfectly prepared for her as if she had never left.

As soon as her coach was announced, Kitty made her

way to the entrance. They always offered her a wheelchair, although she had not needed to use one for years. It was as though nobody believed she was able to get better rather than worse.

"Oh, we'll miss you, sweetie," the head nurse said, adjusting Kitty's bonnet.

"And I shall miss you," Kitty replied. "Everyone is so kind to me here, I feel truly at home. I cannot wait to return for my next rest."

"Unless you require further treatment," the nurse remarked.

Kitty felt a slight concern. "I am in no pain, I hope I shall not need treatment at least until the end of the year."

"I hope so too, my dear," the nurse replied.

Kitty made her way to the coach, where her last case was being firmly tied to the roof of the vehicle ready for the long journey home. Inside the coach sat a maid and Kitty's travel bags by her feet. She was ready to attend to anything that Kitty needed on her trip home.

As the coach pulled away and rolled down the hill towards the docks where the ferry would be no doubt just arriving, Kitty looked out of the rear window.

It was always a little sad to see the resort disappear into the distance. But she also knew that she would be back before long. Her father would not allow her to go more than a few months without treatment. She huffed a breath of indignation. She did not need it.

As a young girl, she had needed vast amounts of medical care. Nobody had dared think that a child her age could be suffering rheumatism, and it only dawned on them when she was six that she had been suffering from it her entire life.

At six, she was barely able to walk, and always in intense pain at her knees, ankles and back. So much so that she rarely left her bed. She was restricted to a wheelchair until she was ten.

But even as she grew stronger and healthier, her father seemed to refuse to acknowledge it. It was getting to a point where she was receiving treatments she did not need, just to comfort him. She lived an active life and enjoyed long walks around their property. She wasn't a little girl anymore.

Her mother's death had really affected Kitty's father. He was always protective of Kitty, but when her mother passed away he became even more overbearing. From that point onward he went from simply guarding her when she was in pain, to treating her as though she were made of the thinnest crystal.

And no matter how effective her treatments were, no matter how well she felt, he insisted on steam baths, massages, special oils and ointments—anything that was recommended. Although she was tired of this, she did not complain. She smiled, accepted her treatment, and told him how much better she felt after them. She couldn't hurt him.

She had been only eight when her mother had passed, and it left a deep scar on her heart. He may be overbearing, but Kitty would do anything to make her father happy. And it made him happy to treat her rheumatism. It gave him a purpose in life.

It was a peculiar situation, where he could not bear to see her in pain, but he couldn't believe that she was ever not in pain. He needed her to be in pain so he could treat her, so he could look after her. And she needed to play along just so she could see him smile.

And yet now she was growing weary of it. She wanted freedom. She wanted to marry. She wanted to go out and watch the races, go to balls, walk with her friends and do all the things that normal young ladies did.

As the sun set on the first day, she could already feel her

knees trying to seize up, and began lightly exercising them as she sat there, so they would not get stiff as she slept. She would have to sleep on the ferry at first, and the cabins were small and cramped. It was best to go in as relaxed as possible.

The journey was long, and it always made her joints stiff. But she knew that once she was home she would limber up in no time. Her condition was nowhere near as debilitating as her father seemed to believe.

She could not sit too still for very long, and she could not travel far. But the only reason she ever had to do either of these things was to receive treatment. If she simply stayed home she would not have to worry about such matters.

But her father would never understand that.

As the sun dawned on the sixth day, Kitty was pleased to wake up and see the fields outside their village. Home at last. Due to the lack of inns on the last stretch of their journey she had been forced to sleep two nights in the coach, and she looked forward to her own cosy bed.

She saw the usual bright barn that meant there was only an hour left to go.

"Please pack up my books," she said to the maid.

The maid smiled. "Of course, mistress."

As the maid packed away Kitty's books and assorted travel items, Kitty looked out of the window and tried to spot the usual landmarks as they rolled by, counting down the minutes until she was home.

It was barely seven in the morning as they finally pulled up outside her home. The gardens were in full bloom, and the mansion was glimmering with dew in the sunlight. It shone like something out of fairy land.

An enormous, bearded, gruff man walked out, still in his bed coat, a broad grin stretching his plump, furry cheeks. Kitty waved at him through the window as the coach pulled up at the bottom of the stairs.

The driver descended from his seat and opened the door for Kitty. She made sure both her legs were feeling strong before standing up and stepping out of the coach. The last thing she wanted was to fall over and scare her father.

Once firmly on solid ground, Kitty all but threw herself into her father's arms. "I have missed you so much, daddy," she said, feeling her heart rest easy now she was safely home.

"I have missed you too, my dearest. Now, come indoors, it is cold. We must get you a nice, filling breakfast," he insisted.

He was just as obsessed with making sure she ate enough as he was with her treatments. Although she did not need much nourishment due to her fairly inactive lifestyle, he would become so worried when she didn't finish the enormous plates she was served, that now she had taken to dropping some under the table for the dogs.

"How is my little girl after her journey? Not too sore?" he asked as they sat at the table, an enormous plate of cold pie, cheeses, and bread in front of both of them. Baron Langley had a glass of wine, and Kitty had her usual spiced tea, an Eastern remedy for her pains, according to Dr. Allen.

"I am feeling quite well," she said with a smile.

"You seemed stiff when you walked in," her father replied sternly.

She knew she couldn't get away with lying, but she still tried. She didn't want to cause him undue concern. He was very good at worrying excessively all on his own.

"I am always stiff after my journey, you know this, father," she insisted. "I shall be right as rain in a day or two."

"I hope so, because I would like to attend a gala on Sunday. Your friends will be there," he said, taking a hearty bite of cheese.

Kitty politely listened and, as he was distracted, dropped some pie to her feet, where the dogs, silent as though understanding their complicity, quickly made it disappear. "That would be lovely, father," she replied.

"I was thinking that perhaps you could meet a few nice young men there," Baron Langley said. "I know how much you want to meet an appropriate suitor, and maybe this time it shall happen."

"I do hope so," Kitty replied.

Her father nodded. "I have been thinking, and I know you do not like me to think of this, but I have been thinking about what may happen when I am no longer here for you. And I think you need a good husband, to care for you."

Kitty just smiled. She knew what would happen. It was what always happened. She would hit off wonderfully with a young man who was handsome, funny, educated, wealthy, and witty, he would go to her father to ask to court her... and then her father would say something about her illness and they would never see the young man ever again.

She had stopped caring about this, to be honest. She used to aspire to marry well, have a beautiful wedding, and bear many children. But as man after man had been scared away, she had given up. At least, contrary to her father's fears, she knew she would be able to care for herself when she was all alone.

Kitty dropped some cheese under the table as she ate some bread. She could feel the dogs' tails wagging against her shins as they enjoyed their breakfast.

"I think the gala is a wonderful idea," she said again with a nod.

"Good, good. I shall inform Duke and Duchess Haskett that we shall attend. But now you need to get plenty of rest," her father said with a warm smile. "Otherwise you shall be in no shape to attend the gala."

"It is not for a few days, I shall be fine," Kitty reassured him, gently resting her hand on his arm.

"Yes, but you must rest for a few days," he insisted. "You need to stay home and build up your strength. I know how badly you suffer when you overdo it."

She smiled and nodded.

CHAPTER 2

Sitting by her window, Kitty felt very much a prisoner in her own home. This was something else that always happened. Whenever there was even a hint that she was under the weather, she was stuck at home. Her father could not fathom that she might be unwell one day and better the next. In his mind, every little ache required a week of convalescence.

The sun shone beautifully outside, the garden looked so bright and fragrant, and she would have to just watch from her stuffy bedroom.

She heard a knock at her door. "Who is it?" she asked.

"Just me," her father said from the other side.

"Come in," she offered.

The door opened and he walked in, smiling proudly as he saw her resting by the window.

"I know that you do not like resting here too much. So that you do not suffer the lack of company, I have invited a friendly young man for dinner," he said, sitting down in the armchair opposite her.

Kitty felt excitement welling up in her chest. This would be perfect! "That is wonderful news," she replied. "Who is he?"

"Someone by the name of Josiah Morton. I met him at an event last week. Lovely young man, his title slips my mind, but he seemed like the sort who might take good care of you."

"I am sure he is wonderful," she replied. "I shall choose a dress for tonight."

Baron Langley nodded and stood up, resting a heavy hand on her shoulder. "Just make sure it is not too exposed, I don't want you to get cold."

Kitty smiled. "I shall choose one with long sleeves," she replied.

"Good girl," her father said. "I shall ensure that dinner is excellent for tonight." And with that he left the room.

Kitty was just happy to be able to while away the hours

trying on dresses, now that she had an excuse. It was something to do.

She eventually selected her best dress, a pretty pink number that highlighted her chestnut locks and bright blue eyes. After finding the right shoes and jewellery to go with it, she laid them out carefully on her bed, then returned to her seat by the window.

Staring out at the bright green fields, the wispy clouds dancing in the blue sky, and the little birds swooping past her window, she wondered what this young man would be like. However much he seemed intent on scaring them away, her father had excellent taste when it came to her suitors.

Dinner time arrived and, dressed and made up, Kitty felt like she was royalty. She smiled at her own reflection as she walked past the mirror and out of her bedroom. Ordinarily her father wouldn't even let her leave the room when she was "recovering". This was a wonderful exception.

"You look like a little doll," her father said with a proud smile.

Kitty beamed. "I am glad. Is he here yet? I would love to meet him."

"He is not, but he will no doubt be here soon," Baron Langley replied. "So we must make sure we are ready to receive him properly."

Sure enough, just as they made their way downstairs, a young man was shown in by the butler. He was very tall, with dark wavy hair, bright eyes, and a sharp, handsome face. He smiled warmly as a maid took his coat and hat to be hung up somewhere.

"Master, mistress," the butler began, "Duke Josiah Morton is here."

She had not expected that. A Duke. And at his young age too! Duke Josiah Morton was almost the ideal. Handsome, young, wealthy, and powerful. Provided he was also a charmer to talk to, she would have no trouble getting along with him.

"Charmed to make your acquaintance," Kitty said, making eye contact with him.

Sitting down for dinner, Kitty smiled politely at him. She could almost melt as he smiled back, he was so handsome. "I am pleased that you were able to make it."

"Well, when a Baron says he has a pretty young

daughter looking for suitors, I do like to oblige," he replied. "I am only sad that you were not at last week's ball."

Kitty looked aside. "I am afraid I was away, but I shall be at Duke Haskett's gala this weekend, if you shall be there."

"I may," he replied. "You really are lovely, I am astounded that you do not yet have any suitors," Duke Morton said, grinning at her.

She nodded. "It is a little complicated. But I am away a lot. Most young men are not prepared to handle that."

"What a coincidence, I am away a lot also. I suppose we could try and travel together," he replied.

"I am not sure that you would want to accompany me on my travels," Kitty said with a nervous giggle.

"And why would that be?" Duke Morton asked, sipping his wine.

Kitty could feel her face hot with shame. Ought she to hide this from him? It would not be right, surely? And yet she knew what happened whenever she mentioned her condition. Or better said, whenever her father mentioned her condition.

It was probably better to get it out of the way. As quickly

and as casually as possible. If he was going to ignore her, then so be it. But there was no point letting him build up hope and interest only for him to back away as soon as he found out.

Besides, it wasn't as though her condition would scare away *everyone*. She was not so ill. Someone would eventually look past it and understand her.

But before she could say anything a maid marched in and curtsied low before her.

"We have a letter for you, mistress," the maid said, holding out a tray with a letter on it.

"Thank you," Kitty replied. Taking the letter and turning it over, she saw a deep brown wax crest had sealed it. "Father, may I take this to the hallway to read? It may require my immediate attention."

Baron Langley raised an eyebrow a little. "Of course, but please return as soon as you are done."

Kitty left the room. She couldn't read this in front of her new suitor. She knew where it was from based on the seal. The resort. She opened the letter and read it. Just a confirmation that her treatment would not be for another six months, unless rescheduled, as she was doing very well. Kitty sighed in relief.

"Maid?" she asked softly, so as to not be heard on the other side of the door.

The maid, who had followed her out of the dining room, patiently waiting for further instruction, walked up to her. "Yes, mistress?"

"Please leave this letter on my father's desk, for his records," Kitty said. "And thank you for bringing it to me."

The maid curtsied. "Of course, mistress. I shall see to that immediately."

Kitty was happy. She knew her father would no doubt reschedule, but it was always good to hear that her health was robust. Even if her father wouldn't believe it.

Re-joining her father and the duke, she curtsied before sitting down.

"What was that?" her father asked. "Nothing important?"

She shook her head. "Not at all."

"If it requires my attention, I can—"

Kitty shook her head again. "It is all arranged."

"I see, was it from the resort?" her father asked.

"Oh, it is nothing, just my treatment has been rescheduled," she replied without thinking.

"Treatment?" Duke Morton asked, raising an eyebrow. "Whatever for, you seem right as rain?"

Kitty smiled, feeling a sweat break out on the back of her neck. From the looks of it he was not the sort of man to take these things lightly. "It's just a little care I require for an ailment I have had since I was a girl. It doesn't cause me much trouble."

"And you cannot say what that ailment is?" he asked.

"I am not sure why I should have to," Kitty replied defiantly. "It clearly does not affect me in my day to day life."

"I am not sure I could marry a young lady who is going through *treatment* for something," the duke said, an eyebrow rising again in suspicion.

Kitty sighed. "That is your choice to make, though I do believe it is foolish to dismiss someone on grounds of her health alone," she said somewhat bitterly.

"I am not sure it is worth my staying for dinner," he replied.

"Now, now, let's not be too hasty," Baron Langley said, slight panic creeping in his voice.

"I have some matters to attend do at home," Duke Morton replied, standing up. "It has been lovely seeing you again, and I hope I shall see you soon."

Baron Langley sighed in resignation. "Of course, I hope that you are able to attend to all the matters you need to."

Duke Morton nodded and smiled. "Thank you. Do not worry about seeing me to the door, I am sure I can find my own way."

"I am sorry to have troubled you, Your Grace" Kitty's father said, settling back into his seat as the duke left. He looked down at his plate.

Kitty could tell her father had lost his appetite. This was a bad sign. This was always a bad sign. When he was comfortable and happy, he was always hungry. When he did not eat, something was wrong. He kept staring at his plate until they heard the front door close. Duke Morton, like many before him, had been scared away.

Kitty sighed.

Baron Langley glared at Kitty. "Why would you say something so blatant in front of our guest, Kitty?" he said, exasperated. "Now he shall not want anything to do with you."

"I- I was not thinking," Kitty replied. "You mentioned the resort and I- I am so sorry, father."

"The resort is not a problem. People attend resorts all the time for perfectly innocent reasons. It is the treatment we did not want him to know about yet. And you had to mention it," he said bluntly, pushing his plate away. "I am not hungry. You have spoiled my dinner."

"Well ordinarily it is you who cannot keep quiet about my condition," Kitty replied angrily. "Why do you think all my last suitors left, father?"

"They need to find out sooner or later," the Baron replied. "After all, with your condition we cannot exactly keep it a secret. But there is a time and a place to reveal these things so that good men are not scared away by the idea of courting a woman who is so frail."

"Pray, tell me then," Kitty replied, "when is the right time and place. Because I am not sure if you have noticed, father, but every suitor has left, no matter when or where you have told him."

She knew this hurt her father and she shouldn't have said it. But she was not about to sit there and be blamed for her own lack of suitors. Her father's face grew red with rage.

"Perhaps at the gala I shall meet a man who does not

mind, but so far they have all been resistant to courting me for that very reason," she added.

"No, young lady, you shall not attend the gala. You may come along and wait in the front room as everyone else enjoys themselves," he replied.

Kitty felt a pain in her chest. "Daddy, please don't," she started. "I shall behave, I am sorry. I do not know what came over me. Just allow me to—"

"No," her father said bluntly. "No, you have disrespected me and you need to learn."

Kitty felt her heart sinking as she realized what she had just done to herself.

CHAPTER 3

The gala would have been wonderful if she had been allowed to attend. She watched from the front room of the Duke Haskett's mansion as the guests paraded up the stairs, each more elegantly dressed than the last, laughing, smiling, and ready for a long night of drinking, socializing, and dancing.

Kitty could hear the cheer outside the door to the front room, wondering if she got closer to the door whether she would be able to make out the conversations taking place. But then she would not be able to see them marching in.

Everything looked so luxurious, so exciting, so beautiful. She should be out there, or, better yet, already in the ball room, wearing her sapphire blue dress, spinning and dancing until she was giddy with joy.

Instead, dressed fairly plainly, Kitty sat holding a book in the front room, trying to eavesdrop on the guests as they arrived. She would not be able to listen in once everyone was there. The dancing was taking place at the other side of the vast mansion, and she could barely hear the music.

But people had been arriving for the past hour, and already the crowd was thinning and slowing. Soon everyone would be dancing in the ball room and she would just have to sit in the front room and read a book, like a child waiting to be sent to bed.

As the last coach pulled away and the last beautiful dress waved in the breeze and disappeared through the front door, Kitty curled up tighter in her window seat and finally opened her book.

Before she could even begin reading, the door opened with a slam, startling her.

A young woman walked in, sighing in exhaustion. She turned to the left and arranged her hair in the mirror, before inspecting her face, her jewels, and the fit of her dress. She was oblivious to the fact that she was not alone, so Kitty picked her book back up and began reading it quietly, as though she also had not noticed the other woman.

Nevertheless, she watched over the edge of her book as this beautiful young woman, with a crowded arrangement of silky, shiny, thick black hair, mellow blue eyes, and a sensual gait, preened herself in front of the mirror.

As Kitty turned the page, an abandoned book mark slid out and landed on the floor with a whisper. It was loud enough. The lady turned around and scanned the room.

Then her eyes landed on Kitty. "I beg your pardon, I did not see you there," she said with a nervous chuckle.

Kitty shook her head. "It is quite alright, I was absorbed in my book. I am Kitty Langley," she said.

"I am Delilah, Delilah Sinclair," the woman replied.

Sinclair... Kitty knew that name from somewhere, though she couldn't quite put her finger on it. It was something important, and yet as soon as she felt she was about to recall it, it slipped her mind.

Delilah had returned to her reflection and was aligning her necklace so that the clasp was once again behind her neck.

"Why are you not dancing? At first, I thought you were

a member of staff, you are dressed so plainly, but your clothes look far too expensive," Delilah observed, walking over to the fire place, sitting down before it, and slipping her feet out of her slippers.

Kitty was surprised she could tell from that distance. "I am the daughter of Baron Langley," she replied. "But I am not allowed to attend the gala."

"Oh, I see. Are you still a little young?" Delilah asked, placing her bare feet on a little footrest and sighing in relief. "I didn't take you for a child."

"Not at all. I was going to be there, but I had an argument with my father, and it is my punishment to not attend the gala," Kitty replied.

"That must have been a serious matter," Delilah said, finally leaning back in her chair, looking into the fire.

"It was," Kitty replied. "He had invited a Duke round for dinner, and was hoping that the young man would show some interest in me. But I accidentally mentioned my condition, and he would not have left faster if he had a pack of wolves chasing him." She laughed nervously. "That happens a lot, though."

"A condition, eh?" Delilah asked. "I understand that. My own father suffered from chronic stomach and chest pains. The doctors said he had a growth inside him which could not be removed. These things do get in the way of your life, and the life of your family. Not everyone is prepared for that."

Kitty shrugged. "That is just it, there is nothing to be prepared for. I am managing my condition myself. I do not need a husband to care for me like some invalid. I am perfectly capable of looking after myself. But my father does not believe so, and insists on my getting all sorts of treatment. Which, naturally, means all my suitors need to find out about the treatment, and that puts them off."

"So you are not seriously ailing, or dying?" Delilah asked a little flippantly.

"Nothing so serious, although my father seems to believe I am at constant risk of coming to harm," Kitty replied. "I can hardly believe that the man who spends half his life talking about how ill and frail I am has punished me for even mentioning my illness."

"I suppose it is not an easy thing for him to manage. On the one hand he needs to defend you, but on the other he wants to make sure you marry the right man," Delilah replied. "All fathers are a bit like that."

Kitty pursed her lips. "I suppose so. But my father has a justification for acting this way."

"And your mother?" Delilah asked.

"She passed away when I was a little girl. I think my father is more protective because of it," Kitty explained.

"It must be difficult," Delilah said, nodding. "But I am sure that you persevere."

Kitty felt her heart warm a little towards Delilah. "I do my best. It's easier now I'm not quite as ill as I used to be. I used to be such a sickly child. My father doting over me was just what I needed back then. But now I am a grown woman. Sometimes... sometimes it feels as though my condition has moved from being a physical burden to being an emotional one."

"How so?" Delilah asked.

"I used to hurt, and my joints were stiff all the time. But lately I only have the odd bad day. Most of the time I am no less capable than any other girl my age. And now I must pretend to still be ill, and go along with my father's beliefs, which is ruining my marriage prospects. If I were to act as well as I feel, my father would be saddened by the fact that he does not need to care for me." Kitty sighed and sank back further into the window seat.

It was odd to talk to a stranger about this, but she felt better for talking to this wonderful young lady. She noticed that although there was a ring mark on her finger, there was no ring.

"Tell me a bit about you, seeing as you know my life story now," Kitty said. "Are you married?"

Delilah pursed her lips. "I am not." Then, she fell silent.

Kitty paused, waiting for Delilah to add something else. Especially considering the little white line left behind from wearing a wedding ring many years. But she said nothing.

"Are you engaged yet?" Delilah asked suddenly, before Kitty could say anything else. "You look about the right age."

"Like I said, my father manages to scare all my suitors away. Or, well, I did so this time. But generally it is him," she replied. "I don't think any one of them stayed for long enough to get to know me as a person."

"Oh," Delilah said, sounding a little disappointed. "I would have thought that, what with you being so pretty, at least one would have given you enough time to prove yourself. I have trouble believing that all young men would be so superficial."

"Alas, it seems that they are," Kitty replied.

"You will find the right man eventually," Delilah said

with conviction. "There is no doubt plenty of men out there who would give their right arm to be married to someone as lovely as you."

Kitty laughed nervously. "No young man would have me, not as I am now. Between my treatments and my father's exaggeration of my illness, none have been brave enough to stay."

"And why would you want to settle for the sort of man who runs for the hills when he faces even the smallest challenge? If you ask me, your circumstances are a blessing, as they will drive away all but the most serious of suitors," Delilah mused.

"And what if nobody is serious?" Kitty asked.

"Then would you not rather be a spinster, than married to a coward? I know I would," Delilah replied with a smirk.

Kitty just sighed.

"But that is beside the point. The right man will come along, you'll see," Delilah insisted. "And he shall be everything you ever dreamed of and more."

Kitty smiled. Delilah was such a wonderful person. How could she be so warm, so kind, so encouraging to someone she had only just met? Although they had barely been talking half an hour, Kitty felt a strong affinity for Delilah, as though she were discovering a sister she had never had.

"Thank you for being so kind to me," Kitty said softly.

"Not at all, I am just telling you the truth. Sometimes we cannot see the truth since our emotions get in the way of our senses, hiding things that are in plain sight. So, like a blind person, we need to have the truth described to us, so that we will recognize it," Delilah explained.

"So you truly believe one day my prince will come?" Kitty replied with a laugh.

"I do, I honestly do," Delilah said.

"I just wish he would hurry up. Or I shall be a hundred on my wedding day," Kitty replied.

"But perhaps then you would both be so old that your ailment will be of no concern to him," Delilah said. "I am sorry," she added hastily, "that was in poor taste."

Kitty laughed. "No, it is also true. Perhaps when I am not so young I can find a man who understands me. Or perhaps, if I look after myself well, I shall soon be considered in excellent health for my age."

Delilah laughed too now. "Perhaps so. You just wait and see. He will find you."

A head of shiny blonde hair stuck in through the door. "Delilah, come back to the dance. Duchess Haskett is asking after you."

Delilah nodded and the blonde head lingered in the doorway, beckoning excitedly with a lily-white arm. "I must go," Delilah said, turning to Kitty. "I've had a chance to rest my feet and made a friend. I hope I shall see you again soon."

"I also hope we shall meet again soon," Kitty replied, watching as Delilah slipped her perfect little feet into her slippers and all but floated out the door.

She was so in awe of Delilah's grace and beauty that she did not pick up her book again until the door had clicked softly shut.

CHAPTER 4

Several weeks passed and slowly Kitty's father forgot about her disobedience and she enjoyed some of the few freedoms that he did not consider "too much" for her. She was now able to go out into the garden, free run of the house including the dogs' room, and, most importantly, to entertain guests a couple of times per week.

Although her heart still yearned for more, for now she was just glad not to be stuck in her room with nothing to do but read. She loved her books, but even at the resort she enjoyed more variety than one room and a shelf of books day after day.

Her friend, Duke Haskett, had come to visit her shortly after the gala, and his wife, Mary, had promised to spend more time visiting Kitty. She was a wonderful woman, and kept true to her word, regularly stopping by with flowers, books, sweets, and little trinkets, to brighten up Kitty's day.

Dr. Allen was not exactly company, but it was nice to have him around. He rarely had much work to do with Kitty, as most days she needed no care at all, but he would make sure he was seen to administer oils for her joints, and to prepare her special herbal teas, to let Baron Langley see that Kitty was looked after.

Baron Langley too was more present, and he spent long days talking to Kitty, reading to her from his paper, and teaching the dogs new tricks, much to her delight. Although it got frustrating at times, in some ways it was nice that he still saw her as his little girl

Whereas many young women did not have a relationship with their father as they grew older, instead bonding with their mother, Kitty had grown very close to her father. And not having any male heirs to pass the title onto, Baron Langley was pleased to teach Kitty all about his responsibilities and rights.

She would listen to him intently, imagining herself in the future as a spinster, Baroness Kitty Langley, fulfilling the same position.

So she was not short of good company.

But the person who Kitty longed the most to see had not yet made an appearance. Helena Keats, her childhood playmate, was still very ill.

They had met through Dr. Allen, before he became their private family doctor. Back then he was a consultant for five families in the area, and one day, when visiting his office, Baroness Langley had bumped into Lady Keats. Although Lady Keats was several ranks below Baroness Langley, the two of them found they had much in common and soon became the best of friends.

Which meant that Kitty and Helena would play together a lot as children.

Both being sickly, they never left the playroom, and barely did anything, but they enjoyed it. It was nice to be able to play with another child that had their own energy and movement restrictions.

With time, Kitty had learned that Helena could not move her legs effectively or breathe very well because at the age of two a cart had run into her, crushing the lower portion of her back and ribs. She had regained some mobility, but would never walk normally again.

They found solace in one another, but whereas Kitty

grew stronger and stronger as she received increasingly effective treatments, Helena only got worse and worse. It reached a point where Helena became bedridden, and besides the odd walk in a wheelchair, she barely left her house any more.

Nevertheless, they had remained friends. Although not as close as they were before, they never forgot one another and remained in contact through letters, visiting each other as much as possible.

But Helena had neither stopped by nor written a letter inviting Kitty to visit in all the time since she had returned. And now Kitty was worried.

One night she woke up with a sense of dread. As though something absolutely terrible had just happened. She sat bolt upright, unable to get back to sleep at all. Something was very, very wrong.

As soon as she heard him walking down the hallway, she threw on her bed coat and went to find her father.

"Daddy," she said, walking into the drawing room, "have we not had any news from the Keats family at all?"

"Not a bit, I'm afraid. I suppose they are busy. Or in London again," he replied.

"But it has been nearly three weeks since I returned," Kitty sighed. "Surely they should be home by now?"

"I am not sure, I have not heard much from them," Baron Langley said. "Not since you last left for the resort, at any rate. I am sure they are simply busy. Helena's condition does require a lot of upkeep. More than yours. No doubt they will reach out to us when they are ready for visitors."

"Or perhaps their letters have been lost in the post," Kitty replied.

"If you are that worried, how about you write to her?" Baron Langley said. "You have permission to use my study before breakfast, to compose the letter."

Kitty felt a little excited. The study was not always open to her. "Thank you, I shall do that immediately."

Her father's study was a big, brown room with not much light and not much room to move around in. It was so full of different files, books, and stationary items, Kitty sometimes wondered if he had just bought an entire book store.

Settling into the vast leather chair behind the desk, Kitty sat down to pen a letter for Helena. The post would arrive later that morning, so perhaps she would be able to send it with the mail man.

"My darling Helena,

I hope that my letter finds you well. It is only that I have returned from my treatment at the resort and I was wondering if you should perhaps like to visit. Or perhaps I should visit you?

Please write back to me and let me know how you are!

Your dear friend, Kitty."

Folding it into the envelope and rushing downstairs, she got to the door just as the post man knocked. At the second knock she swung the door open, startling him and causing him to drop the letters he was holding for them.

"I have a letter for you to take with you," she said.

He shook his head a little. "And I have a letter for you, miss," he replied, leaning down and picking up the three envelopes from the floor. "Two for your father, but one for you."

They exchanged letters and as he walked off, Kitty's heart beat faster. Perhaps this was from Helena? Then she could rest easy, knowing her friend was well.

Kitty looked at the letter in her hand. The handwriting was, sadly, not Helena's. It wasn't that of anyone she knew, for that matter. The letters were big, looping, and beautiful, in a thick ink which left folded ribbon-like lines behind, like an inscription beneath an artist's drawing.

Kitty put her father's two letters on the dresser beside the front door and tore her own letter open.

"*Dearest Kitty,*

Please forgive me, I have asked Duke Haskett for your address as I need your assistance most urgently. My little brother has foolishly injured himself whilst riding down country roads last night. He is in great pain and needs someone to care for him.

Unfortunately, he rejects all medical care. No matter what I have said or done, he stubbornly refuses to have a doctor or nurse care for him. It is only after arguing with him the better part of the night that he agreed to a normal person, with some experience handling such conditions, becoming his in-house nurse.

The problem now is that I do not know of anyone else who could perform this task. And then I thought of you. You have lived with aches and pains much of your life. Perhaps you would be able to persuade him to care for himself? And to nurse him back to health?

I know it is a lot to ask, but my little brother really needs help, and it may be the only way of assisting him.

I beg of you, please consider my request.

Yours sincerely,

Delilah Sinclair."

Kitty was so surprised she read and re-read the letter a few times over. She didn't even hear as her father walked into the hallway.

"What have we here? Why are you standing by the front door? There are cracks under the door, you will catch cold," her father said.

"I have received a letter from Delilah Sinclair," Kitty said. "But it's ridiculous."

"That name rings a bell," Baron Langley remarked. "I think Delilah Sinclair was present at the gala on the night you were punished."

Kitty nodded. "Yes, she came and spoke to me. Seemed a lovely young woman. A friend of yours?"

"No, she was someone important, I can't quite put my finger on it… What is she like?" Baron Langley asked.

"Very tall and graceful, black hair, basically stunning," Kitty said. "She's very warm and friendly too, so happy to talk to me even though she did not know me."

"Red dress, very thick hair and blue eyes?" Baron

Langley asked.

"That is her, yes."

"She is not so young, Kitty, but I know who you mean. She was talking to some very important people at the gala," Baron Langley remarked. "What has she written to you about?"

"She says that her little brother has injured himself and needs someone to help look after him and nurse him back to health, and she is asking me," Kitty explained.

"Do you wish to go?" Baron Langley asked.

Kitty did not hesitate. "I would love to. She seemed so nice, and it would be something new for me. Besides, how could I let a little boy down? The poor child is no doubt suffering, and must want someone to sympathize with him."

"Do you really wish to do something so sudden?" her father asked, taken aback. "It may be dangerous, and you will be living away from home. I wouldn't be there to care for you."

She could hear pain in his voice. She knew he wanted her to say it was scary and she didn't want to go. But she couldn't lie to him. She needed to seize the moment.

"I just wish for a little freedom," Kitty said meekly. "Just to be able to go out and do things with other women. Even if this is a bit unorthodox, I would enjoy it."

"I see," Baron Langley replied.

"Do you... do you not want me to go?" Kitty asked.

"I do not want you to go. I would rather keep you here, where I can see you and look after you. Nevertheless, I think it would be very good for you to go and help her. It would help improve your standing, and you would also be in the company of people who you consider friends," he replied.

"So I may go?" Kitty asked, astonished.

"Of course you may. It is just a friend and her little brother. And your friend is a woman of standing. It is a fantastic idea to move in with them a while, and teach them from your own experiences," her father explained.

Kitty grinned. "Thank you so much, daddy," she replied.

"Besides, that is just the sort of thing which your mother used to do. And her recklessness led to me, and to you. I can put my faith in that," he said, hugging her.

"I doubt I shall find love, but at least I may find fulfilment," she replied.

"As long as my little girl is happy, I do not care," he said.

CHAPTER 5

Kitty was relieved to find out that Delilah Sinclair did not live very far. Although she had always dreamed of setting off on her own adventures, actually going somewhere unfamiliar concerned her. She had only ever experienced her home and the retreat ever since she was a little girl. It was nice to know that even though she was going on an adventure of her own, she would be within a two-day journey from home. And besides, a longer coach ride might have upset her joints. Two days, stopping at an inn on the way, was no trouble at all, and she knew she would be able to move normally as soon as she got out of the coach.

As they drove in through the gates, Kitty was taken aback by how well Delilah Sinclair lived. Her father had not been wrong when he assumed she was someone of importance.

The estate was quite a bit more than she had expected. The grounds stretched out so far, and were so full of exotic plants, it felt like she was moving into another country, all owned by Delilah's family. As the building itself became visible through the final row of silver birch trees, Kitty spied some enormous, spiky plants arranged around a fountain so vast she wondered if it carried a year's worth of water or five.

Stepping outside, Kitty felt tiny in front of the huge white pillars and the looming doors of the house. The driver carried her bags up the stairs and rang the doorbell as she made her way up the steps more slowly, taking in every little feature, every carving and every accent, on the face of this magnificent building.

The door opened slowly and a servant guided them both inside. The building was as amazing inside as out. The walls and floor were gleaming marble, and the marble stairs were adorned with a rich red carpet, held down by weighty metal bars so it hugged each individual step. The furnishings were deep mahogany, and items from around the globe clung to every wall, shelf, and table. An elephant's tusk, a Turkish carpet, a bear skin rug, and a vast brass gong were the biggest items Kitty could see, but around them cluttered countless smaller artefacts.

And yet before she could go and look at them, Delilah appeared at the top of the stairs, looking relieved.

"I am so glad you could make it!" Delilah said, gliding down the stairs and embracing Kitty warmly.

"I would not refuse you," Kitty replied. "It is clear that you need my help, and I shall endeavour to do everything you need me to do."

"Anything you can do at all is a blessing," Delilah said. "He refuses all sorts of treatments. Doesn't trust doctors at all. I'm at my wit's end."

"And where is your brother now?" Kitty asked.

"In his room, in bed," Delilah said.

"Can he move at all?" Kitty asked.

Delilah shrugged, exasperated. "I have no idea. He *won't* move, but the doctors can't even inspect him to see if he needs some support or if he is just tired."

"I see," Kitty said. "Is there any reason for this?"

"He is sulking," Delilah replied, shaking her head. "But I have no doubt that you shall get through to him in no time." She began walking up the stairs. "Come with me, I shall introduce you to him."

"What is his name?" Kitty asked. "And why do you think I can get through to him?"

"Augustus," Delilah said. "And he doesn't listen to doctors. But you are not a doctor. You are just another person who has experienced joint problems."

"So it is his joints?" Kitty asked.

Delilah looked aside. "Yes, when he was found his back was twisted and his knee was completely out of place. They managed to reposition everything before he came to, but now he refuses any and all examination to determine the state of his insides. Here we are."

They arrived in front of a tall, dark, ornate door, where Delilah stopped and knocked. Nobody inside said anything. She knocked again. Still no reply.

Delilah shrugged, swung the door open, and ushered Kitty in, following close behind her.

It quickly became apparent to Kitty that although he was younger than Delilah, Augustus Sinclair was not a little boy. In the bed lay a man, of at least thirty years, with thick black hair and a day of stubble, fast asleep between the pillows.

The blankets had slid down to his waist, revealing that he was wearing nothing but a light vest on top. A vest which was stretched at the arms and neck, revealing broad shoulders and a muscular, lightly hairy chest. A vest which clung to him so tightly that Kitty could see each outlined abdominal muscle, and even his belly button.

His chest rose and fell steadily with each breath. He stirred a little. The blankets slid down further, revealing a part of his flesh between the bottom of his vest and the top of his long johns, his hip bone and taut muscle fully in view.

"Great. He is sleeping," Delilah said quietly. "We may do well to leave the introductions until later. He hates to be woken up. Come, let's get tea and discuss what you can do to care for him."

"But, he is a man," Kitty replied nervously.

"Yes, he's my brother," Delilah said with a quiet giggle. "Did you expect a woman?"

Kitty tried to look away from him, her face growing warm. "I simply... I had assumed that he was... I thought he was a boy," she stammered nervously. "You *did* say he was your younger brother."

"Yes, younger by five years," Delilah said, "but very

much a man. Will that be a problem?"

"I am not sure I can be a nurse to an adult man, Delilah," Kitty explained. "It is improper. My reputation will be ruined."

"Nonsense," Delilah replied. "All you are doing is keeping an eye on a friend's brother. You shall not be in a room alone with him, you shall sleep in your own room at night. You will administer him medicine and nothing else. It is a very noble thing for the daughter of a Baron to do for an Earl."

This also took Kitty aback. "An Earl?" she whispered to herself. Her eyes landed on the beautiful man lying in the bed at the far end of the room. That man was an Earl? He looked so rough, so unkempt, so rugged. She would have taken him for a noble's mischievous son, perhaps, but not for a man with a title all of his own.

"Besides, nobody will know," Delilah continued. "It will be between the four of us and the doctors, nobody else."

"The four of us?" Kitty asked hesitantly.

"Yourself, your father, myself, and my brother, of course," Delilah responded. "Nobody else needs to know."

Kitty sighed. "I am not convinced of this, Delilah. It

seems wrong."

"It is not," Delilah insisted. "Please, I beg you, please help us."

Kitty could feel Delilah's words pulling at her heart strings. But then she glanced at the sleeping man again. Earl Augustus Sinclair. He was too attractive, too desirable. There would be talk. "Promise me nobody else will ever find out," Kitty said.

As they spoke, Earl Sinclair's eyes fluttered open and landed on the two women. For a moment he seemed a bit dazed, then he focused on them. Kitty looked into his dark eyes and saw something she had not seen before. A strange combination of pain and desire, as his eyes scanned her figure. He smiled groggily and pushed himself up on the pillows.

Then he winced with pain and let out a groan, collapsing back, only sitting up a little straighter than before.

Kitty blushed, noticing that the movement had further pulled up his vest, revealing much of his hard, chiselled stomach, shining with a faint layer of perspiration, heaving with his pained breaths. She looked away and tried to fix her eyes on a painting across the room, but they kept being drawn back to that naked flesh.

"You are both making far too much noise," he said, closing his eyes. "Go away if you shall bicker."

"Do not be like that, brother," Delilah replied. "She is the girl I told you about. The Baron's daughter, the one with rheumatism. She has very kindly offered to look after you, so that you do not have to go to a hospital, and now you are going to scare her away with your rudeness."

Earl Sinclair just groaned in what seemed like a combination of frustration and pain. He cracked open one eye. "Very well, she may sit with me." He made no effort to move, or to cover himself.

Kitty looked to the bedside, where there was an empty chair. She had just wanted to leave. But something about him stirred something in her. The pain was something she knew, something she understood. And his stubbornness reminded her of her own father. She wanted to help him. She wanted to take away this beautiful man's pain. Someone who looked so wonderful did not deserve to wear such a pained expression.

Striving not to look at his bare stomach and hips, Kitty sat down beside Earl Sinclair's bed. "How are you feeling today? Your sister said you had an accident last night," she began.

"I am feeling rotten, I am in agony, and those bird-witted doctors must have done something horrible to my back because it feels broken from top to bottom," he replied, turning his head to face her, making eye contact.

She wanted to reply, but she tried to feel more compassionate. "I understand. It must be unusual for someone who was once healthy to experience so much pain all of a sudden. A bad day takes even me by shock."

"What do you do on a bad day?" he asked.

"I rest," she replied. "There is nothing more to do. The body heals itself very well, but it needs rest. Unless you want some ointments—"

"No," he interrupted her. "No ointments. No herbs. No pills. Nothing of the likes. I will not have some snake oil salesmen trying to poison me just so they can charge to cure me."

"You do not trust doctors?" she asked. "Very well, we shall use no medicine."

His lips curled into a soft smile. "Ah, so you understand me, do you? Very well, then. You may be my nurse. But if you insult me or undermine my pain I shall fire you."

And with that he sank into his pillows, almost

immediately falling back asleep. Kitty stood up, trying not to look at his bare stomach again as she walked over to where Delilah was.

What a curious man he seemed to be already!

In some ways he reminded her of her father. He was gruff and stubborn, and he would only have things his own way. He was commanding her as though he believed he had a right to, and yet she felt compelled to look after him, if only because through all that stubbornness she could spot a hint of fear, of weakness, that he was trying to defend.

And yet in some ways he reminded her of her mother, especially after the illness, when she was despairing, had lost all her faith in medicine, and turned to God to either cure her or take her from this Earth.

"So, shall you stay, or am I forcing him into hospital?" Delilah asked as they walked out of the room.

"I shall stay," Kitty replied.

**Do you want to read more?
Click on the link below!**
http://abbyayles.com/AmBo6-Bo5

THE LADY'S GAMBLE

CHAPTER 1

Regina Hartfield concentrated on her stitches. Elizabeth was banging away at the pianoforte just one room over. It was threatening to disturb her calm.

She did feel rather bad. It wasn't Elizabeth's fault she couldn't play well. And she wasn't trying to disturb anybody. But every time it gave her such a headache.

"Elizabeth!" Natalie entered the room. Her hair was only half done up. "For the love of all that's holy would you stop! You can hear it through the whole house!"

The pianoforte stopped. Regina breathed out a quiet sigh of relief.

"Honestly," Natalie grumbled. Then she spied Regina. "Oh, darling, you must start getting ready!"

"I don't think I shall be going tonight."

"But you must!" Natalie looked crestfallen. Although part of that might have been her half-done hair. "Regina, everyone will be there."

"Precisely." Regina focused back on her stitching. The idea of being among such a large crowd of people for hours terrified her.

"Have you told Father?" Natalie asked.

Regina didn't answer. She was a horrible liar. And she hadn't told Father. She'd tactfully avoided the subject of tonight's ball all week.

She had been hoping that, being ensconced in the side parlor, she could avoid Father. Then when it was time the flurry of her four elder sisters climbing into the carriage would disguise her lack of presence. By the time Father realized she wasn't there they would hopefully be halfway to the ball. Far too late to turn back for shy mousy Regina.

It was too late for that now. Natalie would be sure to tell Father.

"I think that you should go," Natalie maintained. "It's always such fun."

"For you it is," Regina replied. It was widely maintained that Natalie was the prettiest of the Hartfield sisters.

Regina supposed that depended upon one's taste. Natalie was the only sister with blue eyes. That helped her to stand out, certainly. Paired with a sweet, heart-shaped face and dark red hair, every man in the county wanted to marry her.

Personally, Regina preferred the cat-like green eyes of her other sisters. Not that Regina took after them. She had red hair like all of her sisters. Gotten from Mother, God rest her soul. But Regina had boring brown eyes and far too many freckles. She was tiny as well. Elizabeth liked to joke about Regina being the runt of the litter. What man wanted to dance with a girl when he had to crane his neck down to look at her?

It wasn't her looks that truly made Regina reluctant to go to the ball. She just didn't like people. And all that exercise. She wasn't the adventurous type. A quiet evening stitching and reading suited her just fine.

Not that Father would see it that way.

"It would be fun for you as well if you would make an effort," Natalie replied.

"I'm sure that stitching would be just as fun for you if you made an effort," Regina pointed out.

Natalie sniffed. She'd always hated stitching. "I'm going to finish getting ready. You should as well. Elizabeth!"

Elizabeth appeared, looking peevish. Elizabeth was the second youngest and had taken to it like a martyr. Her red hair was orange and fiery to match her temper and her green eyes were always flashing.

"It's hours yet, Natalie, I don't have to get ready."

"You should start now. You know your hair takes longer to tame."

Elizabeth had also inherited their father's tight curls. It did make her hair rather difficult to get under control.

"Not all of us need half a day to make ourselves fit enough to be seen by society," Elizabeth replied.

Regina focused back on her stitches. She really didn't want to be privy to another spat between Elizabeth and Natalie.

"You could learn from my example. Perhaps then someone would ask you to dance a second time."

Regina shrank a little farther back into the chair. Luckily the spat was ended when Bridget entered the room.

Bridget was the oldest of the five Hartfield sisters. She was also Regina's favorite. Although, it wouldn't do to tell any of her other sisters that. Bridget was everything that Regina wished she could be. Bridget was confident and tall with pale creamy skin and a serene face. She had dark red hair and quick green eyes. Furthermore, she was wickedly funny, well read, intelligent, and could make anyone love her. Natalie was the prettiest Hartfield, everyone said, but Bridget was the wittiest and the most well-liked.

"Elizabeth, please go and get ready." Bridget didn't raise her voice. She didn't need to. "I'll join you in a moment. Natalie, could you remind Father that he needs to speak to the gardener?"

Natalie and Elizabeth looked like they knew exactly what Bridget was doing but they hurried off anyway. Everyone always did what Bridget asked.

Meanwhile Regina was pretty sure that if the house was on fire, nobody would listen to her if she told them to get out.

Bridget smoothed out her skirt and sat down on the settee next to Regina's chair. "That's a lovely set of stitches."

"They're for the Lord and Lady Morrison."

Bridget smiled. "We shan't be seeing them for another two months, at the masked ball."

"Yes, but I want it to be perfect." Regina focused down on her stitches. She'd chosen the flowers for their meanings. They all meant some version of love and devotion, wishes for a happy marriage.

Bridget placed her hand carefully over Regina's. "Darling. You are quite accomplished at that."

"It's merely practice."

"Precisely." Bridget's voice was gentle. "I think that if you practiced just as much at your social skills as at your needlepoint, you needn't find it all so intimidating."

Regina set aside her sewing. She wasn't going to get any more done today. Not if Bridget got her say—and she always did.

"I simply never know what to say," Regina admitted. "I always say the wrong thing. And the men are terrifying. They all think they know better than I do. And they're loud and pompous and I can't bring myself to look them in the eye. Everybody gossips and says nasty things about one another. About Father and about Mother sometimes as well."

Bridget sighed and squeezed Regina's hand. "Father is a good example of how not to deal with grief. And what does it matter what they say about Mother? We know the truth. And they know the truth as well. They just like to pretend otherwise when they're bored and there's nothing else to discuss."

Regina waited. She knew that there was more Bridget wanted to say by that look of discomfort on her face.

Sure enough, after a moment, Bridget spoke again.

"I don't like the idea of you being alone all the time, darling."

"But I'm not alone. And I won't be for quite some time. Unless the four of you have gotten engaged and neglected to tell me so."

Bridget chuckled. "Now darling, you know it won't be long for any of us. Natalie will be off as soon as she finally chooses one suitor."

Regina allowed herself an indelicate snort. Natalie choose just one out of the many men who danced attendance? Not likely.

Bridget leveled her with a stern look. "I have had a talk with Natalie myself about her future."

"Did she listen to a word of it?"

"She shall, if she knows what is good for her. A woman who is known as a flirt quickly goes from many suitors to none at all."

Regina didn't think that Natalie would be inclined to believe this advice until it actually happened to her.

Bridget continued. "And you know that Mr. Fairchild is only waiting for his aunt to pass so that he may marry Louisa."

"His aunt has been stuck with one foot in the grave for two years. Is Louisa willing to wait another two before she passes?"

Louisa, their second-eldest sister, had the carrot-colored hair of Elizabeth but none of her younger sister's fire. Louisa was the gentlest of all of them. It was no wonder she was the first to have been proposed to, even if it must be kept secret for the time being.

"You know as well as I do how quickly one's health can take a turn for the worst," Bridget replied. "Elizabeth will not lack for suitors long, either."

"If she can find one that will put up with her temper."

"She's a spirited girl. She likes riding and long walks. She enjoys trips to town. Many men would pay dearly for such an active and athletic wife. Just you watch, when the shooting season starts and she is in her element, she will have men to admire her."

"And what of you?" Regina asked. She squeezed Bridget's hand in return. "I doubt there is a man on Earth good enough for you."

Bridget laughed fondly. "You give me too much credit."

Regina blushed and looked down at her lap. Their mother had died in quite distressed circumstances. A longtime friend of their mother, had been injured in a riding accident. Mother had raced to his side.

Some said that they were having an affair, but Mother had looked upon the man only as a brother. He had called her 'sister' in his letters to her. Regina had called him Uncle.

Mother's desperation to take care of the man she saw as family had its consequences. She had been caught in a downpour and continued on. She had arrived in time to make the Earl's last few days bearable. But while he lay dying, she was also ravaged. The rain had given her pneumonia.

She had passed away only a week after the Earl. His estate had been far from home and her family. They hadn't had the chance to say goodbye.

Regina had been quite young at the time. Bridget had immediately stepped up as head of the household and as Regina's caretaker. A governess was well and good but did not replace a mother's care. Bridget had provided that.

In her secret, jealous heart of hearts, Regina did not want Bridget to marry. She did not want to lose the woman who was more like mother than sister to her.

"I admit," Bridget said, "My taste is quite discerning. I have turned down quite a few young men."

Each time that Bridget had turned down a man, Regina had breathed a sigh of relief.

"But that state of affairs cannot endure forever," Bridget said. "Already Father berates me for my stubbornness. And I am not entirely impossible to please. There will be a man for me, darling. And when that happens, you cannot endure this great big house alone."

"But Father will need someone to run the house," Regina protested. "I can serve in that. I have assisted you often enough. I like keeping the books."

"And we are both well grateful for it," Bridget teased. She ruffled Regina's hair. "But your place is not here. You must come into your own. You must be a mistress of your own place. And that can never truly be while you are here."

"Did Father put you up to this?" Regina was well aware that Father despaired of finding her a husband when *all you do is sit*—his words, not hers.

"Father might go about it the wrong way but he worries because he cares. And no, he did not put me up to this. You should know better than to think my opinions come from anyone except myself."

Regina could see that her sister was not moving on this matter. "But what if I find no man to suit my tastes?"

"Well then tell me your tastes. I shall help find you a man to suit them."

Regina thought, but she could not think of a single thing. "I do not know."

"Think on it then," Bridget said. "And when you know, tell it to me. We shall find you someone to protect that gentle heart of yours, darling."

She patted Regina's hand and stood. "Now, come. I have a delightful frock for you for tonight. It shall bring out your fine eyes."

Regina didn't think anything could be done to improve

upon her appearance. But neither could she bear to dampen her beloved sister's spirits. So she allowed herself to be led upstairs.

Perhaps, she thought, this ball would be bearable.

CHAPTER 2

Regina had a headache.

The music and lights from the ball only made the throbbing in her temple intensify. Everyone was talking too loudly. It was all a cacophony.

She had allowed Bridget to dress her in a dark blue dress. The fabric was silky to the touch. Bridget had instructed the maid to do her hair up and they'd put a powder on her face to cover much of her freckles.

Looking in the mirror, she had thought she almost looked pretty. Perhaps the ball wouldn't be so bad.

Now she was in the thick of it and it was as awful as she'd remembered.

Natalie and Elizabeth were out on the dance floor. Natalie was laughing, catching hands and tossing them away in turn. Elizabeth was dancing intensely, locking eyes with her partner like a dance was a challenge.

Louisa was sitting off with some close friends and talking. Holding court, more like. Louisa was gentle and quiet and yet it drew people to her. All her friends sat around with bated breath as she talked.

Regina could see Mr. Fairchild hovering nearby. Obviously wanting to ask Louisa to dance—and obviously unable to. Until his wealthy aunt passed he could not let his favor be known. Poor Louisa, Regina thought. To love someone and be unable to have them. At least Mr. Fairchild loved her in return.

Bridget was about somewhere. Regina craned her head, searching for her. Perhaps she could persuade Regina to call up the carriage to take Regina home. The men about would undoubtedly offer her sisters a ride home when they found them without one.

As Regina made her way through the ball to find her sister, she began to hear whispers. At first, she feared it was about Father again. The gambling habit he'd developed after Mother's death was appalling. Many said it was only a matter of time before he gambled away his estate.

But no, they spoke of something else. Regina listened for a moment.

"Is he really here?" Someone asked.

"Oh to be sure, I saw him over by the foyer. I couldn't bring myself to greet him."

"He's quite intimidating, isn't he?"

Regina wondered who they were talking of. She pushed onward and caught a flash of dark red hair. Bridget!

She hurried forward. Bridget was talking with a man that Regina had never seen before.

Charlotte Tourney was just to the side. Regina came up to her. "Who is that man?"

"Who, speaking with Miss Bridget?"

Regina nodded.

Charlotte was the best person to approach for gossip. She did not disappoint Regina in this matter. "That is the Duke of Whitefern."

"How have I never before seen him?"

"He's quite the mysterious figure. I know hardly a thing about him. Other than his title and that he is heir to a massive fortune. But of course he wasn't born into the latter."

"Oh?" Regina asked. She kept watching her sister and the Duke. She couldn't see the man's face but she was certain he must be enamored of Bridget. What man alive wasn't?

"I heard that his family was quite destitute when he inherited the title. It's said his father was a poor businessman. The Duke had to earn it all back. And he had extraordinary luck about it. If you know what I mean."

"I'm afraid I don't."

Charlotte gave Regina a pitying smile, as though she thought it was sad that Regina didn't know. "Gambling, my dear. He's said to be a master with cards."

Now Regina knew why the smile was pitying. Because of her father. She drew herself up as best she could. Her stomach quaked. "I suppose he has good luck indeed, then."

"Indeed. Not much else is known of him. He is quite good looking but nothing is known of his connections or his family. Of course there is speculation. I heard that his mother was a French duchess."

Regina hummed noncommittally. Not that it deterred Charlotte.

"I also heard that he's won a dozen duels. Nothing to corroborate any of this, but it is rather fanciful, don't you think?"

"Um, yes, rather like a novel," Regina stuttered, and turned to approach Bridget. This headache really was monstrous.

She walked up and cleared her throat politely. "I beg pardon, but I'm afraid I must have a word with my sister."

The Duke of Whitefern turned and Regina's breath caught in her throat. He was tall, though not as tall as some men that she knew. He had dark hair and warm blue eyes. Regina had grown up with Natalie's clear, bright ones. She hadn't known that blue eyes could seem so warm and inviting.

It was more than simply a matter of being handsome—which he was. His entire face was firm, solid, as though he had been carved from stone. The warmth she saw in his eyes seemed quite at odds with the intimidating look of that face.

Regina found herself at a loss for words. He scared her,

somehow. But not in the usual way. She couldn't put a name to it. Still, he scared her.

"Lord Harrison," Bridget said. "Allow me to introduce my youngest sister, Miss Regina Hartfield. Regina, this is Lord Harrison, the Duke of Whitefern."

"It seems that beauty runs in the family," Lord Harrison said. He bowed, taking Regina's hand to kiss it. Warmth spread from the place where his lips had touched.

It made Regina want to snatch her hand away, but she didn't know why. It must have been the headache.

Or perhaps it was the fact that he had inferred that she was beautiful. She did not appreciate flatterers, even less so when the flattery was untrue. She knew what she looked like. Irritation surged up within her, startling her.

"I apologize for the interruption," she said. "May I speak to my sister for one moment?"

"Certainly." Lord Harrison bowed and parted.

"Another suitor, I suppose?" Regina asked. She couldn't help herself. She wasn't quite sure why Lord Harrison was provoking such an emotional response within her. It was unusual.

"He intends to be, I am sure," Bridget said. "I have met

him at other balls and he has made his regard for me clear."

"But you do not like him? He is a Duke."

"He has made his money as a gambler, and we have quite enough of those in our family already," Bridget said firmly.

Regina nodded, secretly quite pleased. She knew it was childish but she really did not want Bridget to marry just yet. "May I take the carriage home? I have the most awful headache."

"You will have to ask Father about that."

That was what Regina had been afraid she'd say. "Where is he?"

"Where else? In the side parlor."

Regina nodded. Gambling again. "If he says yes, do you say yes?"

Bridget nodded. "None of us shall want for offers of a ride home. Mr. Fairchild will take us all if no one else. But Father is not a young, pretty woman."

"Mr. Fairchild will take him as well as Louisa."

"Perhaps. But it's one thing for a young lady to ask a gentleman for a ride home after a ball. It's quite another for an older gentleman to ask another. There is the matter of his pride."

"Very well." Regina sighed. "I shall ask him."

She left Bridget and made her way to the side parlor. It was like stepping into another world. The rest of the house was brightly lit and crowded, filled with noise. The side parlor was done up in dark reds and dimly lit. It was smaller as well, so that the eight men inside seemed to dominate it.

Regina knew all of the men assembled. Lord Harrison was standing off to the side and was the only man she knew by name only. The others she knew both in personality and reputation.

Father was seated at the table with three others. The ones on either side of him were rather young men, a Mr. Charleston and a Mr. Denny. Both looked rather crestfallen.

The one seated directly across from Father—he made her heart sink. Her headache fled completely to be replaced by an awful coldness in her gut.

It was Lord Pettifer.

The man had proposed to Bridget a couple of years ago. He'd only known her for ten days. Bridget had turned him down and he'd called her the most awful names for it.

Natalie had told Regina later on that the man was a terrible rake. He was rumored to have left the daughter of a groundskeeper in the family way up north. He was certainly an unashamed gambler. Unlike most men who pretended they bet only a little—even when they bet a lot—Lord Pettifer boasted of how much he had staked and won.

Lord Pettifer had reason to boast, apparently. He was a veritable card shark. Or so Natalie had told her.

And now he was facing off against Father. Father, who was an awful gambler and had taken up cards as a way to get over his wife's death.

Regina felt a hand at her elbow and looked up into the blue eyes of Lord Harrison. "You shouldn't be in here," he said quietly.

"I know that women aren't allowed," she protested. "I simply have to speak with my father."

"It's not only because women aren't allowed." Lord Harrison's voice was surprisingly soft. There was something else in there too, a protectiveness. "This isn't a good time."

"I only want to ask him a question." What on earth was the matter?

There was a cry from the table. Regina knew that sound—it was her father.

She shoved past Lord Harrison, who was far too surprised to stop her. "Father?"

Father looked very pale, staring at the cards on the table. Lord Pettifer looked far too pleased with himself. Smug, even. Regina thought he looked like a rat.

"It appears as though I've won after all," he said.

Father looked like he might faint. Regina hurried up to him and put her hands on his shoulders. "Father? Are you quite all right?"

"This must be the youngest of your lovely daughters," Lord Pettifer said. "My deepest condolences."

Deepest condolences? Regina looked from Lord Pettifer to her father. "What's going on?"

"Lord Hartfield." It was Lord Harrison. "If I may escort your daughter out?"

Father nodded, still pale and distracted. Lord Harrison turned to Mr. Denny. "Denny, if you'll get Hartfield some water here. Pettifer, do us all a favor and collect your winnings and leave."

"I don't understand." Regina stood firm. "Why must you offer condolences?"

"Regina, please leave," Father said faintly.

"No." She startled herself with how firm her voice sounded. "I want to know what is going on."

"What is going on," Lord Pettifer said, standing, "Is that you are about to find your circumstances wildly changed."

He held up his winnings. There was a wad of notes, a ring, and a piece of paper.

Regina looked closer. No, it wasn't just a piece of paper. It was signed. She squinted until she could read it.

I, Lord Hartfield, do will the holder of this paper the rights and lands owned by me according to the laws of the gentry.

Her father had gambled everything.

And he had lost.

CHAPTER 3

Her knees nearly buckled and only a warm, strong hand at her elbow kept her upright. She looked up to see Lord Harrison looking at her with his brows drawn together. He seemed concerned.

"You should follow me, Miss Regina," he murmured.

Regina yanked her arm away. She had no idea where the impertinence came from. She was never like this. "Father. Have you truly gambled away our lands?"

Lord Pettifer gave an exaggerated sigh. "I did tell him I had a good hand."

"Which you always say when you have a bad one!" Father bellowed.

Regina wrapped an arm around Father's shoulders. He was working himself up into a state. "Father, please, don't yell. Come with me and we'll get you sorted."

"There is no sorting," Mr. Charleston snorted.

"Hold your tongue," Lord Harrison instructed. "Pettifer. Leave. Lord Hartfield, do sit down. Miss Regina if you'll come with me."

"Go," Father said. His voice didn't even sound like his. It was shaking and frail. Regina had never heard him sound so old.

Lord Harrison took her by the elbow again and this time she allowed it.

"Surely this is not legal," she whispered.

Lord Harrison led her out of the room and through to the front door. "It doesn't matter."

He opened the front door and the cool night air hit her face. Only as the wind passed over her face did she realize how hot she had gotten. She was practically shaking.

"Just lean back here." Lord Harrison helped her to lean against the wall of the house. "There now."

Regina looked up at him. "Why does it not matter if it isn't legal?"

Lord Harrison looked away from her. There was light spilling out of the windows of the house on one side. On the other, there were the pearl-white beams of the moon. Both sources coupled with the shadows to play over Lord Harrison's face and place him in contrast: one-half golden and lit up, the other half silvery pale.

Regina wondered which side was true. He looked oddly warm on one half and cold and calculating on the other. It reminded her of the fairy stories Bridget would read to her when she was a child. There were stories about fairy kings in them. They'd enchant you and then whisk you away and entrap you.

She shook her head clear of such thoughts. They were childish and ridiculous. And if there was a time for such thoughts, it wasn't now. She spoke again.

"If I am to be kicked out of my home and my sisters left penniless, I deserve to know why. Surely my father—"

She cut herself off. She had meant to say, *surely my father is not such a fool*. But that wasn't necessarily true, was it? He had been a slave to the cards for years. Regina had eavesdropped on many an argument between Bridget and Father over the matter.

He had lost thousands of pounds over the years at cards. Was it truly so hard to believe that he would lose their home as well?

Lord Harrison sighed and looked back at her. "Miss Regina. You must understand. It is not legally binding. No judge would enforce it. But there is the matter of honor."

"Honor?"

"Your father made a promise in front of others. He swore to honor that promise should he lose. He lost. To back out now would save his land but impugn his honor. He would be looked at with disdain."

"And he shall be looked at with such high regard once he is penniless and without land?"

Lord Harrison inclined his head as if tipping his hat to her. "You see clearly the conundrum you've been left in."

"That I—" Regina's blood froze.

She worried not for herself. She would not miss the balls and the dinners and the like. There was the fear of what it might take to maintain an income. Begging from friends and relying on charity made her stomach churn with humiliation.

But her sisters... her beautiful, stunning sisters. Natalie would wilt when she heard the news. Mr. Fairchild would never be able to marry Louisa now. Elizabeth's sharp wit and fiery temper would become vices rather than amusing virtues.

And what of Bridget? Her sister had rallied them all together when Mother had died. What man would have her now?

Regina had wanted to keep Bridget all to herself but not like this. Not at this price.

Some of her horror must have shown on her face, for Lord Harrison's brow tightened. "I am sorry, Miss Regina."

Her mind raced. "What is to be done? How can this be salvaged?"

"Salvaged?"

"Yes. Surely there is something that we can do to preserve ourselves."

"Well..." Lord Harrison thought for a moment. "Do your sisters have prospects?"

"My three eldest. One is engaged, although it is not common knowledge. The other two have many suitors."

"Then tell them to accept one of them at once. Have their marriages without delay."

"My sister's fiancé cannot marry her. His aunt will not allow it. If they marry she shall rewrite her will to leave him nothing."

"And will he stand by her when the news breaks?"

Regina shook her head. "I do not know."

"If your sisters marry quickly, their husbands can provide for you and your other unmarried sister. Their reputations and income will preserve you until you can be wed."

"How quickly will the news get out?"

"More quickly than you would expect."

Regina passed her hand over her eyes. This felt like a nightmare. It couldn't possibly be real.

But if this was a dream she wouldn't have been able to conjure up a man like Lord Harrison. She couldn't have dreamt such detail. And she could remember every step she had taken throughout the day.

This was all horribly real.

"I shall have to tell them," she said. Her voice was thick and she swallowed quickly. She would not cry in front of a man she didn't even know. "Father will bungle the whole thing."

"Perhaps in the morning. They will be too exhausted to deal with it properly tonight."

Regina nodded. "Bridget will know what to do."

"Bridget?"

Regina looked up at him. Lord Harrison's eyes had lit up in a look that she knew well. She had seen many a man look at Bridget in that way, and Natalie as well. It was how Mr. Fairchild looked at Louisa.

"My eldest sister, with whom you were speaking earlier. She manages our affairs. She'll know what to do."

Lord Harrison inclined his head again. "Well, please give my condolences to your sister and inform her that should she be in need of a suitor, I stand ready and waiting."

"That is rather bold of you, sir," Regina replied. She blinked, surprised at herself. She was not normally so snappish. Perhaps it was the stress. Or perhaps it was that she wanted to protect Bridget.

Lord Harrison chuckled. "There's a feisty one inside of you yet, Miss Regina. And here I had heard that you were the mouse of the five."

Regina swallowed. She knew that she was plain in features. And she knew that she was quiet. But to learn they called her a mouse…

It stung, honestly.

But she would not be a mouse where Bridget was concerned. "My sister is an accomplished woman," she said. "Only the best of men could hope to win her hand."

"And you clearly do not think I am the best of men," Lord Harrison replied. He seemed amused by this, smiling down at her. Regina shivered at that, but not unpleasantly. He looked striking like this, smiling with the moonlight on his face.

"I think that I do not know you well enough to cast judgment. But if you wish to win Bridget, you'd do well to proceed with more delicacy."

"Delicacy?" Lord Harrison chuckled. "Miss Regina, the time for delicacy is at an end. You and your sisters are, as of now, dependent upon the goodwill of others. You must learn to be bold."

"In speaking plainly to you I think that I am being quite bold."

"Miss Regina." Lord Harrison sighed. He briefly

clenched his hand into a fist in frustration. "I apologize if I have offended you. But my offer is genuine. You and your sisters need the protection of a husband since your father can no longer provide any. I am willing and happy to offer your sister my heart and my home. Please convey this to her if it please you.

"You must understand the danger you are now in. I do not wish to see five innocent women thrown out onto the street. My words may be direct but my intentions are good."

He took his hand in hers. Regina was surprised both by the size of it and how warm it was. It practically encased her own. It felt oddly as though the warmth and weight of his hand was the only thing anchoring her.

Lord Harrison's eyes bore into hers. She felt a bit like a mouse pinned by a snake, except there was no malice in his gaze. "Believe me, I am only trying to help you."

Regina swallowed. "You have helped, sir, and I thank you for it. The night air has done some good. As has your advice."

She took a deep breath to steady herself. "I must get to my father. My sisters shall stay. It will be remarked upon if we all retire so early. I shall take my father home.

Mr. Fairchild will give my sisters a ride back. Then I will speak to them of this in the morning."

"Good girl," Lord Harrison said. He squeezed her hand. "Have a calm head and act quickly. It is the only way to save yourselves."

Regina nodded. Yes. Stay calm and act quickly. She could do that. Or, rather, Bridget could. She felt certain that Bridget would know what to do.

Then she realized with a start that Lord Harrison was still holding her hand. She slid her hand out of his grasp. Immediately she missed the safe feeling it had given her and the warmth it had provided.

"Thank you again, Lord Harrison. I shall take my leave, if I may."

Lord Harrison made a shooing gesture. "Do what you must. And remember what I said."

Regina hurried back into the house. She could feel Lord Harrison's eyes tracking her the entire way. It felt like they were burning into her back.

CHAPTER 4

Regina returned to the side parlor to find that all the men had cleared it. Save for Mr. Denny, who was sitting with Father.

"Mr. Denny, your kindness will not be forgotten," she said, crossing to Father's side.

Mr. Denny stood at once. "Anything for the Hartfields, Miss Regina. Are you quite well?"

"Yes. Lord Harrison forced me to take some night air. It did me some good."

Regina knelt in front of Father. He had sunk back into his chair and still looked pale. He turned his green eyes to her. They looked watery.

"Father," Regina whispered. "Are you quite all right?"

He shook his head. "I have ruined us," he whispered.

"Don't fret," Regina said immediately. Her voice held a firmness she did not feel. "We shall find a way out of this. Never you fret."

She looked up at Mr. Denny. "If I may take advantage of your good nature once more, sir?"

"As I said, anything."

"Would you please find my sister, Miss Hartfield? Inform her that Father is feeling unwell and I have taken him home in the carriage."

As the eldest, Bridget was known among society as Miss Hartfield. The second eldest, Louisa, was known as Miss Louisa Hartfield. Natalie, Elizabeth, and Regina were all known simply as Miss.

Mr. Denny bowed. "I shall inform her. I hope your father recovers. And..." he hesitated. "If there is anything I can do to assist, please inform me."

"Not unless you are willing to marry one of us," Regina replied before she could stop herself.

Mr. Denny flushed. Regina felt rather like bashing her

head against the card table. When had she become so impudent?

"I was only jesting, of course," she said quickly. "I apologize. Think nothing of it. I fear my mind is not at rights."

"No apology is necessary," Mr. Denny replied, just as hasty. He bowed again and hurried out the door.

Well, there was one man she'd just scared away from her family.

"Up you get, Father," Regina said. It took some tugging but she convinced Father to stand on his own two feet. "I'm taking you home."

She got him out to the carriage without much incident. It was only once they were safely inside that Father broke down.

Regina had never once seen her father cry. She had heard him in his study sometimes. After Mother had died, he would lock himself inside for hours. Regina would creep down at night to see if he was still there. If she pressed her ear to the door, she was able to hear quiet sobs.

She had wondered then what kind of love was so deep it

ruined a man. She had then wondered if any man would ever love her like that.

She doubted it.

But now Father was sitting next to her in the carriage and crying. He was doing it quietly without much fuss. Regina would have expected great heaving and sobbing. But her father merely let the tears run down his face.

It was awkwardly silent. Regina had no idea what to say.

When they arrived home she helped him out of the carriage.

"Here we are," she said, speaking to him as if he were a child. "I'll get the front door."

Father looked down at her. "You know you have your mother's eyes?"

Regina stopped and turned to look at him. "Yes. Bridget has said so."

"The prettiest brown eyes, they were. So soft and dark." Father sighed. "I apologize. You must forgive an old man's ramblings."

"You are not so old, Father." Regina took his hand and led him inside.

"I am old enough to be labeled an old fool."

"I suspect Mr. Charleston called you that and I will have none of it. He is a sour man of little fortune."

Father shook his head. "He was right. Regina, I have just ruined us. And I have been ruining us for years."

"Don't say that." She started to lead him up the stairs. She was grateful the servants were abed so none of them saw Father this way.

"I suppose Bridget hasn't told you." Father let Regina lead him easy as a lamb. "My weakness for cards led us close to bankruptcy even before tonight. It was why I have been urging you girls toward marriage.

"I feel as though I am seized by a devil. I cannot stop myself. Each time I see the cards and think, I shall win. I must win. Surely this time... and then nothing but more loss.

"Your poor sister has been at her wit's end. I have promised her and promised her that I would stop. And I have failed. Now you will all perish."

"Now Father, be reasonable. The whole world knows Lord Pettifer is the most disgraceful of men. It is his title alone that keeps him on invitations. It is not as if Natalie ran off to Gretna Green."

Father shook his head. "No man will have you girls now."

"Lord Harrison asked for Bridget's hand even after your losses," Regina blurted out.

Father stopped on the stairs and stared at her. "Did he now?"

Regina nodded. She felt a little as though she had betrayed Lord Harrison's confidence. But then, he had not asked her to keep it a secret. And he must ask Father's permission before marrying Bridget anyhow.

"I am not sure of him," Father admitted. "I have heard the most wild stories. Nothing about him is known for certain. But he has wealth and seems a good man, if mysterious. Bridget could do worse given our changed circumstances."

"I am certain other men will come forward as well," Regina said. She spoke with a confidence she did not feel. "Now come, we must get you to bed."

She helped him get up the rest of the stairs and into his chambers. It felt so odd, as though their positions had reversed: he the child and she the parent.

Father didn't say anything more as she helped him. Not

until he was in bed and she prepared to walk away. Then he caught his hand in hers and said,

"I am glad that one of you took after your mother."

"I have been informed that I am nothing like mother," Regina replied. Elizabeth had hurled that truth at her one day during a fight.

Father shook his head. "No. You and Bridget are like your mother. But you got just a bit more of her, I think."

He raised his hand and gently touched right between her eyes. "Your eyes."

Regina gently set his hand down on the bed and patted it. "Sleep, Father. We shall deal with this in the morning."

She made sure all was taken care of and then went to bed herself. She knew that she should get some rest but for a while she simply couldn't sleep.

She tossed and turned. But everything from the night played back at her. Especially Lord Harrison. She could see his eyes staring straight into hers as he promised that he only wanted to help. She could feel his hand holding hers, making her feel safe.

Regina sat up in frustration. Why should she be

thinking of a man she had just met? It was of Father she should be thinking. Father and her family's future.

She had no inclination to marry. And she did not think her sisters would appreciate being rushed into marriage themselves. To marry a husband for charity? Out of desperation? It seemed so base.

Marriage was to make a good match. It was an economical decision. To marry a man for love alone was folly. But neither was marriage something to be rushed into. It required a careful weighing of pros and cons. It went against Regina's nature to rush herself or her sisters into matrimony.

If only there was a way to get back their fortune and land so that they could rely on Father as before. Then they could marry as other women did, smartly and in proper time. What would society say of them all getting married at once?

Her sisters deserved better than marrying under a cloud of scandal. And Father deserved better than the pity and judgment he would receive.

If only she could think of a way.

Regina distantly heard the sound of the front door. She checked the clock. Her sisters were back earlier than expected.

There was the sound of thumping feet and then the door to her bedroom flew open.

It was Elizabeth, her green eyes all but glowing and her chest heaving.

"Regina!" She snapped. "Care to inform me why Mr. Denny just proposed to me?"

Oh dear.

CHAPTER 5

The sisters all met in Bridget's room.

Louisa sat quietly on the bed, propped up with pillows. Elizabeth paced back and forth. Natalie was curled up on the windowsill. Bridget was on the edge of the bed next to Louisa.

Regina stood in the middle. It felt a little like she was on stage.

"Spare nothing," Bridget told her.

As simply as she could she told them what had happened. Elizabeth uttered many words that a lady shouldn't know. Natalie clapped a hand over her mouth. And Louisa burst into tears.

Bridget merely stayed silent.

When Regina had finished she looked to her sister for guidance. Before Bridget said anything, however, Louisa cut in.

"Charles can never marry me now," she whispered through her tears.

"There, now," Bridget said, patting Louisa's knee soothingly. "Mr. Fairchild will not hesitate to wed you. I should say this gives him more reason to."

"If only his aunt would hurry up and die," Elizabeth said with an eye roll. When the other four looked at her, she shrugged. "Don't look so scandalized. You're all thinking it."

"You must accept Mr. Denny," Natalie said.

"I am not accepting a man I hardly know," Elizabeth replied.

"He has an income of ten thousand a year and that's all you need know!" Natalie hissed. "I should think you'd put up with half that a year if the man was fool enough to put up with you."

"Squabbling will get us nowhere," Bridget said. "Elizabeth, please consider Mr. Denny's proposal. He is a good man and has been watching you for some time."

"Watching is not half as good as speaking. If he has been watching me as you say then why not ask me to dance?"

"Because you are a harpy that does nothing but insult the man fool enough to ask you."

"Natalie, enough!" Bridget commanded.

Natalie fell silent.

Bridget drew herself up. "You could do well to improve yourself, Natalie. You cannot treat men as playthings. Pick one, and pick now. The time for indecision is over."

Natalie huffed but said nothing.

"And what of me?" Regina asked.

Bridget looked over at her. Her green eyes warmed and she almost smiled. "Don't fret for anything, darling."

"There's no need to play favorites," Elizabeth said. "She's eighteen, that's old enough to marry."

"And how will it look if all of us marry at once?" Bridget replied. "And if the youngest marries before her elders?" She gestured at Louisa.

Elizabeth had nothing to say to that. What Bridget said was true. Two of them getting married at once would raise eyebrows but not too many. Three or four of them?

Everyone would know the real reason they had tied the knot. The gossip would never cease.

As for age, it was commonly accepted—although by no means a rule—that the elder daughters married first. For Regina to marry before Louisa would provoke spinster comments about Louisa. Comments that her sweet sister did not deserve.

"And what of you, Bridget?" Natalie asked. "Surely you have suitors."

"I have. And I shall think on who would best suit me. I shall have to be married first, if Louisa is not. But there is nothing stopping either you or Elizabeth from entering an engagement."

"Let us face the truth, Bridget," Louisa said. Regina was surprised that she had spoken up. She sounded incredibly tired.

"We must face it. Marriage will save us financially. But it will not—nothing can save our reputations. Especially Father's. It will be years before people will stop whispering about it. Any man who marries us will have to take that on."

"The whispers will die down as soon as the next scandal comes," Bridget replied.

"Our lives will never be the same," Louisa countered. "We shall be indebted to our husbands as most women never are. Our wedding days will be covered in clouds. Father might never be welcomed back into society."

"This is how our lives are now," Bridget said. "Perfect marriages they might not be. But they are all we have. Let us be thankful that we have suitors willing to marry us. Not every woman is so lucky."

Again, Regina wished that there was a way to fix this. If only they could win back their land. That would stick it to Lord Pettifer. Then this cloud wouldn't be over her sisters' marriages. Father could hold his head high again.

If only...

"Then prove it to us," Elizabeth said. "Find yourself a husband."

Bridget thought for a moment. "I shall choose my husband the night of Lord and Lady Morrison's annual masquerade ball. It is in a month's time. Is that acceptable?"

The other three women nodded. Regina didn't. She couldn't. A thought had hit her like a lightning bolt. Her skin tingled and her stomach flipped.

Lord and Lady Morrison's masquerade ball.

There was a way to win their land and money back. There was a way to fix all of this.

She had figured it out.

CHAPTER 6

The girls retired for the night to their bedrooms. Louisa stayed in Bridget's room. They all had their own rooms but Regina suspected that Louisa needed a bit of extra comfort that night.

Regina went back to her bedroom and lay in darkness until she was certain the others were asleep.

When she had waited until she could hardly bear it anymore, she rose. She slid on her robe again and opened her bedroom door.

There was no sound throughout the house.

Do you want to read more?

Click on the link below!
http://abbyayles.com/AmB05-B04

BE A PART OF THE ABBY AYLES FAMILY...

I write for you, the readers, and I love hearing from you! Thank you for your on going support as we journey through the most romantic era together.

If you're not a member of my family yet, it's never too late. Stay up to date on upcoming releases and check out the website for all information on romance.

I hope my stories touch you as deeply as you have impacted me. Enjoy the happily ever after!

Let's connect and download this Free Exclusive Bonus Story!

(Available only to my subscribers)

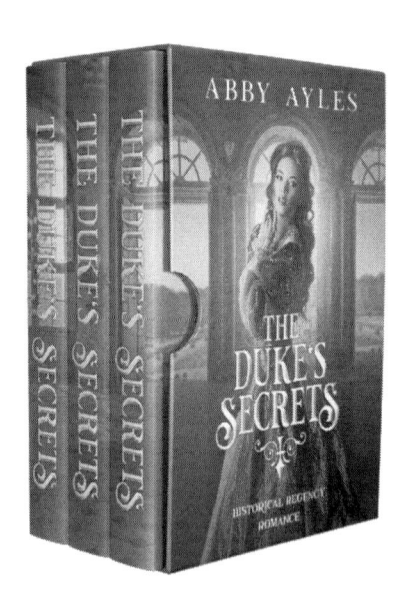

Click on the image or on the button below to get the BONUS
BookHip.com/XNVQAW

ALSO BY ABBY AYLES

- The Lady The Duke The Gentleman
- A Broken Heart's Redemption
- Falling for the Governess
- The Lady's Gamble
- The Lady's Patient

ABOUT THE AUTHORS

Abby Ayles was born in the northern city of Manchester, England, but currently lives in Charleston, South Carolina, with her husband and their three cats. She holds a Master's degree in History and Arts and worked as a history teacher in middle school.

Her greatest interest lies in the era of Regency and Victorian England and Abby shares her love and knowledge of these periods with many readers in her newsletter.

In addition to this she has also written her first romantic novel, **The Duke's Secrets**, which is set in the era and is available for free on her website. As one reader commented – *'Abby's writing makes you travel back in time...'*

When she has time to herself, Abby enjoys going to the theatre, reading and watching documentaries about Regency and Victorian England.

For more information you can contact Abby Ayles Here:
https://manychat.com/l3/abbyaylesauthor
abby@abbyayles.com

Fanny Finch was born in United Kingdom but moved to Denver, Colorado when she was very young. She attended Washington University where she studied for several years and lives with her husband and their bulldog.

Upon leaving university, Fanny found a job as a proof reader for a small press. There, she honed her skills and also met and worked with author Abby Ayles, helping to polish her books to perfection.

But she is also an author in her own right and is working hard to become recognized as such as she starts to publish her own novels through her website. Her genre is in the Historical Regency Romance category and if you like your reading material to be emotionally clean then you will be undoubtedly thrilled by the characters and scenarios Fanny develops.

When she has time to relax, Fanny enjoys listening to opera music and taking long walks in the outdoors. She writes almost every day as well and hopes to produce many more great books in the future.

You can contact Fanny Finch through her website, or download a free copy of her books at:

fannyfinch.com

Fanny@fannyfinch.com

Printed in Great Britain
by Amazon